THE COMPLETE CASES
OF MAX LATIN

THE COMPLETE CASES OF

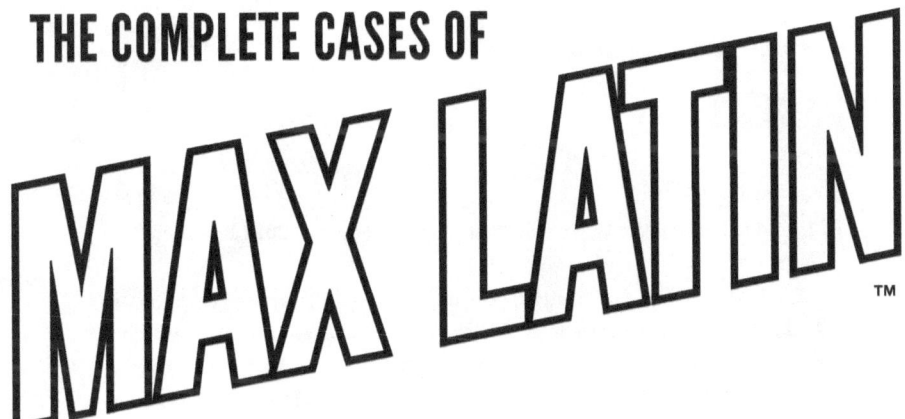

MAX LATIN ™

NORBERT DAVIS

INTRODUCTION BY
BOB BYRNE

ILLUSTRATIONS BY
JOHN FLEMING GOULD

POPULAR PUBLICATIONS • 2022

TABLE OF CONTENTS

INTRODUCTION BY BOB BYRNE

NORBERT DAVIS is considered one of Joseph "Cap" Shaw's *Black Mask Boys:* Those writers who formed the core of the legendary magazine editor's stable. But Shaw only accepted four of Davis' submissions, and one has to think it likely that there were more, but which were rejected. Davis would sell ten stories to subsequent *Mask* editors. Shaw did include a Davis story in his ground-breaking *The Hard-Boiled Omnibus,* but in reality, Davis was much less of a "Shaw guy" than the more commonly identified names, like Dashiell Hammett, Erle Stanley Gardner, Raymond Chandler, Frederick Nebel, Raoul Whitfield, or even Horace McCoy.

One of those five stories Shaw bought was "Red Goose," which Raymond Chandler said impressed him more than any other tale he read when he began his career as a writer. I'd call that high praise!

Davis, who also did westerns, adventures, war stories, and even love stories, both for the pulps and the higher-paying "slicks," wrote and sold hard-boiled stories to the pulps while he was a law student at Stanford. He was doing well at it, and when he graduated he decided rather than taking the bar exam, he would make a living as a writer instead! He never did become a lawyer.

Sadly, he is damned by being remembered as the master of "the screwball hardboiled story." It's not an inaccurate appellation, but it's not particularly rewarding to his reputation. Davis did those kinds of stories better than anyone, as evidenced by his enjoyable Doan and Carstairs novels, which feature the smartest canine in private eye fiction. And he did "straight" hardboiled well, too: check out "Reform Racket," which is Hammett-esque with its political theme. But it is the in-between where I think he nailed it: hardboiled with humor—but not over-the-top.

The Continental Op (Hammett), Carmady (Chandler), Cardigan (Nebel), Race Williams (Carroll John Daly), Jo Gar (Whitfield), Ed Jenkins (Gardner), Bill Lennox (W.T. Ballard), Dal Prentice (Roger Torrey): developing a series character was a viable path to pulp success. So, of course, Norbert Davis didn't follow that route.

Benjamin Martin (1937–1938) did have five appearances in *Detective Tales,* with Dr. Flame (1939–1942) making four issues. John Collins (1942–1943) appeared in *Black Mask* three times after Shaw's departure. I mentioned Ben Shaley, who was in the February, and April, 1934 issues of *Black Mask,* and then, sadly, vanished forever from the pulps.

Davis' most successful ongoing character was William "Bail Bond" Dodd, who appeared in eight issues of *Dime Detective* from 1940 through 1943. Steeger Books has issued the complete Dodd collection in two volumes. Dodd is an excellent example of Davis writing with humor, but not too much of it.

Finally, we come to the irrepressible Max Latin. He's not your typical private eye, and he only appeared in five issues of *Dime Detective,* from July, 1941, through October of 1943. In a twist on the trope, Latin pretended to be absolutely corrupt, but wasn't really as bad as he presented himself to be. Inspector Walters, the weary, cynical, career cop in the series, actually tells Latin a few times that he knows it's partly an act. Latin is suitably offended by this 'positive aspersion' on his character.

In "Don't Give your Right Name" (December, 1941), Inspector Walters confronts Latin after a dead body is found:

> "I know the reason why you never get convicted of any of these things you get pinched for. It's very simple. Because you aren't guilty. You bend the law around like a pretzel, but you never quite break it. Taken all in all, you're generally, almost honest."
>
> "You spread that rumor around and I'll sue you for slander."

There are other comments like that throughout the stories. Latin's bad image is good for business, and he bristles at the allegation that he's better than he appears. You be the judge.

But it's not just Latin that carries the stories. If you are a fan of Rex Stout's Nero Wolfe (and why the heck wouldn't you be?), you know that those stories aren't really about the plots and the crimes to be solved. It's the interplay between the regulars at Wolfe's New York City Brownstone which draws readers back to the stories over and over. It's about Wolfe, Archie, Fritz, Inspector Cramer, Saul, and the rest of the cast, and how they relate to each other. The Latin stories are similar, be it Latin, Guiterrez, Dick, or even Happy.

Norbert Davis was very good at writing characters. He was also very good at writing atmosphere. And he was equally adept at hardboiled and at comedy. That's a lot of strengths to work from. For me, there are three recurring elements in the stories that really stand out: the restaurant, the characters, and Max Latin himself.

THE RESTAURANT & STAFF

GUITERREZ (WE never get a first name) is a top-flight chef and runs the restaurant which bears his name. That establishment, along with Guiterrez and his head waiter, Dick, is a fixture in the series.

Max Latin comes across like a not-official private investigator, though we learn in a later story that he is duly licensed. He doesn't have an office; he operates out of a back booth at the restaurant. By the end of the first story, we realize that Latin actually owns the place, but not openly. That explains why the staff does what he tells them to, and why his booth is always available for him.

Early in the first story, "Watch Me Kill You!," a prospective client comes to Latin's booth and Guiterrez says to him, "Did you know that Latin is nothing but a crook? Did you know he just today got out of the county jail, cell three, north tier?"

When the man replies that he thought Latin was a private inquiry agent, Guiterrez adds, "Also a crook. But you probably are, too."

Now, Latin had, in fact, just gotten out of jail that day, but Guiterrez' tone is set. He consistently runs Latin down as a crook. He hates his customers and tries to get rid of them any way he can. But it's always packed at his place, because his food is so good. And it enrages him that his patrons wolf down his food. He wants them to savor it: to slowly enjoy it.

The place is a dump. The ceilings are sooty, and the tables and booths are nothing special. The staff is loud, insulting and gives poor service. Guiterrez, his disdain for his customers, and his attitude towards Latin, are a treat in every tale.

Dick, the headwaiter, is another full-blown character, always of interest in his scenes. We first meet him as "A waiter wearing a baggy grease-stained coat that was at least three sizes too large for him and an apron that would have served for a circus tent...."

It's anybody's guess whether he will pull a plate, a ridiculously expensive bottle of brandy, or a huge knife out from underneath his voluminous apron. He has a propensity for removing cork bottles with his teeth and making insulting comments to his boss. It's impossible to imagine the place without him.

Guiterrez' is always a place we like to read about, though I'm not sure about actually eating there.

THE CHARACTERS

GUITERREZ AND Dick are integral to the scenes at the restaurant. And we'll get to Latin. But Davis populates the series with a plethora of strong characters. Detective Inspector Walters, Homicide, provides the police presence in the series. He knows Latin is constantly up to something, though as mentioned, that Latin isn't as 'bad' as he seems. He's a good cop, who has worked too hard, for too long. He's worn down by all he's seen, and it shows on his face. When he discovers that he's going to have to deal with the wealthy and influential Patricia Wentworth Craig, he says he'll have to walk soft and talk small. "It seems like they could put me out to pasture or something in my old age."

He is honest, and does his best, though he is a bit too prone to chasing after Latin: Walters tells him that he is minding his business when he follows Latin around. In "Don't Give Your Right Name," Latin impersonates Walters, and introduces the detective as his subordinate. It's an enjoyable scene with Walters, who is a gruff, but likable, character. He appears in all five stories, and he more than pulls his weight.

Patricia Wentworth Craig, the client's husband in the first story, is one of my favorites. Her imperious attitude is wonderful. Telling Walters that she has no doubt Latin is guilty of killing someone, she says, "You will see to it that he is hanged, of course. Good evening." To her, it's a done deal. She instructs him to use the third degree on Latin, and guarantees that no one will object. She absolutely dominates her scenes.

In "You Can Die Any Day," Rene and Raymond play two criminals Latin hires to scare a woman. Yep—you read that right. They are brothers, and not your typical heavies. Davis again gives us compelling characters to provide depth. They're hired through Happy, who runs the garage where Latin rents his cars. Happy lights up his scenes and is a fun addition to the stories.

"Give the Devil his Due's" Count Fidestine Fiolo and his unamorous pursuit of future heiress Hester Zachary makes for a terrific story. That story also gives us madame-gone-straight Rosie Fitzgerald, who absolutely could have been a recurring character in any pulp series. You can picture her running girls in an Old West saloon.

I'd be hard-pressed to name one of Davis' contemporaries who was better at fleshing out an array of recurring and varying characters in pulp tales. Of course, there were only five Latin stories, so it's a small sample. But this element absolutely shines through. And the author is worthy of recognition for it.

MAX LATIN

WHICH BRING us to the star of the series. At the beginning of that first story, Latin is just out of jail for helping to "recover" some stolen goods which he may well have arranged to be stolen in the first place. He was arrested for compounding a felony, though the District Attorney's Office couldn't prove it. The same crime is discussed in regards to the case he's hired for in the next story. Questionable ethics are absolutely part of Latin's persona.

Referred to as a private detective on the shady side, he replies, "black as night." The stories are replete with Latin's own intimations that he's "crooked as a swastika." His shady reputation plays a part in the clients approaching him in all five stories. Walters is more right than wrong about the PI, though like all private detectives, Latin operates "out there" on his own. And I would say that secretly disposing of a body and not reporting it is a questionable activity.

A private eye like Latin certainly needs a lawyer on call, and that's Abe Moscowitz. You can believe his client causes some work for him. He is amusing in a brief appearance in "Don't Give Your Right Name." He deserved more time in the series, and is another example of Davis' ability to consistently create strong supporting characters—not an easy accomplishment in the short story format.

Latin's interactions with Guiterrez are something to look forward to throughout the stories. And his personality, sometimes benevolent—more often, self-serving—

makes for an interesting protagonist. I think that the Latin stories are Davis' best work, and Norbert Davis is on my Hard-boiled Mt. Rushmore. Hopefully you'll enjoy them. It truly is a shame there are only five.

And a bit of a warning: In Latin's world, and indeed, throughout Davis' work, villains get their comeuppance. And in the world of the hardboiled pulps, that includes violence. Women get hit, just like men. Davis punches out a woman in "Don't Give Your Right Name." It turns out she's a murderess, and she attempts to kill Latin a couple different ways, but he does cold cock her.

To end on a lighter note: Davis never met an adverb he didn't like. He uses more adverbs per page than any other pulpster I've read. For a guy getting paid by the word, he had no use for Stephen King's advice. Latin doesn't smile, he smiles glumly. Guiterrez doesn't just go through the back door to the kitchen, he slaps violently through it. Dick doesn't nod. He nods slowly. A maitre d' shivers realistically.

So, enjoy the exploits of Max Latin, and keep an eye out for those adverbs. They're deliciously everywhere.

WATCH ME KILL YOU!

AN ASSIGNMENT AS ART BUYER
IS A NEW ONE FOR LATIN, THE
SHAMUS WITH A SHADY REP—
BUT HE SOON DISCOVERS THAT
EVEN MURDER CAN COME UNDER
THE HEAD OF FINE ART. SORTING
AMONG THE RARE EXHIBITS—A
ROLYPOLY ART-DEALER WHO'S
AS CROOKED AS A SWASTIKA,
A SULTRY SCULPTRESS, AND A
BLUE-BLOODED PATRONESS WITH
A BROW-BEATEN MATE—THE
BRANDY-DRINKING "THIN MAN"
UNCOVERS A COUPLE OF COOL
KILLERS WHO'D PUT A HARDENED
GUNSEL TO SHAME.

CHAPTER ONE
LATIN IN ART

GUITERREZ CAME out of the kitchen in a cloud of steam and slapped the heavy metal swing door violently shut behind him. He was a tall man with a dark, bitterly disillusioned face. He was wearing a white jacket and a white apron, and he had a chef's hat crushed down over his right ear. There was a towel wrapped around his neck, and he wiped his forehead with its frayed end, glaring at Latin.

"What was the matter with it?" he demanded.

Latin was sitting in the last one of the row of narrow high-backed booths. "Matter with what?" he asked.

"My spaghetti *à la crème à la Guiterrez.*"

"Nothing that I know of," said Latin.

"Then what did you send half of it back for? I suppose it ain't good enough for you? I suppose they feed you better in the county jail, cell three, north tier?"

"No," Latin said judiciously. "As a matter of fact, they don't. You just served me too much. I'm full."

A waiter wearing a baggy grease-stained coat that was at least three sizes too large for him and an apron that would have served for a circus tent came up and poked Guiterrez in the ribs with his elbow. "Out of the way, boss." He was carrying a bottle of brandy and a glass, and he planked

them down on the linoleum tabletop in front of Latin and
went away.

Latin poured himself some brandy. He was a thin man
with wide, high shoulders. His features were narrow and

The man in the overcoat
fired without the
slightest warning.

carefully expressionless, and his greenish eyes tipped a
little, catlike, at the corners. He had a casual air that was
as smooth and polished as an expensive gem.

Guiterrez turned around suddenly and said: "Well, what do *you* want?"

The pudgy little man who had been trying to edge past him stepped back, startled.

"They—they told me at the door that I'd find Mr. Max Latin in the last booth—"

"That's him," said Guiterrez.

The pudgy man ducked his head in an embarrassed nod. "How do you do, Mr. Latin. My name is Bernard Hastings."

Guiterrez tapped him on the shoulder. "Did you know that Latin is nothing but a crook? Did you know he just today got out of the county jail, cell three, north tier?"

Hastings swallowed. "Why—why, no. I—I thought he was a private inquiry agent."

"Also a crook," said Guiterrez. "But probably you are, too, and if you want to talk to him sit down in his booth. I don't allow people to stand in the aisle around here."

Hastings slid gingerly into the seat opposite Latin.

The waiter in the baggy coat came up and looked over Guiterrez's shoulder. "You wanta eat, chum?"

Hastings said: "No, thanks. I don't—"

"So my food's not good enough for you?" Guiterrez interrupted.

Hastings was looking scared now. "Oh, no! I mean, it isn't that. I've just eaten and—"

"So I suppose you think you're gonna sit here and dead-head and take up my table space while you chat with this crook?"

"Why—why, no," said Hastings quickly. "If I could have a—a drink—"

The waiter produced a glass from under his voluminous apron, reached around Guiterrez and planked it down on the table.

"Drink some of Latin's brandy," Guiterrez ordered.

"But—but I don't like…. If I could have a wine list…." Hastings stopped, staring incredulously at the label on the brandy bottle. "Why! That—that brandy is priceless! You can't buy it anymore!"

"If you don't like it, get out," said Guiterrez. "I didn't ask you to come here."

"But I do like it! I was just startled at seeing it! It's the best—the very best—"

"Phooey," said Guiterrez, and went on up the aisle toward the front of the restaurant.

LATIN POURED some of the brandy in Hastings's glass. Hastings watched him, wide-eyed, and then cleared his throat with a nervous little cough before he spoke.

"Did—did I offend that—ah—gentleman in some manner? I'm sure I had no intention—"

"Guiterrez?" Latin asked. "Oh, he's always offended. Pay no attention to him. He's frustrated."

"Frustrated?" Hastings repeated.

Latin sipped his brandy appreciatively. "Yes. You see, Guiterrez is a very good chef. For twenty years he worked in the top-notch restaurants and hotels, but he didn't like it. All the time he was saving his money so he could start a small, quiet, dignified place of his own where he could serve the absolute best in food, cooked just the way he wanted it to a select group of customers who would appreciate his efforts."

"Why, that's very laudable. I can't see why—"

Latin waved his arm. "Look at this place."

It was one long dingy room with dark-stained walls and beams crossing close against the sooty ceiling. High-backed booths were lined along one side and the rest of the floor space was packed with spindly wire-legged tables. It was still early for dinner, but every seat in the place was taken.

The confusion was unbelievable. Crockery clashed and clattered, a jukebox howled boogie-woogie from the corner, and the cash register clanged with maddening irregularity. Cigarette smoke floated in eye-smarting layers, and Guiterrez was denouncing a tableful of customers in a bitterly despairing voice while they ignored him and kept right on eating. An incredibly shabby army of waiters dipped and swerved between tables with the breathtaking skill of slack-wire walkers, in the meantime shouting orders, threats, and demands for the right-of-way. Conversational babble throbbed in the thick air like the beat of an immense drum.

Hastings said: "I noticed the atmosphere seemed rather— But certainly Mr. Guiterrez can't complain about the amount of business—"

"Oh, yes he can. That's what's the matter. There's too much business. Guiterrez insults his customers, gives them terrible service, makes them stand in line outside whenever it's raining, but he still can't get rid of them. The food he serves is too good. The customers don't mind putting up with a few discomforts if they are allowed to eat it."

Hastings shook his head. "It seems very strange. But if he *really* wanted to get rid of some of his excess customers, he could just stop serving such good food for a while."

"He can't help making it good. He's an artist."

"Oh," said Hastings, nodding as though that explained everything. "An artist. Yes, I see. Artists are indeed incredible people. I can't understand…. But Mr. Latin, I wanted to talk to you about my wife."

"Yes," said Latin. "Five hundred."

Hastings stared at him. "Eh?"

Latin elaborated: "Yes, I will get evidence that will enable you to divorce her, and it will cost you five hundred dollars unless I have to fake the evidence and then the price is seven-fifty."

"But—but it isn't that at all! I mean, I'm very happy. I mean, I don't want a divorce!"

Latin poured himself more brandy. "Oh. Well then, what *do* you want?"

HASTINGS TOOK a deep breath and started over again. "Mr. Latin, you were recommended to me by Walker and Crenshaw, my attorneys. They told me that you were very clever and absolutely—ah—unscrupulous."

"Right on both counts," said Latin complacently.

"Yes, I see," said Hastings in an uncertain tone. "Well, anyway, my wife is Patricia Wentworth Craig."

Latin put his glass down carefully. "Who?"

"Patricia Wentworth Craig."

"The girl with the money bags?"

"My wife is the possessor of an extremely large fortune," Hastings admitted with dignity.

"Yes, indeed," Latin agreed. "Fifty million dollars. I thought you said your name was Hastings."

"I did, and it is. Due to her enormous business interests and to the legal complications in which they result, she thought it best to retain her maiden name after we were married. It is less confusing."

"Yeah," Latin said absently. "I heard she had a husband kicking around somewhere. How'd you do it, anyway?"

Hastings's lips tightened. "I beg your pardon?"

"How'd you hook her? I've always wanted a wife with fifty million dollars. How do you go about getting one?"

Hastings's round face was red with indignation. "Mr. Latin, if you *please!* My wife married me because she loved me and I loved her. Her fortune had nothing whatsoever to do with it. I assure you that I am myself by no means a pauper. I have never touched a cent of my wife's money and never will!"

"Them that has gets," Latin said gloomily. "All right, what did you want to tell me about your wife?"

"If you'll let me talk without these constant interruptions. My wife's father had a brother who, instead of being as honest and energetic and astute as my wife's father, was nothing but a bum and a loafer all his life. He died years ago of acute alcoholism. He had one son."

"I'm right with you so far," Latin said.

"This son's name is Winston Wentworth Craig. He's an artist. I mean, a real one. He paints pictures."

"All right," said Latin.

"My wife collects pictures—modern paintings in particular. She has a most extensive collection—very valuable."

"It would be," said Latin. "Go on."

"It seems," Hastings admitted reluctantly, "that Winston Wentworth Craig is a very good painter. He's had many exhibits, and his pictures are in all the most famous museums and art galleries and collections. My wife wants some of them in her collection."

"Why doesn't she buy them?"

"Because Winston Wentworth Craig won't sell her any."

Latin blinked. "Why won't he?"

Hastings wiggled on the hard bench. "Well, you see, Winston Wentworth Craig's father spent most of his time trying to sponge money off my wife's father. When he managed to get any he dissipated it in riotous living. Winston Wentworth Craig came to my wife several years ago and asked her to finance him while he studied in Paris. She refused to give him any money, and I'm afraid she— ah—laughed rather rudely at his ambition to be an artist."

"I'm beginning to get the idea," said Latin.

Hastings made a harassed gesture. "How could she know he was going to turn out to be good? He has many of his father's—ah—less desirable characteristics, and she thought naturally that this art study business was just an excuse to get enough money from her to loaf a year or two. But her refusal made him angry, and he's a very vindictive sort of a person. Now he refuses to sell her any of his pictures."

"So what?" Latin asked.

HASTINGS LEANED forward earnestly. "Don't you see? My wife, over a space of years, has built up a reputation as an authority on modern paintings and as a sponsor of it. Now this uncouth person, Winston Wentworth Craig, goes around telling everyone who will listen that she is merely a rich ignoramus who knows so little about art that she can't recognize talent even in her own relations. It's horribly humiliating. People *laugh* at her!"

"How too bad," said Latin.

"Also," said Hastings, ignoring the comment, "he tells people that she can never acquire any of his work, even with all the money she has, and naturally other collectors— who are envious of her—ridicule her for that reason. It is vital, Mr. Latin—*vital*—that she acquire some of Winston Wentworth Craig's pictures!"

"I can see that," Latin said gravely.

"I want you to get some of those pictures for her."

"Steal them?" Latin asked in a bland voice.

"No!" Hastings said emphatically. "Of course not! My wife will pay any price he asks. I want you to get him to consent to sell some to her."

"I hate to do myself out of a job," Latin said, "but this seems pretty silly to me. All your wife has to do is to buy one of Craig's pictures from some other collector or dealer or museum. With her money, that shouldn't be very difficult to accomplish."

"Please, Mr. Latin!" Hastings snapped. "Do you think my wife is such a fool she didn't think of that long ago? Craig won't permit anyone to sell her one of his pictures."

"After he once sells a picture to someone, the picture belongs to the buyer. The buyer can resell it to whom he pleases. Craig couldn't prevent that."

"Oh, yes he can!" Hastings said angrily. "You don't know how maliciously clever he is. He claims that he has a reversionary creative interest in every picture he paints."

"A what?" Latin asked.

"A reversionary creative interest. There is no such thing. I think he just made it up himself. But he says that the mere thought of one of his pictures being in my wife's possession would be such a mental torture to him that he couldn't paint any more and that he would sue her for a million dollars on the grounds that she was robbing him of his talent and means of livelihood."

"He wouldn't get very far."

Hastings tapped the linoleum tabletop. "Far enough, Mr. Latin! Far enough! He couldn't win any such fantastic suit, of course. But he certainly would file it. He's just the type. And if he did file it, the newspapers would get hold of it and put it all over the front pages. Can you think of the dreadful humiliation that would mean for my wife? The whole country would laugh at her!"

"Oh," said Latin.

"So," Hastings said earnestly, "Winston Wentworth Craig must consent to sell her some of his pictures! Her reputation as an art patron and her peace of mind are at stake! And she must obtain those pictures at once! At once!"

"Why?" Latin asked.

"Because she is having an exhibition of her collection at the Keever Art Gallery in just three days. That exhibition would not be complete without some of Craig's pictures. All of her enemies will laugh at her if she doesn't have some of her own cousin's paintings in her collection. If she doesn't, they'll know why. Craig has seen to that."

"I see," said Latin.

HASTINGS SAID impressively: "My wife is willing to pay up to five thousand dollars for each Craig picture you can get him to consent to sell her."

Latin sat very still. "I thought you said five thousand dollars per picture."

"I did. They are selling currently for about a thousand dollars apiece."

"One thousand," Latin said dreamily. "Five thousand. Mr. Hastings, you've made yourself a deal. I'll get Craig's consent to sell her some pictures if I have to kill him doing it."

"Oh, no!" Hastings said, horrified. "Mr. Latin! Please! Nothing like that!"

"Half kill him, then," Latin compromised.

Hastings looked very doubtful. "Mr.—ah—Guiterrez said you had just gotten out of jail. He was—ah—joking, no doubt?"

"He never jokes. I did just get out."

"Oh," said Hastings uneasily. "And—ah—what were you charged with?"

"Compounding a felony."

"I'm not familiar with legal terms—"

Latin said: "I was charged with paying some gentlemen to return some jewelry they stole from a client of mine and forgetting to ask the gentlemen what their names were or where the police could find them."

"Did you—ah—do that?"

"Certainly not," said Latin. "I merely paid a reward for the return of some jewelry that had been inadvertently lost."

"Lost." Hastings repeated vaguely. "Stolen. Reward. Buying back. It doesn't seem to me there is very much difference…."

Latin smiled. "Just the difference between sitting here and sitting in the county jail, cell three, north tier, that's all."

"Oh," said Hastings. "Well—please look into this matter at once, Mr. Latin. Time is of the very essence. I can't over-emphasize the importance—"

"I'll get right on my horse."

"Winston Wentworth Craig lives at 345 B, Greene Street. You'd best go there now. He works at night, and he's never there in the daytime. I haven't mentioned it, but

WATCH ME KILL YOU! 15

he has an—ah—unpleasant disposition. He can be most insulting—"

"So can I."

"Then I'll leave you—"

"Not without paying for that brandy, you won't," said Guiterrez, suddenly appearing beside the booth. "And I know how much you drank, too, because I marked the bottle. It'll cost you just three bucks."

"Three dollars!" Hastings exclaimed. "But I only had one very small—"

"So you want an argument, do you?" said Guiterrez. He called to one of the waiters: "Dick, go out in the kitchen and get me my cleaver. The sharp one."

Hastings swallowed. "Well, on the other hand, rather than make an issue—"

"Three bucks," said Guiterrez. "Count it out on the table and no back-chat."

CHAPTER TWO
MURDER FOR ART'S SAKE

GREENE STREET had once been a cowpath, and the city fathers had never taken the time or trouble to straighten it out and brush it off and make a modern thoroughfare out of it. Now, as it always had, it wandered in draggling loops between the river and the sullenly massive factories of the industrial section, crossing more conventional streets at any old careless angle, making blocks as weirdly shaped as the pieces of a jigsaw puzzle. It was old and lazy and tattered and nobody cared, least of all the people who lived on it.

The cement blocks that made up the narrow sidewalk had risen in some places and sunk in others, and Latin had the impression of climbing up and down a flatly elongated stairway. The dusk hid the soot streaks, and the houses were all the same depressed gray color, squatting close together and silent, down a little from the street level.

Latin found 345 by the process of counting from the corner. It was a thin starved-looking building with brilliantly artificial light gleaming through the tall windows on its second floor. There were no lights downstairs, and Latin groped his way down three cement steps and along a narrow brick walk to the front porch.

A cigarette tip made a sudden bright red dot in the black shadow of the front door, and a woman's hoarsely pleasant voice said: "What do you want, sonny?"

Latin tapped the brim of his hat politely. "Looking for Winston Wentworth Craig."

"He doesn't live here."

"I'm still looking for him."

A light switch snapped, and a bulb in the porch ceiling glowed with weary brilliance, revealing the woman who was standing in the doorway. She had brown hair that was cropped carelessly short and tousled like a boy's. There were blue shadows under her eyes, and her lips were twisted into a cynical half smile. Her cigarette was in a long ivory holder, and her long fingernails were stained a dark bloodred. She was wearing a cotton hostess coat and open-toed sandals. She regarded Latin with a detached, disinterested air.

"Shall I advance three paces and give the password?" he asked.

"Try it, and I'll stick this cigarette right in your eye."

"Which eye?" Latin asked curiously.

"The left one, I think."

"That's O.K., then. The left one's my glass eye."

Latin came up the steps and on the porch. The woman was lounging against the edge of the door, and she didn't move, but she did smile a little.

"Hello," said Latin.

She nodded her cropped head. "Hello. What's your name?"

"Max Latin."

"Latin," she repeated thoughtfully. "There was a Latin in the papers the other day—also in jail."

"I'm that one."

"I thought so. Private detective on the shady side, eh?"

"Not shady," Latin denied. "Black as night. Got any minor crimes you'd like committed? I'm cutting prices these days because I owe my lawyer some money."

"I'll think it over. Why do you want to see Craig?"

"Who's asking?"

THE WOMAN smiled more broadly. "Nan Carter. You can call me Nan if you want to be formal. The reason I'm curious is that I'm holding off process servers and bill collectors and such vermin until I can pry some back rent out of my distinguished tenant, Mr. Winston Wentworth Craig."

"You wrong me," Latin told her. "I'm an earnest student of the arts, and I am here to purchase paintings in large quantities."

"Who sent you?"

"Remind me to tell you all about it sometime when I'm not busy."

Nan Carter blew a long plume of smoke at him. "In other words, Patricia Wentworth Craig."

"That would be about it."

Nan Carter said: "Craig won't sell her any of his pictures nor let her buy any. Don't you know the setup? He's a genius, or so he claims. Temperamental and like that. He wouldn't touch any of her money. He scorns it. He'd rather borrow from all his friends and forget to pay them back or let me put his rent on the cuff for six months straight."

"I'll change his mind for him."

"How?" she asked.

"I've got a wonderfully persuasive personality and also a pretty fair left hook."

Nan Carter watched him thoughtfully. "Rough stuff, huh? I sort of figured you for that sort of a gent."

"If people get between me and a nice juicy fee, is it my fault if they get trampled in the rush?" Latin asked reasonably.

"No," Nan Carter admitted, "and I think perhaps our dough-heavy friend has finally figured the right way to approach her dear cousin. He's nasty, but he's yellow as a daisy. The stairs are right there. There's no lock on the studio door. Don't bother to knock. Just go in and make yourself at home."

Latin went through the door and along the short length of hall and up the steep, shadowy slant of the narrow stairway. At the top there was another and shorter hall with the black well of back stairs at the far end of it. There was a door midway along the hall, and Latin went to it, turned the knob quietly and pushed it open.

The bright light from inside the studio jumped at him, blinding him momentarily, and then he caught the whole scene in one flashing split second and stepped quietly into the studio and pushed the door shut behind him.

The partitions had been knocked out and the whole upper story of the house was one enormous room with its ceiling the high, peaked slant of the roof. There was an easel against the far wall with powerful daylight floor lamps set in front of it, their reflectors focused so there would be no slightest shadow on the canvas it held.

The man was lying in front of the easel, crumpled up there, with his blue painter's smock making a bright pile of color against the dull black of the floor. His face was turned toward Latin, and his eyes were wide and bulging and glassy. There was no blood, but the man was dead.

LATIN STOOD against the door apparently relaxed, while he turned his head slowly a little at a time, searching the shadows that clung in the corners of the big room. On the other side of the easel there was an open window, and through it Latin could hear the faraway hum of traffic and see the faint glow of lights from the uptown district.

There was no sound and no movement in the studio. After a moment Latin walked quietly across to the limp form in the blue smock and knelt down beside it. He felt one of the man's bony wrists, and it was warm in his hand, but there was no faintest pulse.

Latin pursed his lips and began to whistle soundlessly to himself. He started to get up and then stopped, staring at an object under the easel.

It was a woman's shoe. A dancing pump delicately made of thin strips of crisscrossing red leather with a high, stilt-like heel. Latin took a handkerchief from his pocket and, using it to cover his hand, carefully picked the slipper up.

It was an expensive one, handmade for a short high-arched foot, and Latin was looking inside it for the maker's name when he heard the hinge on the door squeak softly.

Latin moved with instant, catlike coordination. He flipped the slipper out the open window, came up to his feet and pivoted, crouching warily.

"Hold it right there," the man in the doorway whispered.

Latin stayed rigidly immovable.

The man in the doorway was small and slight, and the overcoat he wore made him seem more so. The overcoat was enormous. It looked as though it had been made for someone three feet taller and two feet wider. It hung in shapeless heavy folds, the skirts brushing the floor. The high collar was turned up and fastened with a strap across the front, hiding everything of the man's face but a pasty white triangle from his chin to the bottoms of the huge dark-lensed glasses he wore. He had a black flop-brimmed hat pulled down over his forehead.

In his right hand he was holding a thick stubby-barreled automatic. He moved it warningly and then reached behind him with his left hand and carefully closed the door, holding the knob so the latch wouldn't click.

"What did you throw out of the window?"

"You guess," Latin invited.

The man watched him in silence for a second, the lenses of the glasses like shiny blacked-out portholes. "Move over to your right a little," he ordered in the same soft whisper.

Latin moved one step sideways and then another. The other man began to move, too, following the opposite rim of the invisible circle that separated them. He moved in light, mincing steps, as gracefully as a dancer.

"Stand still now."

Latin obeyed. The other man had reached the easel. He stood with one foot on either side of the blue-smocked body on the floor. Still watching Latin, he leaned down and began to grope behind the easel with his left hand.

There was a little scraping clatter, and he brought his hand out holding three small, square canvases.

"Don't move," he whispered, and he began to travel sideways on his mincing circle toward the door.

Latin suddenly realized what was getting away from him. "Oh, no," he said. "No, you don't. I've got first call on those pictures. Put them down."

The man in the overcoat stopped, and his tongue flicked over the thin red of his lips.

"I mean it," Latin said. "You're not walking out of here with those pictures."

THE MAN in the overcoat fired at him without the slightest warning. Latin flopped flat on his face on the floor, kicked himself over and rolled frantically for the wall. The automatic whacked three times more, and the bullets dug into the floor on both sides of Latin with sinister little snaps.

Latin banged into the wall and sat up, flipping his own stubby .38 out of the waistband of his trousers. He was just in time to see the studio door close and hear the latch snap with quiet finality.

Latin heaved himself up and charged across the studio. He was blind, fighting mad, and he jerked the door open again heedlessly and jumped out into the hall.

He could see down the front stairs into the empty front hall, and he whirled around and headed for the rear stairs. He had reached the top when the little man in the overcoat materialized out of the shadow against the banister and extended a leg deftly in front of him.

Latin tried to hurdle it and didn't quite get over. He caught one ankle, and he went headfirst down into the blackness of the stairwell. He managed to half turn while he was still in the air, and his back smashed against the banister with breathtaking force.

He hit the stairs, sprawled full length, did two complete forward somersaults, and landed at the bottom of the stairway in an awkward heap. For a while he couldn't get up and he couldn't breathe, and red-streaked blackness whirled around inside his head like a pinwheel.

From the front hall the automatic whacked sharply again, and Nan Carter screamed. A door slammed shut.

Latin got up and fell down on the stairs. He started to crawl upward, still clutching his revolver. His legs wouldn't work properly, and he slipped back two steps for every three he climbed. He kept right on going, clawing himself along by main force and clumsiness.

Finally he poked his head above the last step. Looking at him from the same level on the front stairs was the face of Nan Carter. Her cropped hair was even more tousled now, and her blue-shadowed eyes were wide.

"My God!" she said hoarsely. "What—what—"

Latin got up the rest of the steps and leaned against the wall for support. He made three attempts and finally managed to gulp air into his lungs.

"Where'd he go?"

"You're asking me, are you?" Nan Carter said, also drawing a deep breath. "I don't know, and I don't care, and I hope he stays there from now on. I heard the shots up here, and I opened my door to take a look. He was right in front of me. He shot once. That was all the hint I needed. I slammed the door and ducked."

"Did he—have pictures?"

She stared at him incredulously. "Pictures! Are you punch-drunk? He might have been carrying battleships on both shoulders for all I know. I just saw that gun. What in the devil were you two doing up here?"

"Call the police," said Latin. "Craig's dead."

Nan Carter gasped. "Dead!"

"Yes. Got a telephone here?"

She was still staring incredulously. "Dead? Telephone? Yes. Downstairs in my apartment."

LATIN FELT his way along the hall and went rubbery-legged down the front stairs. There was a neat round bullet hole in the panel of Nan Carter's apartment door. She opened it, and Latin went into a small cluttered living room and plopped himself down on the divan with a sigh of relief.

"The telephone is over there," Nan Carter told him, pointing to it.

"You call," Latin said, "I'm out of wind. The number is Madison 5050. Tell them that Craig's dead and somebody just tried to use me to make it two of a kind."

She dialed the number while Latin held his head in his hands, both palms tight against his temples, trying by main force to dispel the fog that seemed to shroud his brain.

"They're coming," Nan Carter said, hanging up the receiver.

Latin looked up, wincing when the light from the floor lamp hit his eyes. "This Craig—did he have an agent? Anyone who sold his pictures for him?"

She nodded blankly. "Yes. Name of Haggerty. You need a drink or a doctor or something."

"Drink," said Latin.

She opened a wooden-doored corner cabinet and brought out a flat pint bottle that was half full of cheap whiskey. Holding it in both hands, Latin upended it and took three big swigs. The whiskey was as fast as it was rough. It went down his throat like a powder train and started a raging fire in his stomach, but it took the shroud off his brain instantly.

"Whew!" he said, catching his breath again.

Nan Carter took the bottle away from him and had a drink out of it herself.

Latin said: "Have you got a directory? I want to look up this Haggerty's number."

"Two of them are written on the wall, there above the telephone. Craig was always calling Haggerty, trying to get advances. One is his office and the other is his home. I don't know which is which."

Latin found the pencil-scrawled numbers and deciphered them. He called the first, and he could hear the buzz of the phone ringing at the other end, but there was no answer. He tried the other, and after the second ring a weary feminine voice answered.

"Hello?"

"Can I speak to Mr. Haggerty, please?" Latin asked.

"He isn't home."

"Can you tell me where I can get him?"

"Hah!" said the feminine voice. "That I certainly cannot. He's out drinking somewhere with his ratty artist clients."

"When he comes in, please tell him that one of his clients—Winston Wentworth Craig—just died, and that he'd better scamper down to Craig's studio as fast as he can."

"I'll tell him if he ever comes home and he's not too drunk to understand when he does."

A siren began its eery song somewhere close as Latin hung up the receiver.

CHAPTER THREE
LATIN EXPLAINS

DETECTIVE INSPECTOR WALTERS, Homicide, was a tall, gauntly somber man with a face that was long and lined and cynical. He stood now with his arms folded across the hollow of his chest, gloomily watching the medical examiner work on the sprawled body in the blue smock.

The medical examiner stood up at last and nodded at his two assistants. "O.K., boys. Haul it off."

"Well, what?" Walters asked, as the assistants rolled the body on a stretcher and covered it with a sheet.

"He's dead," said the medical examiner, "or did you know? The reason he's dead is because someone was unkind enough to break his neck for him by giving him a very nifty rabbit punch with some instrument with a protuberance on it about so square."

He held his thumb and forefinger about three-quarters of an inch apart to illustrate.

"A hammer?" Walters hazarded.

The medical examiner scratched his head. "No... I don't think so. Maybe a very light tack hammer. It was a very sharp blow with something that wasn't very heavy. The murderer knew just exactly where to hit to snap a spine. I couldn't have done a neater job myself."

"How about that?" Walters asked, pointing to a rusty hammer the fingerprint men had left on a chair.

"No. It's too big and too heavy."

"Hell," said Walters, disappointed. "The boys didn't find anything else around here…. How long has he been dead?"

The medical examiner didn't even bother to reply. He simply looked disgusted.

Walters sighed. "Well—anything else?"

"He was a junkie."

"Can you tell what brand?"

"Either morphine or heroin, with the odds on morphine. Call me up after the autopsy and I'll tell you more."

Walters nodded, and the medical examiner went out after his assistants and their loaded stretcher. Walters stood in front of the easel staring at the picture it held, rocking back and forth gently. The uniformed patrolman on guard at the door lounged lazily against the wall, exploring his teeth with a sharpened match. The studio was silent except for the gentle squeak-squeak of Walters's shoe soles.

Finally he turned around and said: "How do you feel now?"

Latin was sitting on the edge of the models' platform holding his head in his hands. "To be frank," he said, looking up, "not so hot. I've got bees buzzing in my belfry."

Walters turned back to the picture. "What do you think of this here?" He tilted the picture so Latin could see it.

"Pretty good," Latin said.

It was a portrait, almost completed. It was unmistakably a likeness of the man who had been lying dead in front of it, and it was a startlingly good one. It had a vigor and a sweep that was lifelike. The eyes were half closed, and the mouth was twisted into a cynical little smile.

Walters observed: "He looks like he was amused because somebody popped him, and I wish he could speak up and tell me who it was, because if the bird that did it sneaked up behind Craig while he was painting, then this Craig in the picture was certainly watching him do it. Kind of a funny thing for a detective to think of, isn't it? I mean, a guy in a picture watching the guy he's the picture of get the old socko."

"Very funny," said Latin sourly.

"A little confusing," Walters admitted. He shrugged. "Oh, well. Off to work we go. Suppose you start talking, Latin. Don't lie any more than is absolutely necessary."

"He," Latin said, pointing at the picture, "is and was Winston Wentworth Craig, and he's the first cousin of Patricia Wentworth Craig."

Walters opened his mouth and shut it. "Oh-oh! The one with the heavy dough?"

"That one."

WALTERS SIGHED. "Then it's up to me to walk soft and talk small, I suppose. Why do I always have to get stuck with the hot ones? It seems like they could put me out to pasture or something in my old age. So what were you doing up here?"

Latin said: "Patricia Wentworth Craig hired me to buy some of Winston Wentworth Craig's pictures—or rather, her husband did."

Walters looked skeptical. "Come, come. You'll have to get a little more speedy than that, Latin."

"Fact," said Latin. "Winston hated his dear Cousin Patricia because Patricia had refused to lend him dough so he could study art, so he studied it anyway and got to be good. Then he refused to sell her any of his pictures and needled her by telling everyone that the reason he wouldn't was because she was too dumb to appreciate them."

Walters looked more skeptical. "I'm listening, but not for much longer."

"Patricia collects modern art, and she's giving an exhibit of her collection in a couple of days. She had to have some of Cousin Winston's pictures in the exhibit, because if she didn't everybody would boob her. She hired me to come down here and talk Winston into selling her some."

"Nuts," said Walters. "The crunchy kind. Why didn't she just—"

"Yes, yes," Latin interrupted. "She couldn't buy any of Craig's pictures from anyone else, because he said that would cause him great mental agony and he'd sue her."

"He couldn't—"

"He could start suit, and if he did the newspapers would blow it up big, and that would mean that the general populace would give Patricia the horse laugh along with all the artists and art collectors who were already doing it."

"Ummm," said Walters. "This all sounds very much on the corny side to me."

"Not necessarily. Get the setup. Here's a dame that has probably always been able to buy anything she wanted in the world and in addition is very proud of herself for being an expert on modern art. This Craig cousin of hers was attacking her on both fronts, and people were giving her the old snicker because of it. People aren't supposed to laugh at you when you have fifty million dollars."

"I ain't laughing at her," said Walters. "So maybe this is true and they hired you to get the pictures. But why? You don't claim to be an expert, now, do you?"

"I'm crooked. They figured I'd chisel the pictures out of Craig with one of my snide tricks. I would have, too."

Walters rubbed the lobe of his ear, squinting. "You know, when I was a kid back in Iowa there used to be a banker in town who called himself Honest John. One fine day he went south with about thirty thousand dollars worth of deposits."

"Very interesting," Latin commented.

"Yeah. Ever since then I've doubted people who go around claiming how honest they are. I think maybe that works backwards sometimes, too."

"Such as how?" Latin asked.

"You. You talk about bein' crooked so much, I doubt if you are. I think that's just your front. I think maybe you're honest."

"That's slander," Latin said indignantly. "I'll sue you. I'm as crooked as a swastika."

"Uh-huh. You may be a trifle speedy on the turns, but I think that's as far as it goes. But let me tell you that if the boys in the district attorney's office ever catch you in a corner they're going to tear your ears off. They're pretty griped about you slipping out of that compounding a felony rap. So you came up here to buy pictures—then what happened?"

"Craig was lying dead on the floor."

"See any deadly weapons around?"

"No," Latin said.

"All right. Go on."

"Here's where the story really gets ripe. I'd no more than found out the guy was dead, when in comes a little gent in dark glasses and a big overcoat and sticks me up and grabs some of Craig's pictures. I tried to argue with him, and he started blowing at me. I know that sounds—"

WALTERS'S EYES looked narrow and shiny. "Little gent in a big overcoat and dark glasses. Did he have a pan that looked like it had just been pushed in a flour barrel and a flop-brimmed hat and sport a Spanish mail-order automatic?"

Latin stared at him. "Why, yes."

"McTeague!" Walters snarled. He paced back and forth across the studio, muttering profanity.

The policeman on guard at the door had straightened up alertly and was watching Latin.

"What's what?" Latin asked.

"We're not funning now," said Walters. "I want that little weasel, and I want him bad. You heard that a cop named Gardner got killed a couple of months ago?"

Latin frowned. "I remember something about it. Trying to stop a store holdup, wasn't he?"

"No. That was just for the papers. He was on guard at a school crosswalk on the north side. There'd been reports coming in from that school and others that some of the kids were acting funny. The doctors thought maybe it was dope of some kind, although we couldn't shake anything loose from any of the kids. So the cops were keeping an eye open. Gardner spotted this funny-looking guy with a candy wagon prowling around the school grounds, so he strolls over to take a look. He didn't even have a chance to say hello. The guy just started shooting. Five times he let go, and the fifth one got Gardner in the stomach. The guy was this McTeague you saw."

"Five times," Latin said. "And only one hit. How close was he to Gardner?"

"About ten feet."

"That's lousy shooting. I figured that it was a miracle he missed me, but now I'm not so sure."

"He killed a cop," said Walters coldly. "A damned good cop. We want that baby. Can you tell me any more about him."

"No. Except that he talked in a whisper. He did know his way around this studio, though. Probably he was the one who was furnishing Craig with dope. Why don't you ask the doll downstairs if she knows anything about him?"

Walters nodded at the policeman in the doorway. "Go get her."

They waited for a moment, and then Nan Carter came in the studio ahead of the policeman. She still wore her cotton housecoat, and she was smoking another cigarette in her long ivory holder. She looked quite cheerful and a little bit intoxicated and she nodded her cropped head casually at Latin and said: "Hi. Are you pinched?"

"Not yet," Latin said. "This is Inspector Walters. This is Nan Carter, Walters."

Walters said: "I'd like to ask you about what happened here tonight."

"Plenty, ain't it so?" Nan Carter inquired. "Well, let's see. Latin came along and asked for Craig, and I stalled him a bit because I figured that girl might have sent him over to put the bite on Craig, and I wanted first chance at any money he might have for his back rent."

WALTERS ASKED: "What girl?"

"She used to model for Craig. She got into trouble, and she claimed Craig was the cause of it all. I don't doubt that he was. He was a trifle on the rat side. She pestered him for weeks, trying to get him to marry her or give her money. I used to ring his doorbell when I saw her coming, and he'd dodge out the back way."

"She been around lately?"

"No. Not for the last week or so."

"What's her name?"

"Mona something or other. She didn't kill him if that's what's worrying you. She was crazy about him, and besides, she wouldn't have nerve enough."

"I'll just look her up, anyway," said Walters. "O.K. Go on with your story."

"Well, Latin came up here, and he hadn't been here a minute before the war broke out. I'd gone in to powder my nose, and I heard people stamping around and shots and the house falling down in general, so I opened my door to see what was going on. That little rat of a McTeague was right in front of the door. He shot and I ducked—but fast."

"McTeague," Walters repeated casually. "So you know his name?"

Nan Carter looked surprised. "Of course. He came around here every week."

"Good friend of Craig's, eh?"

She shrugged. "I guess so. He seems slimy enough to qualify. Anyway, he paid me some of Craig's back rent once."

Walters was watching her narrowly. "How did that happen?"

"I just asked him for it, and he paid."

"You're a liar," said Walters.

"Tut, tut," said Nan Carter amiably.

"You knew Craig was on the dope, and you also knew McTeague was selling it to him. You shook him down."

"Did I, now?" Nan Carter said.

"Yes. Instead of reporting McTeague to the police."

"Shame on me," said Nan Carter, and blew a long plume of smoke in Walters's face.

Walters reached out and slapped her hand. The ivory holder and its cigarette flipped through the air. The holder snapped in two when it hit the floor. The policeman stepped forward casually to put his foot on the cigarette.

Walters said: "Don't get smart with me."

Nan Carter's eyes looked heavy-lidded and sleepy. "Just for that I'm not answering any more questions."

"You will," Walters promised grimly. "Keenan, take her down to the station."

The policeman came forward and put his hand on Nan Carter's arm. "Come on along, now."

She fell into him. She did it very neatly and so quickly that she slid down to a sitting position on the floor before he could catch her. She sat there and beamed placidly up at Walters.

"Carry her," he ordered quietly.

Keenan bent down and picked her up without the slightest effort. He carried her across the studio, and as she went out the door she flipped her hand at Latin in a casual farewell salute.

Latin cleared his throat. "I wouldn't, if I were you."

Walters's face was set grimly. "I want McTeague."

"You haven't got anything to hold her on. She'll hang a suit for false arrest on you."

Walters jerked his shoulders irritably. "I suppose so. Oh, hell!" He went to the door and whistled shrilly. "Keenan! Bring her back up here."

CHAPTER FOUR
A LADY GETS A LIFT

KEENAN'S FEET thudded on the stairs, and he carried Nan Carter back into the studio and stood there holding her.

Latin said: "Nan, Walters is a little on the edgy side. McTeague's a cop shooter, and Walters is very anxious to get a grip on him."

Nan Carter looked at Walters inquiringly.

"All right," said Walters. "I apologize, and I'll buy you another holder."

She smiled. "Never mind. I've got a dozen. I just don't like being slapped around. You can put me down now, mister. Thanks for the lift."

Keenan stood her on her feet and went indifferently back to his station at the door.

"Well?" said Nan Carter. "Ask me more. I honestly didn't know Craig was a dope fiend. I thought there was something wrong with him, but that never occurred to me. I really did shake McTeague down, though. Craig used to throw parties all the time, and they were really dillies. I came to one once, and I left fast. I'm not easy to shock, either.

"Craig used to show dirty motion pictures to his lovely guests. I had McTeague tagged for that racket, although I wasn't sure. I thought it was worth a throw, though. I was broke. So I put it up to him. I sort of leered like they do in the movies and told him I wanted some of Craig's rent."

"What happened?" Walters asked.

She shivered. "He paid. Fifty dollars. Didn't say a word. He just stood there and looked at me for about five minutes, as though he was measuring me for a coffin. I was good and scared. I kept out of his way after that. I got the idea he could be a very nasty proposition if he wanted to be."

"He is," said Walters. "You don't know how lucky you were that he didn't do more than look."

"Oh yes, I do," said Nan Carter. "I'm getting the chills all over again."

"Did Patricia Wentworth Craig or her husband, Bernard Hastings, ever come up here?" Latin asked.

"She did—once. She and Craig had a whopper of a row. He threw her out finally. I mean—threw. Hastings came around a dozen times or so. He and Craig got very, very chummy."

"Chummy?" Latin repeated, puzzled.

"For a while. It was easy to figure out. Hastings thought he could butter up Craig and get on the good side of him and persuade him to sell some pictures to Patricia. Craig knew that was the idea. He just played Hastings along— drinking his liquor and borrowing money from him and letting him pay for the parties, and then when he got tired, he gave Hastings the razzberry and kicked him out. That Hastings is soft-brained, if you ask me. He should have known Craig would see right through him. Craig was no fool. What killed him, anyway?"

"Someone hit him on the back of the neck and broke his spine," Walters answered absently.

Nan Carter looked at Latin with raised eyebrows.

Latin shook his head. "Not guilty. He was laid out like a rug when I arrived."

"Was the back door locked?" Walters asked.

"Never," said Nan Carter.

Walters nodded. "I want that McTeague. Anything more you can tell me about him?"

"No," she said. "After the rent incident I didn't want any part of him. Latin said he was a cop shooter. You mean he killed a policeman?"

"Yeah. I want him."

"What else do *you* know about him?" Latin asked curiously. "You just said he downed Gardner."

Walters was frowning. "He had his reasons. The doctors were right. The kids were getting dope—morphine—and he was selling it to them. He had it fixed up in candy. Very clever fellow. The kids talked fast afterward, because Gardner was very popular with them. McTeague had told them that the candy contained caffeine and that it would pep them up for examinations and stuff, but that they shouldn't let on to anyone because even if the stuff was perfectly harmless, parents would be apt to be sticky about it. You know how kids go for secrets like that, and so did McTeague."

Nan Carter looked a little sick. "Morphine—to kids—"

"Yes," said Walters. "Very, very little of it. Not enough to make them goofy—but enough to give them a lift and enough to put them on the habit if they kept at it."

THEY WERE silent for a second, and then Walters nodded at Nan Carter.

"If you ever see him again, get behind something solid and start screaming. But be sure what you're behind will stop a bullet, because he'll shoot."

She shivered. "Right-o."

Someone shouted something from the lower floor, and Keenan, the policeman on guard at the door, put his head out into the hall.

"What?"

The voice below shouted something else and Keenan turned back to Walters.

"There's a guy down below who says his name is Haggerty. He wants in."

"He's Craig's agent," Latin explained.

"Send him up," Walters ordered.

Keenan relayed the order, and feet thumped raggedly on the stairs. A fat little man with a red, round face came puffing through the door. He was carrying a cane, and he braced the rubber tip of it on the floor in front of him and leaned the soft bulge of his stomach against it for a support, regarding them all.

"Hah!" he said explosively. "I told him a good many times he was such a louse he ought to go and kill himself, but I never thought he'd do it."

"He didn't," said Walters. "Somebody broke his neck for him. Is this actually Haggerty, and is he actually Winston Wentworth Craig's manager, Miss Carter?"

"Yes," she said. "Hello, you greasy bloodsucker."

Haggerty took off his hat, revealing close-cropped red hair. "Miss Carter. It is delighted I am to see you, even in such sad circumstances."

"You and your phoney Irish dialect. Will you kindly go to hell with my best regards?"

Haggerty beamed at her. "Your wish is my command, and indeed it surely is, my dear."

Nan Carter turned to Walters. "Through with me now? Being in the same room with this fat rat makes me queasy."

"All through," said Walters, "for the moment. Stick around down below."

She sauntered out of the door.

Walters waited until her footsteps had gone down the stairs and then said to Haggerty: "She doesn't seem to like you."

"A pity," said Haggerty. "Indeed, it saddens the heart of me to the point of breaking."

"Why doesn't she like you?"

Haggerty smiled benignly. "And your name, sir?"

"Inspector Walters. Homicide. Why doesn't she like you?"

"It is indeed a great pleasure to make your acquaintance, sir. She does not like me because I won't act as her agent."

"Why won't you?"

Haggerty waggled a fat forefinger at him. "Indeed, my dear Inspector, for the one best reason of all, of course. Her stuff won't sell, and it won't sell because it is no good."

"What does she do—paint?"

"No, no. She's a sculptress—she says. All impressionistic and very, very lousy."

"Why did you come here tonight?"

"Someone called me and asked me to."

"I did," said Latin.

"What for?" Walters demanded.

"Business," said Latin. "Can I talk to him alone?"

"Ha, ha," said Walters.

Latin shrugged. "Haggerty, my name is Latin."

HAGGERTY BLINKED eyes that were a bright steely blue in spite of being slightly bloodshot at the corners. "Indeed? The gentleman who had some slight—difficulty over some stolen jewels recently?"

"Yes."

"Well, well," said Haggerty thoughtfully.

"Do you have any of Craig's pictures now—on sale?"

Haggerty rubbed his chin. "In a manner of speaking, yes. That is, he had three finished that he was going to deliver to me tomorrow."

"Deliver to you to sell as his agent?"

"Right, sir."

"You can't be an agent for a dead man."

Haggerty grinned. "Ah, yes. The deal was completed before his death. I advanced him money and the title of the pictures passed to me then. I have contracts to prove it. He was just holding the pictures temporarily because he wanted to put some finishing touches on them."

Latin pointed to the easel. "Is that one of them?"

"No. It isn't completed, and wouldn't be worth much if it was, as I told him. Who wants to look at an artist's face? But Craig liked himself, even if no one else did."

"I want to make a deal with you," Latin said. "I want you to sell me those three completed pictures for a thousand apiece. That's the current market value for them."

"Ah, no," said Haggerty merrily. "They'll double in value, now there's to be no more of them. If you'd like to bid—"

"No. Take my offer or get nothing."

"Nothing?" Haggerty inquired. "Now I think not, indeed. I'll take the pictures, and there's a strong market—"

"Where are the pictures?" Latin asked.

Haggerty pointed with his cane. "Right over—" He turned around to look at Latin. His smile was strained at the corners now. "They're supposed to be under that easel. He always kept the completed ones there."

Latin shrugged complacently. He said nothing.

Haggerty's smile was completely gone. "And what is this now, please?"

"I'll be fair about it," said Latin. "Fifteen hundred apiece and five hundred to you for acting as my agent on the resale. Take it or leave it."

Haggerty's blue eyes opened wide. "Indeed, now. But the pictures are really mine, sir. I took title as security for the money I advanced to Craig."

"All right," Latin said. "Hunt for the pictures."

Haggerty puffed out his fat cheeks and sucked them in again. He looked calculatingly from Latin to Walters and back to Latin again.

"They're not here?"

"No," said Latin.

"Are they in your possession?"

"No."

"I warn you that I can identify them."

"Go ahead," Latin invited indifferently.

"And you, sir," said Haggerty to Walters. "A police officer, do nothing but stand there—"

"I'm doing more than standing," said Walters, watching Latin narrowly. "I'm listening, and what I hear I don't like so very well. Where are those pictures, Latin?"

"McTeague took them, like I told you."

"Yes. And where they are, McTeague will be. I want that McTeague. Where, Latin?"

"I don't know."

"Latin," said Walters very softly, "don't get in between me and McTeague or I'll run you down. I mean it. Do you know where he is?"

"No."

Haggerty cleared his throat. "On due consideration, Mr. Latin, I think I'll take your kind offer and thank you."

"Right," said Latin.

"Latin—" Walters said warningly.

The voice shouted from the hall below, and Kennan put his head out the door again.

"What?" He listened and relayed the information to Walters. "There's a guy and a dame downstairs. Say they're related to the stiff."

Walters groaned. "Send them up—politely, Keenan, very politely. In fact, you may go down and escort them, Keenan. Remember to salute."

"And remember you're my agent," Latin said to Haggerty.

Haggerty put his smile on again. "Ah, yes. And I think matters become slightly clearer."

"Do you?" Walters asked sourly. "I don't."

BERNARD HASTINGS and a woman came in the studio ahead of a suddenly deferential Keenan. Hastings looked really scared now. His plump face was a yellowish white, and he stared right and left with fearful bulging eyes, as though he expected a gory body to leap at him out of any corner. When he saw Latin, his eyes bulged even more, and he flicked a tongue across lips that were suddenly dry and colorless.

The woman with him said in a harsh, high voice: "Who is in charge here?"

Walters stepped forward. "Inspector Walters, ma'am. Homicide."

"I am Patricia Wentworth Craig."

She wouldn't have needed to identify herself. Her thin, arrogant features were pictured in the papers as often as the most popular movie star's. She was blond and tall and very erect, high-shouldered, and she walked and talked and looked as though she was sure she was better than anyone else and that everyone knew it. She was wearing a long chinchilla coat with a black formal dress under it. She had a diamond bracelet a good two inches wide on her left wrist. It was the only jewelry she wore.

"Yes, ma'am," said Walters.

She looked at Haggerty. "What are you doing here?"

Haggerty bowed. "Endeavoring to help in my humble way, dear lady."

She shrugged in disgust and pointed at Latin. "Who is he?"

Hastings said in a croak: "That—that is the man—"

"What man?" she said impatiently.

Hastings swallowed. "The one—Latin."

She looked Latin up and down. "I see. Then you've apprehended him already, and there's no need for us to stay. My husband is a fool, Inspector, and you'll have to excuse him."

Hastings winced but made no effort to deny the accusation.

"Yes, ma'am?" Walters said cautiously.

"Yes. This man Latin is a criminal. He just got out of jail, as you probably know. My husband, in his stupid way, decided for some reason to hire Latin to purchase some pictures from my cousin. My cousin refused, for reasons that are none of your affair, and Latin killed him, intending to steal some pictures from him, I have no doubt. You will see to it that he is hanged, of course. Good evening."

Walters cleared his throat. "Well, ma'am, we're not so sure Latin killed your cousin."

She swung back toward him. "What? Nonsense! If he didn't, who did?"

"Well, we don't know yet."

She stared icily. "Don't be a fool. Of course Latin killed him, and naturally he'd deny it. You police have what you call a third degree, haven't you? Well, use it. *Make* him confess. No matter what methods you use, I'll see to it that no one ever objects to them."

Latin looked at Haggerty. Haggerty was grinning. Latin's greenish eyes began to glow slightly.

Patricia Wentworth Craig was examining the portrait on the easel. "I'll take that one, and Haggerty, you will deliver any other pictures you have to me at once."

"Indeed?" said Haggerty politely.

"He hasn't any," said Latin.

She looked at him. "Did you speak?"

"Yes, Your Majesty. I said Haggerty hasn't any of Craig's pictures. He did own three of them, but he sold them to me. I'll sell them to you for five thousand apiece, in accordance with my agreement with your husband."

She laughed mockingly. "Five thousand! What utter and complete absurdity!"

Hastings said: "But, my dear, I—I did—"

"Be quiet!"

Hastings swallowed hard and remained silent.

"Five thousand," Latin said blandly.

"You must be a fool as well as a murderer," said Patricia Wentworth Craig coldly. "You have nothing to show in writing, and in this state a contract involving a sum of more than five hundred dollars is not enforceable unless it is in writing. I can buy all of my cousin's pictures I want now for a quarter of five thousand dollars."

"On the other hand, no," said Latin blandly.

SHE REALLY looked at him, as though she were seeing him as a person for the first time. "Why can't I?"

"Well, you *could*. But I'd have to sue you if you did."

"Sue me for what?"

Latin smiled. "Well, you see Craig's pictures are unique. They are pictures that Patricia Wentworth Craig—the richest girl in the world—can't buy. That gives them a special value, which was why I invested in them. Now if you should buy some of his pictures—from someone else—then that would reduce the value of the pictures I have, because they wouldn't be unique anymore. So I'd have to sue you for what I'd lose, and if I did I'd have to explain in my complaint just why you couldn't buy any of Craig's pictures while he was alive."

Haggerty blew out his breath in a long sigh, and Walters began to whistle softly to himself.

Patricia Wentworth Craig hissed at her husband: "You stupid oaf! Did you have to tell him everything you knew?"

"I—I—," Hastings said miserably.

"Five thousand," Latin repeated.

She was biting her under lip. "All right. When and where will you deliver them?"

"I won't. You'll come and get them when and where I tell you."

Patricia Wentworth Craig's thin face was white now, and the rouge showed up in ragged red patches on her cheekbones. "All right," she whispered. "But you—you—" She drew in her breath, turning to Walters. "Is he under arrest?"

"Latin?" Walters asked. "Well—"

"If he is, release him at once."

"Yes, ma'am," said Walters meekly. "Have you—changed your mind about him killing your cousin?"

"Of course, you fool. Release him."

Walters nodded at Latin. "You're released."

"Thanks a lot," Latin said mockingly.

Patricia Wentworth Craig turned on her husband. "Well, what are you waiting for? Take me out of here, you blundering numbskull."

"Yes, my dear," said Hastings quickly. He escorted her to the door as carefully as though she were made of spun glass.

Walters waited until they were gone and then took off his hat and wiped his brow with the palm of his hand. *"Whee!* Join the police and have more fun! It's lucky I didn't have you under arrest, Latin. I wouldn't want to cross that dame. She's really as neat a dose of pure poison as I've ever seen, and she could probably get me thrown off the force before I could light a cigar. I think you're going to be a sorry man, Latin, if you play any of your cute tricks on her."

"Five thousand dollars a picture," Haggerty said in a dreamy voice.

"Don't get any ideas," Latin warned.

"Ah, no," said Haggerty, beaming. "No, indeed."

"Do you know a guy by the name of McTeague?" Walters demanded. "Friend of Craig's?"

"No," said Haggerty.

"Well, I guess I'll be running along," said Latin.

"I wish you would," Walters informed him. "You're certainly not much help to me."

CHAPTER FIVE
McTEAGUE MEETS
HIS MAKER

IT WAS an hour later when Latin came into Guiterrez's restaurant again. The crowd had thinned now, and the place wasn't quite so noisy or confused, but almost. Latin sat down in his favorite booth, and he hadn't been there more than five seconds when Guiterrez came through the metal swinging door that led to the kitchen and glowered at him.

"I was hopin' maybe they tossed you in the jail again," he said. "I bet you they got cell three, north tier all cleaned and ready for you by this time."

Latin nodded absently. "Is Pete here?"

"Washin' dishes."

"Tell him to go down to 345 Greene Street and wait outside until the police leave. Tell him to telephone you here when they go and also to find out whether they leave anyone on guard. Tell him to keep out of sight."

"Tell—tell—tell," said Guiterrez sourly. "Suppose you tell me who's gonna wash the dishes."

"You."

Guiterrez swelled up. "Me! I'll have you know that I was the master chef—"

"All right. Throw the dishes away and buy new ones. In the meantime, bring me a telephone."

The little waiter in the baggy, grease-stained coat came up with a bottle of brandy and a glass and put them down on the table in front of Latin.

"Get him the telephone, Dick," Guiterrez ordered. "He's pretending like he's important again."

Guiterrez stamped back through the swinging door into the kitchen, muttering to himself. Dick brought Latin a portable telephone, and Latin plugged in on a concealed connection behind the chintz curtain at the rear of the booth.

He sat for several moments, staring absently upward at the smoke layers that floated under the stained ceiling. Finally he nodded once to himself and dialed the number of Haggerty's home.

The phone rang several times, and then the same weary feminine voice said crossly: "Well, hello?"

"Has Mr. Haggerty come home yet?" Latin asked.

"Hah! Twice, no less! You'd think this was the Grand Central Station, the way he comes and goes. He isn't here now, if that's what you want to know."

"Can you tell me where he is?"

"Hah! Your guess is as good as mine. He *said* he was going to his office, but if you want him you might as well start looking in the nearest gutter."

"Thanks," Latin said.

He pressed down on the breaker bar to cut the connection and then dialed Haggerty's office. The repeated buzz in his ear indicated the phone was ringing at the other end of the line, but there was no answer. After about the tenth ring, there was a click and then, instantly, another. The buzzing ceased, and the line hummed emptily.

Latin pursed his lips thoughtfully. He dialed a third number, and instantly a voice bellowed cheerfully in his ear:

"Hello there! Happy's All-Night Garage!"

"This is Latin, Happy."

"Ah, now! Hooray! You're out, eh? I knew you'd do it! I told my wife they couldn't keep Latin in their flea-trap jail on a bum rap like that. Murder or arson or bank robbery or something decent, I said, why sure. That would be all right, I told her. But this compounding a felony stuff, I said, why that's chicken feed for Latin. He'll spit right in their eye, I told her. Hooray! I'm glad you're out!"

"Thanks, Happy. Send the black coupé around."

"Coming up!"

HAGGERTY'S PLACE was on Claghorn Street, right in the middle of the city's financial district, and it looked as out of place there as a hobo jungle camp would have. The office buildings and stores around it were pale and austere and dignified, but the whole front of Haggerty's store was one gaudy splash of bloodred enamel that glistened sinisterly even in the dim light of the street lamps.

There was a wide bronze door in the middle of the enamel. On one side of the door, futuristically cockeyed letters spelled the word *Haggerty,* and on the other one the word *Art.*

Latin, drifting past in the black coupé, decided that Haggerty was probably a pretty good salesman. At least, he knew enough to come where the money was and how to advertise himself and his wares in a spectacular manner when he got there.

Latin parked the black coupé midway in the next block and walked back. He stood in front of the brass door for a moment, looking both ways. The street was deserted.

There was a bell beside the door, but Latin didn't ring it. He tried the catch on the bronze door, and it opened with a smooth, soft click.

He pushed the door open and looked into the dim, narrow length of the store. At the back there was the faint glow of light coming through a partially closed door, but there was no slightest sound. Latin stepped inside and closed the door noiselessly behind him.

The darkness was thick now, and soft, heavy with the smell of turpentine. Latin drifted toward the light, his feet soundless on the thick carpeting. There was still no sound, no sound at all.

Latin felt a queer prickling sensation between his shoulder blades, and he stopped and stood still for a full minute, listening. He was frowning in a worried way, and finally he drew his stubby .38 from the waistband of his trousers and balanced it casually in his right hand.

He went forward step by step. The door was just in front of him, and he reached out his left hand, fingers rigid, and pushed it slightly.

It moved on oiled hinges. It moved back like the slow unrolling of a stage curtain and revealed a square, small office with white plaster walls and two narrow blue rugs slantwise in the shape of a lopsided T on the black polished floor and thick blue drapes that covered windows in the far wall.

It revealed Haggerty sitting behind a square desk in the corner. Haggerty's fat face was like a white, strained moon with the bristly red halo of his hair gleaming above it. He was staring at the door with his bloodshot eyes popped impossibly wide.

"Hello," Latin said, and stepped inside the office.

Haggerty heaved in his chair. *"Gaah!"* he screeched in one wordless, breathless sound and fell over backwards into the corner, chair and all.

Latin dropped flat on his face on the blue rug. The drapes blew out as though a gust of wind had caught them, and the smack of the first report blended with the crash of Haggerty's chair going down. The bullet hit the door on the near edge and slammed it shut.

McTeague slid out from behind the drapes, as deadly and quick as a cobra. He fired three times more in a blasting stutter of sound. Two of the bullets went wide to Latin's left and the third tapped his hat and tipped it neatly on the back of his head.

Latin fired once, and the report was a solid bump of sound after the chattering racket of McTeague's automatic. McTeague made a shrill little sobbing noise. He came one step and then two toward Latin, as mincing and neat as ever, and then he collapsed, and the thick folds of his overcoat seemed to settle and blend into the blue of the rug under him, and he lay very flat and small and motionless there.

THE ECHOES rang deafeningly in Latin's ears. He was sitting up now, breathing in short gasps through his mouth. Very slowly the white moon of Haggerty's face rose above the horizon of the black desk. His eyes, like jiggling coordinated marbles, moved from Latin to McTeague and back to Latin.

"Oh," said Haggerty in a thin, sick voice.

Latin leveled his revolver. "Don't try to duck behind that desk again. I'll shoot through it."

Haggerty's voice went up to a hysterical squeak. "No, man! Don't!"

"How did you know I was coming in here?"

Haggerty gulped. "Bell. Rings in here when the front door opens. He—he heard. He had his gun on me. Said—said he'd shoot if I warned...."

Latin stared at him silently.

There were big beads of perspiration on Haggerty's forehead. "Man! You—don't think that I—I would—"

"I guess not," said Latin.

He got up, and Haggerty did, too. Haggerty moved like a man in the last stages of some wasting disease. He fumbled his chair upright and sat down in it with a thump.

"Is he—is he—"

"Dead," said Latin.

Haggerty found a big silk handkerchief and began to mop at his brow with it. "And a good thing it is, indeed! I was sitting in here, you understand, as peaceful and innocent as a newborn babe, when in he came like a snake out of the weeds with that gun of his leveled at my head...."

Latin was looking at him, and Haggerty's voice died away to an unintelligible mumble.

"Liar," said Latin.

"Now indeed, sir!" Haggerty protested hastily. "Indeed and I may slip slightly from the strict path of truth on occasion, but I swear—"

"You were trying to gyp me."

Haggerty gasped in horror. "I? Haggerty? Gyp you?"

"Yes. McTeague called you up and told you he had three pictures of Craig's. He described the pictures, and you knew which ones they were. You knew they were the ones you had agreed to sell me. But you thought you could void the sale because it wasn't in writing and then go and sell them to Patricia Wentworth Craig on the deal I worked out with her and leave me holding the bag."

Haggerty looked sick. "Oh, my dear sir! Oh, please! That would be unethical, not to say dishonest, and I can assure you indeed that the name of Haggerty is no less than the definition of honesty its very self!"

"Got anything else to say before I shoot you?"

"Shoot?" said Haggerty, gaping. "Me?"

"Yes." Latin gestured toward McTeague's still form. "Someone's got to take the rap for this, and I can't afford to. I'm hotter than a firecracker in this town. I think maybe he shot you and you shot him with my gun."

"*Gaah!*" said Haggerty, suddenly becoming incoherent again.

"Well?" said Latin.

HAGGERTY GULPED. "Please, my dear good kind sir! If you will only allow me to speak for one short second I assure you I would never think—No! Wait, wait! I admit it! The very thought of fifteen thousand dollars for three pictures was like a worm crawling in my miserable brain, and when this—this called and said he had the three pictures and would sell them for a thousand apiece—"

"You couldn't resist trying a double cross."

"Right," said Haggerty miserably. "But please forgive me, my dear sir. Don't shoot me in cold blood and leave my poor wife bereaved and destitute—"

"Did McTeague bring the pictures?"

"No!" said Haggerty explosively. "Indeed, and I think the scum had every intention of cheating me by taking my money forcibly and refusing delivery!"

"My, my," said Latin. "It's surprising how dishonest people are. I suppose it never occurred to you to turn him over to the cops and get your money back—after you got the pictures."

"Certainly!" said Haggerty. "It would have been my duty as a citizen, no less! The return of the money I paid, of course, would have been incidental."

"I can imagine."

Haggerty moistened his lips and grinned in a sickeningly shaky way. "What—what—"

"I want to use your telephone."

Haggerty pushed the desk set gingerly toward him. Latin dialed a number, using the stubby barrel of the revolver. Guiterrez's voice answered explosively:

"No! I don't make no reservations over the telephone!"

"Did Pete call in?" Latin asked.

"Oh, it's you!" Guiterrez snarled. "Where are you calling from—cell three, north tier, county jail?"

"None of your business. Did Pete call in?"

"Yes. He said the joint was crawling with cops, but they all went away and didn't leave nobody on guard. Who was the poor fella you knocked off?"

"Good-bye," said Latin. He hung up and nodded at Haggerty. "You're a rat, but you're still my agent."

Haggerty grinned more confidently. "Indeed, it will give me the greatest pleasure—"

"Write out a bill of sale for those three pictures. Describe them, and be sure you describe the right ones."

"But my dear sir, I haven't got—"

"I know where they are. Is there a back door to this place?"

"Yes. On the alley.... What—what do you intend...."

"I'm going to wrap McTeague up in your rug and take him away from here."

"But, my dear man! Suppose the police stop you or—or find out?"

"Then I'll tell them that you shot him and hired me to hide the body."

"Huh!" said Haggerty, losing all his breath in one gasp.

"It would be easy," Latin told him calmly. "Your rug, your office. And this gun isn't registered. I could probably scare up a couple of people who would swear it was yours, too. Just remember all that before you start throwing any more curves around here."

Haggerty's moonlike face was as white as a sheet, and he stared at Latin with a sort of horrified fascination.

CHAPTER SIX
A CORPSE GOES HOME

DARKNESS HAD fallen over Greene Street and left it as shadowy and deserted as it must have been in its earlier days. There were no cars on the street and no pedestrians, and the house at Number 345 looked as somber and black as though it were in mourning for the death that had occurred within it.

Latin parked in front and stayed in the car for several moments, watching the houses nearby. There were no signs of life from any of them, and finally he got out. He maneuvered the slim, light body of McTeague out of the front seat and carried it up the narrow walk and up the steps. He used the keys he had found in McTeague's pocket to open the front door and used them again to open the door of the lower apartment.

He went through the living room where he had telephoned Haggerty such a short, violent time ago, along a dark hallway. He tried two other doors and found a bedroom.

He put McTeague down on the bed and carefully folded one side of the high, thick collar of McTeague's overcoat so that it hid the features.

He stood in the darkness quite a while, looking down at the bed. Then he shook his head once with a little shivering jerk of his shoulders. He could feel the perspiration wet and cold on his face, and his eyes burned dryly. He drew the shades down carefully, turned on the light. He didn't look at McTeague again. He began to search the bedroom.

He found the handmade red dancing pump in the closet, mixed in with a confusing jumble of other shoes. He left the bedroom and went on searching patiently. He found the three Craig paintings tacked to the underside of the kitchen table.

Carrying the pictures, he went back in the living room and dialed Madison 5050 on the telephone, and when a voice answered, said: "Tell Inspector Walters that he will find Mr. McTeague in the lower apartment at 345 Greene Street." He hung up at once and went hurriedly out of the house, shivering a little.

It took him less than ten minutes to get back to the restaurant. He parked the black coupé in the alley and came in the rear door.

Guiterrez was standing in the middle of the big low-ceilinged kitchen. He opened his mouth, preparing himself for a blast of sarcasm, and then shut it again when he saw Latin's face.

"Well?" he said mildly.

"Pete," Latin said.

Pete was a bald, bandy-legged little man with a long drooping mustache. He had been presiding at a long sink piled high with dishes, and he came forward wiping his huge, reddened hands on his apron.

"Yus, Mr. Latin."

"The black coupé is in the alley. Take it over to Happy's and tell him to pull off the wheels and start relining the brakes. If anyone asks, it hasn't been out of the place all day."

"Yus, sir."

Guiterrez glared at Pete, said dangerously: "Get it right, dope, or I'll bounce a cleaver off your thick skull."

Latin was carrying Haggerty's blue rug bundled up under his arm. He handed it to Guiterrez and also gave him the stubby .38 revolver.

"Ditch these."

"O.K.," said Guiterrez.

"I've been here for an hour. When I went out a while ago, I came right back in."

Guiterrez went to the kitchen door, opened it slightly and yelled: "Dick. Come here!"

The little waiter in the grease-stained coat slid in through the door. "Yeah?"

"Latin's been here for over an hour."

"Absolutely," said Dick.

"Fix it so he can get in his booth."

"Yup."

DICK WENT out into the main dining room again. Latin waited next to the swing door. In about ten seconds there was the jangling crash of a tray of crockery breaking. Instantly afterwards two voices began screeching frantically.

Latin pushed the door open. Dick and a tall, bald waiter were face-to-face at the front end of the restaurant, howling insults at each other. Broken crockery lay in windrows around them. Every patron remaining in the place was staring at the disturbance in open-mouthed amazement, and Latin slipped unseen into the end booth.

The argument stopped as suddenly as it had started. Dick came back to the booth, carrying an ashtray full of snubbed-out cigarettes. He put it down in front of Latin and put the clean one that was on the table in his pocket.

From under his huge apron he produced a bottle, half full of brandy, and a glass. He spilled some brandy on the linoleum tabletop, smeared it expertly with the palm of his hand, and made overlapping concentric rings in it with the bottom of the bottle and the bottom of the glass.

He went away without a word. Latin sat quietly, smoking and sipping brandy.

It took Walters about fifteen minutes to get there. His face was tight and hard and savagely strained. He knew where to go. He came hard-heeled down the aisle and stopped in front of the last booth, glowering down at Latin, his shoulders hunched dangerously, his hands pushed deep in his pockets.

"Hello, Walters," Latin said casually.

Guiterrez came out of the kitchen and said: "I don't like cops around here. They stink up the place. You gonna pinch Latin again, I hope?"

"Shut up," said Walters. He was looking at the ashtray and the wet rings the brandy bottle had made. "How long has Latin been here?"

"Too long," said Guiterrez. "Over an hour."

Walters jerked around. "An hour!"

"Sure," said Guiterrez.

"Where's his waiter?"

"Dick," said Guiterrez.

Dick came up and squinted insolently at Walters. "Huh! So it's flatfeet now. Latin sure pals around with crummy characters. What do you want, chum?" he asked.

Walters was breathing noisily through his nose. "Did you serve Latin?"

"Yeah. Me and the other slaves drew lots for him, and I lost. Who wants to know?"

"I do. Let me see your tag."

Dick produced one. "There. See, there's his name and the number of the booth and my number. He had the special dinner with the double broiled steak *à la Gutierrez* and soup and salad—"

"All right." Walters handed the slip back to him. He nodded to Latin. "Let me see your gun."

"I left it at home," Latin said. "If you want to go look, it's in the top drawer of the desk in the living room along with my license to carry it."

"Damn you," said Walters. "You know you've got four or five guns with licenses to fit."

"Oh, no. I lost all but the one."

Walters drew a deep breath. "And I suppose you're having the valves ground on your car?"

"No. I'm getting the brakes relined."

Walters glared at Guiterrez and Dick. "Beat it, you two."

Guiterrez went back into the kitchen, and Dick sauntered toward the front of the restaurant.

WALTERS SLID into the seat opposite Latin. He looked both tired and resigned now.

"All right. You win. I wanted to get that McTeague myself, but I should have known I'd trip over you before I got through. I can't prove anything, and I don't know what good it would do me if I did. Just tell me—off the record—how you spotted her."

"McTeague was a very peculiar-looking gent," Latin said absently. "You see a lot of peculiar-looking gents here and there, but you seldom see one that paints his fingernails dark red."

"Damn!" Walters snarled. "Why didn't you tell me that?"

"Listen, I'd been shot at point-blank and fallen downstairs on my head. I didn't notice it at first myself. I just knew there was something wrong with his hands. I didn't realize what until I saw Nan Carter dialing the telephone when she called the police. Her nails were the same color, but that was no sure sign she was McTeague. That color is popular with women now."

"Go on," said Walters gloomily.

"I got to thinking about it, after what you told me, and the whole setup pointed to a woman. I mean, cooking up dope in candy. Would a guy think of that, or know how if he did? She was on her own. She made trips to Mexico, looking for stuff to make statues of, and she probably smuggled the stuff in herself. She didn't want to risk selling it to regular addicts who might lead the police to her.

"And then the shooting. You know, the ordinary woman thinks all you have to do to kill a guy is point a pistol at his general direction and start blazing away. That's just what she did. She was lucky with Gardner, but not so lucky with me. Any man as quick on the shoot as all that would have practiced up a little bit. And the costume was a giveaway. It covered up too much."

"Ummm," said Walters.

"And she could have pulled the job off tonight very easily. She wasn't wearing anything under that housecoat. All she had to do, after I went upstairs, was to shuck it off, put on the overcoat and hat and some men's shoes and the glasses, pat some powder on her face, and hike upstairs. She grabbed the pictures, shot at me, and tripped me up on the stairs. Then she ran down the front steps, took a shot at her own door, screamed, and ditched the clothes in the closet. She was back in the housecoat and part way back up the stairs before I could pull myself together."

"Why?" said Walters.

"The best reason of all. She was broke. Killing Gardner put the kibosh on the dope business. She couldn't sell any of her work, couldn't even collect rent or money for the dope from Craig. She knew I'd spot that Craig was on the habit, and she knew if I did, I'd get the pictures away from him. She wanted them, because she knew just as well as I did where she could cash in with them. She figured that I was a crook, and that if she had the pictures she could make a deal with me to split what I got from Patricia Wentworth Craig. She figured I was tough enough to make Craig consent to the sale."

Walters sat up straight. "What?"

Latin went on casually: "That's why I made a deal with Haggerty. I figured that McTeague—whether it was Nan Carter or who—would try to deal through him because he had the best excuse for having those pictures. I figured right."

"Wait a minute," said Walters. "Are you telling me that McTeague—Nan Carter—didn't kill Craig?"

"No. She didn't know he was dead until I told her. She thought I'd just smacked him one."

"And—who did kill him?"

"I wouldn't know," Latin said amiably. "I think maybe I'll find out pretty quick, though. How about this Mona party?"

Walters's mouth was open slightly. He shut it and swallowed hard and said: "That was straight stuff. She was Craig's model, and she did get into trouble. She kept after him until just about a week ago. Then apparently she got a lot of dough somewhere. Her landlady told me Mona was sporting a whopper of a roll. Then she just up and disappeared."

Latin's eyes were narrowed thoughtfully. "A big roll. And Craig was broke. Well, well."

"Well what?"

"Nothing," said Latin. He chewed on his lower lip. "Sorry about McTeague, Walters. But she had eight setup shots at me, and that's about all I believe in giving anybody—man, woman or child. She was bound to get lucky again if she kept it up long enough, and she didn't give me much of a chance to sit down and discuss it calmly. I should have told you sooner what I guessed, maybe, but—I wanted those pictures. If they had gotten sucked into Craig's estate I would never have been able to prove ownership over his other creditors. Fifteen thousand dollars ain't hay, Walters."

"No," said Walters woodenly, watching him.

Latin snubbed out his cigarette. "I'm going to be busy for a while. Have dinner on me tomorrow night?"

"What time?"

"About eight, I think."

"All right," said Walters. "I'm getting a little tired of you, my friend. You better make it good, Latin. Damned good."

"The dinner, you mean?"

"No, I don't mean the dinner."

CHAPTER SEVEN
REVENGE IS SWEET

PATRICIA WENTWORTH CRAIG said: "Why, it's dirty! It's a horrible place, really!"

"You're telling me, lady," said Dick, the waiter, confidentially. "You should work here for a while. Rats in the stew, cockroaches in the salad, and the second cook has a slight case of leprosy. If we didn't pay off every week, the health department would've closed us long ago."

Patricia Wentworth Craig stared at him in a sort of disbelieving dismay. She and Hastings were sitting in Latin's booth. It was the dinner hour, and the bedlam was in full swing again.

"You waitin' for Latin?" Dick inquired, leaning over the back of the booth.

"Yes," said Hastings. His round face was shiny with nervous prostration, and he tugged at his collar. "He told us to come here tonight...." He hesitated.

"Where is he?" Patricia Wentworth Craig demanded.

Dick took a water glass from under his apron, polished it carefully on the greasy edge of his coat, and set it down in front of her. "Latin? Oh, he's probably off on a bat. He gets drunk every night that he don't load himself up on marihuana. A very low character, that Latin."

"This is absurd!" Patricia Wentworth Craig snapped at her husband. "Why did he ask us to meet him here? Why can't we see him at his office?"

Hastings shook his head apologetically. "But, my dear, he hasn't got an office."

Latin came down the aisle and nodded to them. "Good evening. Sorry to keep you waiting." He slid into the opposite seat of the booth. "I've had quite a lot of running around to do today." He was carrying a paper-wrapped parcel, and he put it down on the table in front of him.

"This is an impossible place!" Patricia Wentworth Craig snapped. "Mr. Latin, if it is your idea that you can safely humiliate me, I will soon disabuse—"

"No, no," said Latin, smiling. "It was quite important that I should see you here for several reasons."

"With this uproar and confusion, no one can talk—"

"You'll get used to it," Latin assured her. "Have you the money—in cash?"

Her thin lips tightened savagely. "Let me tell you, Mr. Latin, that this is nothing more nor less than the most brazen sort of blackmail, and if my husband hadn't been such a stupid fool as to tell you—"

Hastings said uncomfortably: "But, my dear, how could I possibly know?"

"Water under the bridge," said Latin. "Have you got the money?"

Patricia Wentworth Craig took some bills out of her purse, wadded them carelessly together and threw them on the table in front of him.

Latin straightened them out and counted them. "Thanks. Give her the pictures, Dick."

Dick produced the three canvases from under his apron and slid them across the table. "Lousy stuff, if you ask me," he said judicially. "Now I go for these dames in bathing suits like they put on calendars. Guiterrez has got one in the kitchen that really knocks your eye out."

Patricia Wentworth Craig looked up from the pictures. "Is it really necessary for this—this greasy person to stand here and gape at us?"

"Oh, I can take a hint," Dick said. He strolled back into the kitchen.

PATRICIA WENTWORTH CRAIG examined each of the pictures carefully. "These are Winston's work. All right, Mr. Latin. We'll leave now. You may think that you have put over something very clever, but you'll find that I make a bad enemy."

"Don't hurry," Latin said amiably. "I've got some things I'd like to show you."

He unwrapped the package on the table and revealed two red leather dancing pumps with stiltlike heels and a small square of three-quarter-inch soft pine board. The piece of wood had a black circle painted in the center of it, and the circle and the wood surrounding it was pockmarked with dozens of sharp little depressions.

Latin pointed at the pumps. "Your shoes," he said to Patricia Wentworth Craig. "This one I found on the floor beside your cousin's body. This one was in your shoe rack in your bedroom closet."

Her thin face was chalk-white. "You—dared to search in my—"

"Sure," said Latin. "This board was on the top shelf of the same closet. Look at it. Know what I think it is? A target. Somebody has been using it to practice up whacking people with the heel of a slipper. It's quite a trick. I tried it myself. A slipper is light, you know, and you'd think it was sort of harmless. But if you practice up on your aim a bit and take a real full-arm swing, you can hit damned hard. Hard enough to snap a spine—providing you were an art student before you became an art collector and had studied anatomy and knew just where to hit."

Patricia Wentworth Craig said: "Why you—you—"

"It wouldn't be the first time you and your cousin had come to blows. He threw you out of his studio bodily once and you've handed him a few off-hand slaps at art meetings. You told him a couple of times you'd kill him if he didn't stop telling people you were a dummy about art."

"You fool," said Patricia Wentworth Craig.

Hastings stuttered: "Now see here, Mr. Latin. I can't have—I won't stand—"

"How did you find out Craig was dead last night?" Latin asked casually.

"Ah?" said Hastings. "Why—why, a person who said he was a reporter called to ask if—if he were Patricia's cousin, and I thought you—you might...."

Latin nodded at Patricia Wentworth Craig. "You should learn to manage your temper."

"Do you dare to insinuate—"

A muscle in Hastings's round face twitched spasmodically, but he had control of his voice. "My dear, please don't say anything more. He—he is actually accusing you of murdering Winston. Mr. Latin, I warn you solemnly that this has gone too far for any attempts at evasion on your part. You will find yourself in serious trouble unless you can explain just what you mean clearly and at once."

"You explain. You cooked it up."

THE BOOTH seemed like a quiet, still pocket in the midst of the clatter and racket of the restaurant.

Latin nodded at Patricia Wentworth Craig. "You should learn to control your temper and brush up on your manners a bit, too. Things like this are liable to happen if you don't. Hastings killed Craig, and he had every intention of framing the murder on you. He hates you."

"Slander!" Hastings gasped. "You can't…. Lies!"

"Why, no," said Latin. "You hate her because you once loved her and you married her because you did. But everyone thought you married her for her money—even she did. Everyone made fun of you—and she despised you. She thought you were a nincompoop and a milksop and a dimwit, and she never hesitated to tell you so. She wouldn't even take your name. You were Mr. Patricia Wentworth Craig."

"Lies," Hastings whispered hoarsely. "I won't listen—"

"Yes, you will. You made your own money, and you had a lot of pride in your ability. You didn't like being her stooge. But you never had a chance to show what you could do. She wouldn't trust you to buy a postage stamp, let alone consider your advice on any of her business affairs. But this Craig layout gave you a chance. You decided to show her what a smooth worker you were. You would get on the good side of Craig and get him to sell her some of his pictures. Isn't that true?"

Hastings said: "Well, I—I did."

"Yes. But Craig was way out of your class. You'd never dealt with anyone like him before. If he had just pretended to be taken in and then given you the horse laugh, you could probably have stood it. You were used to being laughed at, but he did a lot more than that, didn't he?"

"I—I don't know what—"

"Mona," said Latin. "She was in trouble and pestering Craig, and he got one of his nasty ideas. At one of those parties of his, he dipped a little morphine in one of your drinks. You passed out. Later he sent Mona around to see you. She told you that *you* were responsible. You were horrified. You couldn't remember what happened. You couldn't prove you weren't. You didn't dare risk the scandal. You paid her off. And then the worst thing of all happened. You went to see Craig again, and he told you the whole dirty scheme and laughed in your face. Not only that, but he threatened to tell his cousin."

Hastings's lips moved stiffly and soundlessly.

"So," said Latin casually, "you killed him. You had read about me in the papers, and you thought I was just smart enough and crooked enough to do a Charlie McCarthy for you. After you left me here, you waited until I started to go to Craig's, beat it there ahead of me, sneaked in the back and socked him with your wife's dancing pump."

Patricia Wentworth Craig laughed suddenly and shrilly. "Why, you poor fool! You're not seriously trying to tell me that silly, stupid Bernard would have either the nerve or the brains to plan anything as elaborate—"

That did it. Hastings's round face was livid with rage suddenly, and he seemed to swell up until the booth was too small for him.

"Damn you," he whispered. "You and your money and your supercilious air and your smirking rat of a cousin. Yes! I killed him! But you can't prove it—you can *never* prove it! I'm stupid, am I? We'll see. We'll see what you think about that when you face a jury. You think it will make any difference what Latin knows? He's a jailbird and a crook. His testimony is worth nothing. I framed you, and you're still framed! I've got letters, evidence, witnesses—everything!"

"Bernard," said Patricia Wentworth Craig in a choked, horrified voice.

Hastings laughed on a cracked, high note. "I'm leaving you—"

"Yeah," said Inspector Walters, coming out of the kitchen. "With me."

Hastings gasped and choked. "You—you can't prove it—"

He stopped, watching with dazed fascination as Latin reached out slowly and pulled the chintz curtain at the back of the booth aside and revealed the round gleam of a microphone.

"Walters and Guiterrez and three or four waiters heard everything you said."

Hastings seemed to melt inside his clothes until he was a fat pasty-faced little man with stiff lips that moved and made no sound.

Patricia Wentworth Craig said: "I see—now. You don't have an office because—*this* is your office. This is your restaurant. You own it. And all these men—they work for you and help you...."

Latin was smiling slightly. "Yes, madam. We have a very nice dinner tonight. Would you like to try it?"

DON'T GIVE YOUR RIGHT NAME

IT'S ALL IN A DAY'S WORK WHEN
THE SHAMUS WITH THE SHADY
REP HIRES OUT TO STEAL A
GLAMOR GAL'S GEWGAWS—BUT
LATIN HAS TO SOP UP PLENTY OF
BRANDY TO BOLSTER HIM WHEN
HE GETS IN THE LINE OF FIRE OF
A BALEFUL BORGIA ON A MURDER
RAMPAGE.

CHAPTER ONE
AN AUTOGRAPH ADDICT

GUITERREZ WAS leaning against the wall beside the front door of his restaurant with his tall chef's hat pushed down over one eye and his hands folded under the bib of his apron. He looked disgusted. There was nothing unusual about that. He always did. He had his reasons, and one of them was getting out of a taxi in front of the restaurant now.

"Hello, you crook," said Guiterrez. "How are you, you chiseler? Have you burned down any orphan asylums or robbed any starving widows today?"

"Not yet," said Max Latin. "But the night is young."

He was a tall man, thin and high-shouldered, and he had the assured, sleek self-confidence of a champion racehorse. His eyes were as cold and smooth as green glass, tipped a little at the corners.

Guiterrez was counting on his fingers. "It seems incredible to me, but you ain't been pinched for three weeks. How does that happen? Did you catch the mayor sleeping with somebody else's wife?"

"No," said Latin. "But I have hopes. What's on the menu tonight?"

"Tonight," Guiterrez answered, "Guiterrez is featuring steamed ragout *à la supreme à la Guiterrez.*"

"Is it good?"

Guiterrez snorted. "Good! It's marvelous! I cooked it, didn't I?" He opened the restaurant door and yelled loudly: "Dick! Here's that thief of a Latin! Be sure you mark the level of the brandy bottle before you give it to him—and with an indelible pencil!"

Latin went on inside, and Guiterrez poked a cigarette into the corner of his mouth and leaned against the wall again. The red neon tubing that bordered the doorway gave his face a satanically dissipated cast.

Another taxi pulled up at the curb, and two men and a woman got out of it. The men were very young and broad-shouldered and husky. They were hatless, and they had crew haircuts. One was blond and the other was brunet. They wore dress overcoats with the collars turned up and white scarfs. They were unmistakably college boys weekending in the city.

"Are you sure this is the place you want to go?" the blond one asked doubtfully.

"It looks dirty," the brunet observed.

"It don't only look dirty," Guiterrez told him. "It is. You won't like it."

The two men stared at him and then decided to ignore him.

The woman said: "I'm certain this is the place. It has an international reputation. The food is divine." She must have been younger, in years, than even her escorts were. Only in years, though. She had a lusciously curved young body very much on display in a striptease-black evening gown with a cut out middle section. She wore a silver fox cape and the diamond bracelet on her left wrist was a good four inches wide. Her hair was dead black, and she wore it in a long sleek bob. Her brown eyes were sultry and languorous, and her mouth was a red, moist invitation.

"This is Guiterrez's restaurant, isn't it?" she asked Guiterrez.

"Yup," said Guiterrez. "I run the dump." He leered at her knowingly. "And how are you getting along with your work, baby?"

The two men looked at each other and then started ominously for Guiterrez.

Guiterrez pushed the door open behind him and called: "Hey, Dick!"

A WIZENED little waiter wearing a black, grease-stained coat and an apron so big that he had wrapped it around himself three times and still had plenty left over appeared instantly. Without saying a word, he took a butcher knife with a blade over a foot long from under the apron and handed it to Guiterrez.

The face of the man in the hamper was a mottled bluish-red.

The two college men stopped short, eyeing the long shimmering blade uneasily. Guiterrez commenced to clean his fingernails with it. Dick, the waiter, watched with a sort of idle interest.

The girl laughed throatily. "Bruce! Bill! Behave yourselves! He's just ribbing you. Aren't you, Mr. Guiterrez?"

"Sure," Guiterrez answered. "I'm one of these here humorists. I'm funny as hell all day long."

The two college men decided they saw the joke. They laughed in a rather pained way.

The girl said: "I've been wanting to try some of your wonderful food for a long time, Mr. Guiterrez. Everybody in town is talking about it."

"Yeah," said Guiterrez. "You got any room in the joint for these people, Dick?"

"I got one table left," Dick said. "But I was savin' it for a big spender. These birds look like cheapskates to me."

Guiterrez nodded. "Yeah. They probably are. But just think what you can watch while you're servin' them." He pointed the butcher knife at the girl.

"You got something there," Dick agreed, popping his eyes admiringly. "Come on, gorgeous. I'll give you and your two poodles my personal attention."

The girl swept her magnificently inviting body through the door with the two college men trailing uncertainly behind her.

Guiterrez spat his cigarette butt into the gutter and sighed drearily. Running feet pattered along the walk, and a youth as skinny and tall as a beanpole staggered up and leaned against the wall beside Guiterrez, panting in exhausted gasps.

"Gobble-glip-glip," he said unintelligibly, pointing toward the door of the restaurant. "Glip?"

"I think it'll rain myself," Guiterrez answered.

The skinny youth fought for breath. "Did—did they go—in there?"

"Which they?" Guiterrez asked.

"Lily Trace. She had—two guys—with her."

"Who?" said Guiterrez.

The skinny youth got his breath back with a desperate gasp. "Lily Trace! The most glamorous girl in the world! Her pictures are in all the papers and magazines all the time!"

"She did look a little familiar, at that," Guiterrez observed. "Yeah, she just went in to eat. Is she a friend of yours?"

"Friend!" the skinny youth echoed, aghast. "No! All her friends are millionaires and people like that! She has a penthouse apartment that rents for a thousand dollars a month and twenty-four fur coats and a hundred thousand dollars worth of diamonds!"

"How'd she get all that?" Guiterrez asked, interested. "Buy it?"

"No!" said the skinny youth scornfully. "Her admirers present her with every luxury she desires."

"They do, do they?" said Guiterrez. "For free?"

"Of course! All she has to do is smile at them, and they grant her slightest wish."

"Is that a fact?" Guiterrez asked. "Well, you live and learn, I always say. What do you want with her?"

The skinny youth looked at him doubtfully, and then backed away a little, getting ready to run. "I want her autograph, is all."

"So," said Guiterrez. "You're one of them cookies, are you?"

HE DIDN'T sound very hostile, and the skinny youth relaxed. He was wearing a ragged sport coat and baggy sport slacks and white shoes that were unbelievably soiled. His small, high-crowned hat had the brim tipped up jauntily in front. His face was pale and bony, spotted with enormous freckles, and he had a desperately serious do-or-die air.

"Sure," he said. "I'm an autograph collector. I specialize in celebrities who aren't in the theater or on the radio or in the movies or like that. I've got over ten thousand famous names in my collection. It's very valuable."

"I wouldn't doubt it," said Guiterrez. "You don't go for actors or actresses, huh?"

The skinny youth was scornful. "Naw. That's cornfed stuff. They're too easy. I pick the hard babies. I'm well known for that. The tougher they are, the better I like it. My name's Steamer. You ever heard of me?"

"Not until now," Guiterrez admitted. "How do you propose to get Lily Trace's autograph?"

"I'll wait here until she comes out and then ask her. If she refuses I'll think up some other gag. I've got lots of them on tap. You don't mind me waitin' here, do you? I mean, lots of guys get tough if they catch us autograph hunters hanging around their joints. They claim we pester the customers and keep 'em from comin' again."

"Is that so?" Guiterrez said thoughtfully. "Pester the customers, huh?"

"Oh, I won't," said Steamer. "Honest."

"Oh, yes, you will," said Guiterrez.

Steamer started to edge away again. "Huh?"

Guiterrez got him by the arm. "Listen, jitterbug. Here's a buck. That's for you if you go inside and start annoying customers in a big way."

"Why?" Steamer asked, still doubtful.

"On account of I hate my customers," Guiterrez explained. "I hate each and every one of them personally."

"Well, why?" Steamer repeated blankly.

Guiterrez scowled ferociously. "Because I sweat and slave over a hot stove all day long to cook them the most beautiful food in the whole world! And what do they do with it? Sit in there and poke it down their gullets like a bunch of pigs at a swill box!"

"They pay for it, don't they?" Steamer inquired.

"Is money everything?" Guiterrez demanded. "No! I'm an artist! I've got a soul!"

"What ought they to do with your food?" Steamer asked curiously.

"Appreciate it! Sit there and savor each mouthful gracefully and gratefully! It's genius they're eating! The genius of Guiterrez!"

"Oh," said Steamer.

"Come along," said Guiterrez.

He opened the door and pushed Steamer into the restaurant. It was a long bare room with a high, smoke-stained ceiling. There were booths along the walls, and the center space was packed with round spindle-legged tables. It was late now for the dinner hour, but the place was full and overflowing.

DINERS WERE hunched over the tables, eating with ferocious concentration, as though they were afraid that if they paused for a breath the food would be snatched from them. They were quite right about that. A mangy horde of waiters prowled around, ready to pounce at the first signs of slackening interest. You had to fight for your food at Guiterrez's.

The noise was terrific. The waiters dropped trays now and then just because they were tired of carrying them. They screamed threats at each other and the customers and orders at the cook. They conducted profane political arguments the length of the room, digressing occasionally to discuss the manners and looks of the diners. A jukebox howled jive from a corner, and the cash register had a bell like a fire gong attached to it.

"Wow!" said Steamer in an awed voice.

Guiterrez shouted in his ear. "Nobody with any brains would eat in a joint like this, would they? I ask you. But look at 'em! I can't get rid of 'em!"

Dick, the small waiter in the big apron, came up and said to Guiterrez: "What's with you now, stupid? You want I should feed this starving fugitive from a rat race?"

"No," said Guiterrez. "He's an annoyer. He collects autographs. Get to work, Steamer."

"Can I get Lily Trace's first?" Steamer asked.

"Sure," Guiterrez said. "She's over there at the side—" He stopped, staring at a small table near the door. "Since when am I running a flophouse here? Who's that sleeping beauty?"

There was only one man at the table. He was slumped down in his chair, head resting in his folded arms. His thinnish blond hair was crumpled and sticky with perspiration, and there was a loose pink roll of fat over the back of his collar.

"He's drunk," said Dick.

"Do tell," said Guiterrez. "I would never have guessed it." He raised his voice to an indignant shout. "So he's drunk! So throw the bum out, you bum!"

"He's got dough," said Dick. "He waves it. I charged him double for the dinners and he didn't kick."

"How many dinners did he have?" Guiterrez demanded.

"Only one. He's got a dame with him. She had one, too. Also he had fifty or sixty drinks. The dame has been tryin' to get him to blow, but he don't want to. She went back to telephone. I think she's calling for help."

"Maybe I could wake him up," said Steamer. "Sometimes when you ask a guy for his autograph, he concentrates and gets sort of sober. Shall I try?"

"Sure," said Guiterrez.

Steamer went over and tapped the drunk politely on the shoulder and began to talk in a low, insistent voice in his ear. For about a minute he got no results. Then the man rolled his head back and forth in vague awareness. Steamer kept on talking and tapping confidentially.

The man heaved himself back in his chair. "Huh?" He had a round, heavily jowled face and eyes that were glassily bloodshot. His clothes were expensively tailored. "What you say?"

STEAMER SLID a piece of paper in front of him and poked a pencil into the vaguely fumbling fingers all in one deft, practiced motion.

"Your name, sir. Your autograph, please."

"Oh," said the man. He scowled at the pencil as though he had never seen one before. He maneuvered it around until he got the point headed in the right direction and made a groping, careful scrawl on the piece of paper.

"Thank you," said Steamer.

He pocketed the slip of paper and headed for Lily Trace's table.

"The kid's good," said Dick. "Maybe we should try being more polite to the suckers, huh?"

"Don't be a Communist," said Guiterrez. "The guy's waked up now. Where's his dame?"

"She's coming. The skinny one, there."

The girl was thin to the point of emaciation, and her eyes were enormous in the white stillness of her face. Her lips were a thin, bright-red streak. She looked like a drawing of one of those impossibly elongated fashion manikins, and her sport clothes had the same slick, professional lines. She walked with a beautiful, practiced grace.

"Come on, Don," she said with determination. "Please."

"One drink," said the man. "Only one. Honest. Then we'll go right away."

"Now!" said the girl.

"One drink!" said the man stubbornly. He looked inquiringly at Dick and raised a finger.

"We're fresh out of everything but Mickey Finns," said Dick. "Be happy to serve you one of them, though."

"Eh?" said the man blankly.

The girl jerked at his arm. "Oh, come on! Please, Don! We *can't* stay here any longer! You can have a drink when we get home."

"Two?" asked the man cleverly.

"A dozen! A hundred!"

"O.K.," said the man. He got unsteadily to his feet. "How much I owe, waiter?"

Dick whipped a bill out of his pocket. "Well, you had two *de luxe* dinners—" He stopped in midsentence, looking at the girl. He drew a deep breath and put the bill away again. "But you paid for them. Don't you remember?"

"Sure, sure. Tip for you."

The man dropped a crumpled bill on the table. The girl picked it up and calmly put it in the pocket of her sport coat, watching Dick as she did it. Dick smiled in a painfully polite way.

The girl took a firm hold on the man's arm and steered him carefully toward the door and out through it. Dick went back to where Guiterrez was standing.

"See that?" he asked. "A man can't even chisel an honest dollar anymore. That dame is pure poison. I'd hate to have her get behind me if she had a knife around anywhere."

"She don't need a knife," said Guiterrez. "She's got fingernails she could cut your throat with. Where'd that autograph bug go?"

"I dunno," said Dick, looking around.

"Must have got Lily Trace's signature and beat it out the side door, I guess," Guiterrez said, shrugging. "Well, there goes a buck, but it wasn't a very good idea, anyway."

"Naturally not," Dick observed. "If you thought of it. Why don't you go back and do some cooking?"

"I'm not in the mood," Guiterrez answered sourly. "I want to be alone."

CHAPTER TWO
HIRED TO STEAL

MAX LATIN was sitting in his special booth, the last one in the line, near the metal swing door that led into the kitchen. Dick stopped beside him and produced a bottle of brandy and a small glass from under his voluminous apron. He pulled the cork out of the bottle with his teeth and put it down beside the glass on the table.

"Screwball is having one of his fits again," he observed.

"Guiterrez?" Latin asked, pouring brandy.

"Yeah. He wants to be alone. So do I—with hot hips over there. Only I'm afraid she comes higher than a gumdrop or a shiny apple."

Latin looked across the room. "I'm afraid so. That's Lily Trace. She's on the expensive side."

"I wonder if she ever gives a benefit performance—for charity and like that?" Dick said speculatively.

"I wouldn't count on it."

"I wish I had more money and less brains," said Dick gloomily. "I got to go to work. Holler if you want me."

Latin sipped at his brandy, enjoying himself. He had the lazy, relaxed air of a sleepy cat.

A smoothly clipped voice said: "Are you Mr. Max Latin, the private inquiry agent?"

"Yes," said Latin, looking up.

The man beside the booth was very tall, taller even than Latin. He had even young-old features that were as cold and sharp as chiseled steel. His eyes were a faded, smooth blue, very light against the tan of his face. He was wearing a dark business suit, and he carried a topcoat over his arm.

"My name is Caleb Drew," he said. "I was informed that you were in the habit of conducting your—ah—business from this restaurant."

"This booth is my office," Latin answered.

"I have a friend who would like to talk to you. If you'll pardon me for a second."

Caleb Drew walked across to Lily Trace's table. She smiled up at him in excellently simulated surprise. The two college boys stood at attention and were introduced to Drew. Lily Trace made a gesture inviting him to sit down. He shook his head and nodded toward Latin's booth.

Lily Trace clapped her hands delightedly. The college boys scowled. Lily Trace got up and took Caleb Drew's arm and let him guide her toward Latin's booth. The college boys sat down glumly and glowered at each other.

"This is Mr. Max Latin," Drew said. "Mr. Latin, this is Lily Trace."

Dick, the waiter, came up and put his elbows on the back of the booth and stared dreamily at Lily Trace. "Latin," he said, "how do you do it, anyway?"

"Get me a couple of glasses," Latin ordered. "Sit down, Miss Trace—Mr. Drew."

Dick took two small glasses from under his apron and put them down on the table. "You go settin' up drinks with that brandy, and Guiterrez will cloud up and rain all over you. That stuff costs sixteen smackers a bottle."

"Go away," said Latin.

"Don't say I didn't warn you," said Dick, obeying. "Call me before the dame leaves, will you? I want to watch her wiggle out of that booth."

Drew said: "The help around here is a little bit—forward."

"I've noticed that," Latin said idly. "Have some brandy?"

"I never drink," said Lily Trace, smiling.

Drew nodded. "Thanks."

Latin poured him a drink. "You wanted to see me, Miss Trace?"

"Yes," said Lily Trace frankly. "I really did want to see you. I like to meet famous people, and you are one of them."

Latin sipped at his brandy. "I've got a long police record, if that's what you mean."

"A lot of arrests," said Drew. "No convictions."

"Bribing juries is an expensive habit," Latin told him. "And with me, time is money. Now you've met me, and we're all happy here together, so what's next?"

"I'd like you to do some work for me," Lily Trace stated. "Some confidential work."

"All my work is confidential—and expensive."

"I'm paying," Drew said.

"Go into your spiel, then," Latin invited.

LILY TRACE lowered her voice to a husky, confidential murmur. "I want you to help me steal some jewelry."

"O.K.," said Latin. "Where and when?"

Lily Trace laughed admiringly. "Oh, I like the way you said that! You're so casual. You'd think you went around stealing things all the time!"

"I do," said Latin.

"Oh," said Lily Trace, surprised.

Drew said: "You'd better let me handle this, Lily. You're a little out of your weight class here, I think."

Lily Trace didn't like that last. She studied Latin with narrowed, speculative eyes. She took a deep breath and stretched the cloth of the front of her dress. Latin sipped his brandy. He was not impressed. Lily Trace chewed on her lower lip, slightly at a loss.

"This is no gag, Mr. Latin," Drew said in his smooth voice. "At least, not the kind you think. Lily doesn't mean for you to actually steal any jewels, of course. She wants it to appear that hers have been stolen."

Latin looked at her. "Insurance?"

"Of course not!" said Drew. "There's no crooked work involved at all."

"Then I don't want to be involved, either."

"Now just a moment," Drew said, losing some of his smooth veneer. "Let me explain, please. Lily wants some more publicity—of the undercover, confidential sort that's so hard to get. Cryptic little hints by columnists and that sort of thing. You know what I mean."

"I've got a rough idea."

"She's not going to report her jewels stolen, and they aren't going to be. But she wants the rumor to get around that they have been—wants people whispering behind their hands about it. You're just the man to handle that."

"I'm listening."

Drew coughed. "Your—ah—reputation...."

"It smells high," said Latin.

"Yes," said Drew, relieved. "She wants to use it. She wants you to put out feelers—inquiries—as though you were trying to buy back her jewelry secretly from the imaginary thieves who stole it."

"Compounding a felony," Latin defined.

"Yes," said Lily Trace eagerly. "But it'll work. Really it will. I know. Everybody will be running around and whispering and pointing and wondering. There'll be hints about it in all the gossip columns. It'll be one of those secrets because they know, and I'll just get all kinds of publicity!"

"And maybe some more jewelry," Latin added.

"Nothing like that is intended," Drew said coldly. "Miss Trace is not accepting any more presents from her admirers. She and I are going to be married."

"Felicitations," said Latin. "My price for this little job of work is one thousand dollars—in advance."

Drew stared at him. "That seems excessive—"

"Unless I have to argue about it," Latin continued in the same tone. "Then the price goes up. It costs money to argue with me."

Drew's face looked white and stiff. He took his wallet from his pocket and carefully counted out ten one hundred dollar bills.

"I judged you'd want cash." He dropped a card on the bills. "There's my address and phone number, if you want to get in touch with me."

"Very thoughtful of you," Latin commented. "You'll be hearing of and from me. You'd better get the jewelry out of sight somewhere. As soon as the police hear that I'm nosing around, they'll come and see you. They might be a little on the rough side. They're mad at me now for one reason or another."

"That will be taken care of," Drew promised.

He helped Lily Trace out of the booth. The two college boys sprang to attention and settled back into despair again as Lily Trace waved to them gaily and went on out of the restaurant with Drew.

Dick came out of the kitchen and leaned over the back of the booth. "Latin," he murmured. "There's a stiff out in the alley. Is it one of yours?"

Latin looked up at him silently.

"No joke," said Dick. "Guiterrez fell over it and grabbed a handful of blood. He don't want to be alone anymore."

Latin slid out of the booth. "Come on."

GUITERREZ WAS holding his hands under the hot water faucet in the sink. He took them out and wiped them on a dish towel and looked at them. They were as clean and pink as a new baby's. Guiterrez shuddered and shoved them under the hot water faucet again.

"That's the kind of thing I run into around here," he muttered savagely. "My customers not only stuff themselves like hogs—they go out in my alley and die on me. Why don't they go home first if they want to die?"

"You sure it isn't just a stray drunk?" Latin asked.

Guiterrez looked at him soberly. "I'm sure. It's a guy, and he's awful dead, Latin. In that dark stretch between the side door and the mouth of the alley. Just beyond where we set the garbage cans."

"Wait here," Latin ordered.

He went out the side door and closed it behind him. The darkness was like a living thing, a heavy menacing weight that pressed coldly against his face. The mouth of the alley, half a block away, was a narrow high rectangle with the streetlights feeble and yellow beyond it.

Latin moved slowly and cautiously forward. His knee thrust against the side of a garbage can, rattled the galvanized lid, and the echoes chased themselves hollowly away from him. He touched a limp, yielding weight with the toe of his shoe.

In the street an auto horn blatted flatly, and gears clashed. Latin took a match from his pocket and snapped it on his thumbnail. Shadows jiggled and swooped weirdly around him, and then the yellow flame steadied as he cupped it in his hands.

The man was lying sprawled on his face with his head pillowed in a slick pool of blood. He looked very flat and thin and deflated. His throat had been cut.

The match flickered out, and Latin struck another. The dead man's clothes had a messy, pulled-around look to them. All his pockets had been turned inside out, the linings hanging like multiple tags pinned helter-skelter to him.

Latin leaned closer to look at his face and then blew out the match. He made his way cautiously back to the side door and went into the restaurant kitchen.

Guiterrez was letting the water from the cold water tap run over his hands. Dick was leaning against the asbestos-covered side of the steak broiler, picking his teeth with a curved paring knife.

"Did you look at him?" Latin asked.

"Oh, no," said Guiterrez. "I felt him. That convinced me that I didn't want to know him any better."

Latin said: "He's just a kid—maybe twenty at the best. Skinny and tall—freckled face. Wearing dirty white shoes and checked slacks and a sport coat."

Guiterrez stared at Dick, his eyes widening. "The jitterbug!"

Dick nodded. "Must be."

"Do you know him?" Latin inquired.

Guiterrez said: "He told me his name was Steamer. He's one of these dopey autograph collectors. He wanted to get Lily Trace's signature. He saw her go in the joint, and he was gonna wait outside. I told him to go on in and brace her inside and pester some of the other customers while he was at it. I think maybe that wasn't such a hot idea."

"He had something somebody wanted," Latin said. "He's been rolled. A nice thorough job."

"Rolled!" Guiterrez repeated, startled. "Why, hell, anybody could tell just by lookin' at him that he wouldn't be carrying any dough."

"Something else, then," said Latin.

THE SECOND cook pushed Dick out of the way and threw steaks in the broiler like a man dealing out meaty, thick cards. The steaks sizzled and smoked and spattered. Guiterrez looked at them and shivered. He put his hands back under the water faucet.

"Did Steamer pester any customers?" Latin asked.

Guiterrez shook his head. "He gypped me. He got Lily Trace's signature and hopped it."

"The drunk," Dick said.

Guiterrez nodded. "Oh, yeah. There was a drunk sleepin' on one of the tables. The kid woke him up by pretendin' he wanted the guy's autograph."

"Did you know the drunk?"

"Nope," said Guiterrez. "He's been here before, though. Quite a while ago, as I remember."

Latin nodded at Dick, and Dick went out through the swing door into the front part of the restaurant. A waiter yelled some unintelligible gibberish through the order slot, and the pastry chef said: "Go to hell. That ain't on the menu."

Guiterrez began to wipe his hands slowly and carefully. "I don't feel so good now, Latin. I'm afraid I pulled that kid into this. I shoulda kept my big mouth shut."

"Forget it," Latin said absently. He was frowning, his greenish eyes narrowed thoughtfully.

Dick came back into the kitchen. "The drunk's been here before—two or three times. But nobody knows his name or anything about him. The dame he had with him called him Don. She's never been here except tonight. The drunk is a big spender. Steamer got his autograph and Lily Trace's. Nobody else's. Then two college cutups beefed with Steamer when he braced Lily Trace. They're just leavin' now."

"Have they got a car?" Latin asked.

"No."

"Go out and tell the taxi driver who picks them up to keep track of them and telephone me here."

"O.K.," said Dick, going out again.

"Get me a tablecloth," Latin said to Guiterrez. "A big one."

"What're you gonna use that for?" Guiterrez asked.

"A shroud."

Guiterrez stared at him, his face paling.

Latin said: "If the cops find that body there, they'll pinch me on suspicion. They couldn't prove anything, but they could hold me for a couple of days. I don't want to be in jail right at the moment."

"You're gonna move him?" Guiterrez asked shakily.

"Yes. Afterwards, I want you to get some ashes out of the broiler—a lot of them—and spread them over the blood and stamp them down."

"Oh-oh," said Guiterrez.

Dick came back through the swing door. "Benny Merkle was the driver that picked up the college guys. I told him what you said."

Latin nodded. "All right. I'm going over and get my car now. You go out in the alley and see that nobody else falls over Steamer. Wait there until I come back with the car."

"O.K., chum," Dick said casually.

CHAPTER THREE
DEATH OF A DICK

DETECTIVE INSPECTOR WALTERS, Homicide, had a yellowish gaunt face and a sourly cynical nature. He had been chasing murderers of one sort or another for twenty years, and he had gotten to the point where he didn't believe what he heard even when he was talking to himself. He sat in Latin's booth and watched Latin sip delicately at a small glass of brandy.

"It's good," said Latin. "Want some?"

"No," said Walters.

It was late now, and the restaurant was almost empty. A half-dozen waiters were playing craps on a table near the cash register.

Guiterrez came out of the kitchen and said: "Listen, Latin. I've told you before I don't like cops hanging around here all the time. People are gonna think I'm running a bookie joint or a hook shop. You know what kind of a reputation cops have. They stink a place up."

Before Walters could think of an answer, Guiterrez went on up to the front of the restaurant and shouldered his way into the crap game.

Walters drew a deep breath and said: "A guy got killed tonight, Latin."

"Only one?" Latin observed. "Hitler must be slipping."

"This guy wasn't in Europe," Walters said patiently. "And Hitler didn't kill him."

"Who did?" Latin inquired.

"That's a coincidence," Walters said. "I was just about to ask you that."

"Me?" Latin said, surprised. "Now listen, Walters, this is getting to be a nuisance. Just because you find a body somewhere—"

"Not somewhere. On the front steps of the morgue."

"That was thoughtful of the guy."

"He didn't put himself there. Somebody else did."

"Not guilty," said Latin. "I don't even know where the morgue is, and besides, I haven't been out of this place all night. You can ask Guiterrez or Dick or any of the waiters."

"Let's not clown around," said Walters wearily. "I know you own this joint and that all these birds work for you. They'd swear black was white if you gave them the nod."

"Prove it," Latin invited.

"I can't. Besides, I've got other things to do. This is just a confidential chat. Do you know anything about this bird that got biffed?"

"Who was he?" Latin asked.

"He called himself Steamer Morgan. He was a private detective and a good one—that is, if there are any good ones."

Latin put his glass down. "A private detective?"

"Yeah. Not a crook like you are, though. At least, he didn't go around talking about it as much if he was. He specialized in getting evidence in civil cases."

"Divorces?" Latin inquired.

"No. Accident cases and damage suits. He was plenty expert—knew a lot about law. He had a swell front for it. He looked like a kid, and he went around acting like a jitterbug and a sort of a screwy young punk. The last type of guy you'd suspect of being a detective. He's sneaked up on an awful lot of smarties with that act. And when he got evidence—it was the kind that held in court."

"Was he working on a case?"

Walters shrugged. "I think so. I'm trying to find out now. He worked undercover and on his own. He didn't keep any records. Somebody searched him before they left him at the morgue. Nothing in his pockets at all."

DICK CAME up to the booth carrying a portable telephone. "One of your crummy friends wants to talk to you."

Latin plugged the phone in on the concealed connection behind the drape at the back of the booth. "Latin speaking," he said into the mouthpiece.

"This here is Benny Merkle, Mr. Latin. I'm the taxi driver that picked up them two guys from your joint a while back. Dick said you wanted to know where they went and such."

"Yes," said Latin. "Go ahead."

"They called each other Bruce and Bill. They didn't use no last names. I drove 'em from your joint to a very swanky dive called the Château Carleton on Vandervort Road. They don't live there. They waked up the janitor and laid down a pound note to get in."

"What then?" Latin asked.

"I waited around, and in about ten minutes they came boiling out again. One of 'em had a bloody nose and the other had a big bump on his noggin. They was plenty mad at some dame they called Lily."

"What did they do next?"

"They had me drive 'em to a liquor store, and they bought a fifth of Scotch. It was good Scotch. They gave me a couple of drinks. Then they asked me if I knew where they could—I mean, they told me to drive 'em over to Katie Althouse's place on Barker Street. They went in there, and they both picked out a girl by the name of Priscilla."

Latin was smiling. "What does she look like?"

"Priscilla? Well, she's sort of dark and kinda built in a big way. She's got black hair she wears in a long bob, and she makes up her mouth in a smear."

Latin chuckled. "All right, Benny. Did you wait for them?"

"Yeah. I took 'em home. They was kinda tired and pretty drunk. I put 'em to bed at the Milton Hotel. I'm there now. You want I should ask some questions about 'em?"

"No," said Latin. "Let it go. Thanks a lot, Benny. Drop in and say hello to the cashier here tomorrow."

Latin put the telephone back in its cradle. He was still grinning.

"Let me laugh, too," Walters invited.

Latin said: "Lily Trace came in here tonight with a couple of college boys. She ditched them and then bounced them when they tried to call on her later. They got mad and went over to Katie Althouse's place and picked out a girl who looked like Lily Trace. As long as they couldn't get the real article they were going to take a substitute."

"They must be dopes," said Walters.

"They've got some fancy company."

Walters nodded. "I don't get it. This café society is away over my head. In my time gals like Lily Trace stayed down by the stockyards and hung red lanterns over their doors. They didn't have their pictures in the society pages waltzing with all the town's best bankrolls."

"Do you know where she came from?"

"No, but I'll make you a bet I can guess how. You want to watch your step with her, sonny."

"What?" said Latin.

Walters said: "Look, Latin. I like you in spite of all your fancy tricks, and I think maybe you're even halfway honest now and then. This little deal you've got on with Lily Trace is going to backfire right in your face if you don't watch your step."

"What deal?" Latin asked casually.

"It didn't fool me any, but some of the boys have got a mad on with you. Especially the district attorney's office. About twenty tips have come in tonight that Lily Trace had a lot of jewelry stolen and that you're dickering either for the guys who lifted it or for her or for both. I knew it was phoney because there were too many tips, but the district attorney's boys aren't that subtle."

"Thanks, Walters," said Latin. "I'll take care of it. I know something about Steamer's death. I don't know who killed him, but I'll find out and let you know."

WALTERS GOT up. "Better hurry a little. I can't hold the district attorney's boys off you forever, and anyway I like to see results for my efforts."

Latin poured himself another drink. "Find out what Steamer was working on if you can."

"Find out yourself. You know more crooked lawyers than I do."

Walters stopped at the crap game to exchange insults with Guiterrez and then went on out of the restaurant. Latin finished up his glass of brandy and lit a cigarette. After a while, he took the card Caleb Drew had given him out of his pocket and looked at it.

It was outsize, made of thick parchment. Engraved on it in jet-black old English letters was the name "Caleb Drew IV" and under that "Investment Counsellor." In the lower left corner was an address Latin recognized as belonging to the Teasdale Building in the downtown financial district and a telephone number. In the lower right-hand corner there was another telephone number.

Latin dialed that number, and after the first ring a voice said politely in his ear: "Gravesend Manor."

"May I speak to Mr. Caleb Drew?" Latin asked.

"He's not in, sir."

"Do you mean that he's not home or that he's asleep?"

"He's not here, sir. He hasn't been in for the last two or three days. Do you wish to leave a message?"

"No, thanks."

Latin hung up and dialed Information. When a courteously long-suffering feminine voice answered, he said: "Will you give me the number of Miss Lily Trace? She lives at the Château Carleton on Vandervort Road."

"One moment, please." The line hummed emptily to itself, and then the long-suffering voice said: "There's no telephone listed under that name, sir."

"You mean it's a hidden number?"

"There's no telephone listed under that name, sir."

"All right," said Latin. "Is there switchboard service at the Carleton?"

"No, sir."

"Good-bye," said Latin. He hung up and poured himself another very small portion of brandy. He didn't drink it. He scowled at it thoughtfully for a while and then dialed still another number.

This time the telephone at the other end rang a long time before the connection snapped and a hoarse, blurred voice said: "Abraham Moscowitz, Attorney, speaking."

Latin said: "This is Latin, Abe."

"O.K. I'm coming." The line clicked and was dead.

LATIN SWORE to himself and dialed the same number again. "O.K., O.K.," said Moscowitz's blurred voice. "Don't get ants in your pants. I said I'm coming. Give me a chance to put on my shoes first, will you?"

"I'm not in jail," Latin told him.

"What?" said Moscowitz incredulously. "You mean those police bums got the nerve to hold you without booking you? Get off the phone so I can call the mayor! I'll fix 'em!"

"Shut up," said Latin. "I'm not even arrested. I want to ask you some questions about law."

"Law?" said Moscowitz. "I don't know anything about law. I'm an attorney."

"Did you ever do any business with a private detective named Steamer Morgan?"

"Nope," said Moscowitz. "He's too ignorant. He won't even commit perjury. Can you imagine a private detective that won't commit perjury? What good is he as a witness?"

"Who does he work for?"

"Baldwin and Frazier, mostly. They are a couple of old dodos with hay in their hair. Sometimes they win a case by accident, but not very often."

"What kind of cases?"

"They got a whole bunch of corporate accounts they inherited from their grandpappies."

"Anything in court now that's hot?"

"They got half-a-dozen appeals floating around here and there. Stockholders' suits. They're always suing for an accounting."

"What does that mean?" Latin asked.

"Oh, that's when the stockholders find out there's no dough in the treasury and they want to find out who spent it and what for. I always say, as long as it's gone—who cares? Some sharpshooter is always rapping suckers for their nickels. It doesn't make much difference who he is or how he does it—they won't get their money back."

"Ever hear of a girl named Lily Trace?"

"*Whee!*"

"Aside from that, do you know anything about her?"

"Nope. I never met her except in my dreams."

"How about a gent named Caleb Drew?"

"Never heard of him."

"He's going to marry Lily Trace."

"Marry her?" Moscowitz repeated, startled. "Say, now there's a smart guy! I never thought of that. A marriage license only costs two bucks, and mink coats come a lot higher than that—even wholesale."

"Good-bye," said Latin. He put the telephone back in its cradle and downed the small drink of brandy. He got up out of the booth and went through the metal swing door into the kitchen.

After a moment Guiterrez followed him. He was carrying Latin's hat and topcoat. Without a word he helped Latin into the coat.

Latin took a stubby hammerless Smith and Wesson revolver out of the waistband of his trousers and dropped it into the side pocket of the topcoat. He took his hat from Guiterrez and put it on carefully.

Guiterrez cleared his throat. "Be a little careful, huh?" he suggested uneasily.

Latin winked at him and went out the back door.

THE GRAVESEND Manor Apartment Hotel was a somber, heavily dignified building in the massive style of a medieval European castle. It had a lobby like a baronial hall, long and narrow, with ornamental beams that were smooth and dark and oily against the high white ceiling. Latin walked down a length of deep red carpet to the small desk in the corner.

"I'd like to speak to Caleb Drew," he said.

The desk clerk was a small, plump man with a benign smile and white hair that floated around his head like a halo. He looked like a casket salesman.

"I'm sorry, sir," he said, as though he really meant it. "He's not in now."

"It's rather important that I see him," said Latin. "Do you expect him soon?"

"No, sir. That is, I have no idea when he'll return."

Latin nodded and frowned as though he were masticating on some weighty problem. Finally he leaned confidentially on the desk.

"May I have your name?"

"Mr. Hammersley, sir," the clerk said, looking faintly surprised.

"Mr. Hammersley, I'm Detective Inspector Walters of the Homicide detail. May I speak to you in confidence?"

"Oh, of course," said Hammersley, impressed.

"Have you ever heard of a man named Max Latin?"

"That person!" said Hammersley. "Oh, yes indeed! I follow the crime news with—ah—considerable interest. A hobby of mine, you might say. This Latin seems to be a very reprehensible sort of a character—always getting arrested for something or other. He's a private detective, isn't he, sir?"

"That's what he claims," said Latin. "But I know him well, and in my opinion he's nothing but a crook. We're very anxious to prove that. He's in trouble right now over the matter of an unexplained murder."

"Murder!" Hammersley repeated, blinking.

"Yes. He has homicidal tendencies. Now, we have heard it rumored that he's done some sort of work for Mr. Drew in the past. Not connected with this business, of course, but we think that Latin might try to get in touch with Mr. Drew, knowing how influential Mr. Drew is, to try to persuade him to lend Latin his influence or even some money."

"I understand," said Hammersley eagerly.

"Have you seen Latin around here? He looks a little bit like me."

"No, I haven't. I'm certain I'd have noticed him if he'd been here. I can recognize his type easily."

"Be sure and notify headquarters if you see him. But I think—knowing the sly, crafty nature of the man—that he will probably attempt to get in touch with Mr. Drew by telephone. I know this is a very unusual request, but will you tell me if Mr. Drew has received any telephone calls this evening while he's been out? I'm sure Gravesend Manor would want to cooperate with the authorities, and this man Latin is really a menace."

"In the circumstances," said Hammersley, "anything we can do…." He fluttered through some telephone call slips and put several on the desk in front of Latin. "You can see that if he did call, he didn't leave his name."

"Oh, he wouldn't use his own name," Latin said, going through the slips. "How about these five calls? They're all from the same person."

"Oh, no," said Hammersley. "They don't have anything to do with Latin."

"I hate to seem inquisitive, but I'd like to be sure—"

"They're all from Miss Mayan. Miss Teresa Mayan. She's Mr. Drew's secretary. She called here repeatedly early this evening, as you see. She said she had to get in touch with Mr. Drew in regard to an important business matter."

"Oh, yes," said Latin. "I wonder. Perhaps she could tell me something about Mr. Drew's business dealings with Latin. It's something I don't like to speak about over the telephone. Do you know where she lives?"

"Yes. At Hadley House. It's on First and Drexel."

"Thank you, Mr. Hammersley," said Latin. "We of the police department appreciate the help of conscientious citizens like you are."

"It was nothing at all," Hammersley said, embarrassed and pleased. "Don't mention it."

CHAPTER FOUR
TARGET FOR TERESA

HADLEY HOUSE went in for the modernistic. It was all as sleek and streamlined as a pursuit plane. Latin got out of the mirror-studded, chromium-lined elevator at the fourth floor and walked down a long hall that had pale blue walls and a dark blue ceiling. He knocked on the door numbered 412.

Teresa Mayan opened it. Latin had never seen her before, but he recognized her at once from the descriptions Guiterrez and Dick had given him. She was the girl who had been with the drunk called Don at the restaurant.

She was wearing a black satin hostess coat that rustled luxuriously when she moved, and her face looked pale and still and thoughtful above it. She was not at all surprised to see Latin. She nodded casually and said: "Come on in."

Latin stepped into the square, low-ceilinged living room and watched her move in her gracefully indolent way to the liquor cabinet in the corner. She poured whiskey out of a squat decanter into two tall, silver-rimmed glasses, fizzed a shot of soda into each. She gave Latin one of the glasses and pointed to the divan.

"Sit down."

Latin sat down slowly, holding the glass in both hands, and watched her. He couldn't quite figure out this approach and he said: "Were you expecting someone—I mean, now?"

"Yes," said Teresa Mayan. "You."

"Do you know who I am?" Latin asked.

She nodded. "I recognized you—from your picture. It's quite a remarkable likeness."

"Picture?" Latin repeated slowly and thoughtfully.

Teresa Mayan smiled at him. "You're quite a clever little lad, but that surprised you, didn't it? You didn't know I had a camera with me, did you?"

"No," said Latin honestly. "I didn't."

"A good one, too. A very good one. Wait." She walked through the doorway that led into the bedroom and came out carrying a large flat square of cardboard. "Be careful. It's still wet."

She lowered the cardboard so that he could see the wet photographic print lying on it. Latin looked and closed his eyes slowly and then looked again.

It was a remarkably good picture of him. Very effective, too. He *was* kneeling down, holding a match in front of him, and the match flame made his features look white and sharp and clear. It also revealed plainly the body that was lying on the ground in front of him, the slick shine of the pool of blood, the pale loosened features of Steamer Morgan, and even a couple of shadowy garbage cans.

"I've got a title for it," said Teresa Mayan. "I'm going to call it 'Caught in the Act.' I think that sort of explains it, don't you?"

"Sort of," Latin agreed. His face looked white and a little strained.

"The camera is specially made for candid shots," Teresa Mayan explained. "Has a beautiful lens. Very fast, very sensitive. A match in a dark alley like that was just right for it."

"I can see that," said Latin.

"I developed the print myself. I have knockdown dark-room equipment here."

"Very handy," said Latin.

"Yes, it is. I got it for Don. I've been keeping him amused by letting him take nude candid shots of me." She smoothed the front of her housecoat. "I make a good nude model if you like them long and limber."

"Oh," said Latin.

TERESA MAYAN laughed at him.

"Still a little at sea, aren't you? I'll tell you how it was. I know that you own that restaurant and that you hang around there all the time and that you're a sharpshooter. It's not as big a secret as you seem to think. And I knew that the dope who runs it for you—Guiterrez—saw me tonight when he fell over the body in the alley. He covered it up—pretending he didn't know there was anyone around and acted scared out of his pants—but he didn't fool me. I knew he recognized me, and I knew you'd find out who I was someway or other and come around and try to black-mail me. I was right, wasn't I?"

"It looks that way," Latin admitted.

"So I acted to protect myself," said Teresa Mayan. "You played right along with me by moving the body. Now I've got more on you than you have on me." She indicated the picture with a forefinger that had a bloodred glistening nail two inches long and pointed like a dagger. "I only developed one negative. I've got a lot more."

"Where?" Latin asked.

"Not here," she said, smiling coolly. "Now you put that print in your pocket and run along home. Take a look at it any time you get more smart ideas about shaking me down."

"O.K.," said Latin glumly. He put his glass down on the coffee table and got up. "I don't suppose it would do any good to tell you that I didn't have any such ideas in mind at all when I came over here?"

Teresa Mayan stood and laughed at him in a lightly amused way.

"O.K.," said Latin again.

He took one catlike step toward her and hit her. His fist didn't travel more than six inches, and it landed with a sharp smack on the hinge of her jaw just below her ear. Teresa Mayan whirled around with a graceful rustle of silk, fell across the divan, and rolled off on the floor. She lay motionless, face down.

Latin dropped instantly on one knee and one hand, like a football linesman getting ready to charge. He was holding the stubby Smith and Wesson in his other hand, and he peered tensely over the top of the divan at the door into the bedroom.

Nothing happened. There was no sound, no movement in the apartment. A minute dragged past, then another. Latin came up out of his crouch and slid into the bedroom and flicked the light switch.

The room was severely modernistic. The bed was low and wide. It had no foot, and the head was one huge mirror. There were a good many pictures of Teresa Mayan on the walls. As she had said, she made a very good nude model if you like them long and limber.

Latin looked in the closet and in the bathroom. He went back through the living room and tried the kitchen. The portable developing outfit was on the tile sideboard next to the sink. Its light-proof hood was raised now, and there were trays and round bottles of developing fluid lined up behind it. The camera was there, too. A pocket-sized German miniature. The back of it was open. There was no film in it and none anywhere around that Latin could see.

Silk rustled in the living room, and Latin jumped for the doorway. Teresa Mayan was still lying in a limp, graceful heap on the floor.

Latin walked over and looked down at her. "The trouble with you is that you've been to too many movies. You're not dealing with Charlie Chan now. I want that negative. Where is it?"

She didn't move.

LATIN LEANED over and picked her up effortlessly and bounced her on the divan. She pulled herself slowly up to a sitting position. There was a little red spot on her cheek where Latin had hit her, and she rubbed it slowly and gently, watching him with eyes that were glistening, narrow slits.

"This isn't going to hurt me worse than it does you," Latin told her conversationally. "In fact, I just love to bat people around. You tell me where that film is or you're going to be in the market for some store teeth. You got yourself into this by being too smart. Guiterrez actually didn't see you in the alley. He really was scared out of his pants. I didn't come around here to blackmail you. I didn't know who you were or that you were anywhere near that alley. I wanted to find Caleb Drew, and I thought he'd probably check in here sooner or later."

Teresa Mayan said: "What do you want him for?"

"I'm working for him."

"You're a liar."

"Certainly. That's why he hired me. I'm supposed to be negotiating for the return of some of Lily Trace's jewelry that hasn't been stolen."

Her eyes looked as lidless and deadly as a snake's. "Why?"

"She wants publicity. I was going to tell Caleb Drew that if she wanted to get it from what I was doing, she'd have to keep her own big mouth shut. If she doesn't quit sounding off everyone will know it's a phoney. Now I want that film. I don't think it's going to convict me of murder or anything like that, but it can make me plenty of trouble. Where is it?"

"Then what happens?"

"We'll talk about that after I get the film."

"It's in the top drawer of the desk over there."

The desk was against the wall next to the door into the bedroom. Latin went over to it and opened the top drawer. He leaned down to look into it, and the bullet that had been meant for the back of his head missed by about an inch and buried itself in the wall in front of his face.

Latin didn't turn around or straighten up. He dived headfirst through the door into the bedroom. As he hit the floor and rolled, he flipped his arm up and shoved the door hard. The sound of its slam was like an echo of the bursting smash of the shot.

Latin rolled on over and came up to his knees, cursing himself soundlessly. Teresa Mayan wasn't wearing anything under the hostess coat, and it didn't have any pockets large enough to hide a gun. But he should have known she would have one cached around somewhere. Probably it had been poked back of the cushions on the divan.

Another report smacked out, and the bullet made a neat white hole in the door about six inches below the knob. It would have taken Latin right in the middle of the face had he been trying to look through the keyhole.

Latin didn't like that, either. Teresa Mayan could call her shots. He knew just as well as if he could see her that she was kneeling in back of the divan, using its top for a rest. From the sound of its reports, he judged she was using a .25 caliber automatic. That meant she had at least five more shots. Under the circumstances, Latin had no slightest urge to open the door.

This was like a motion picture script that had gone haywire. The heroine besieged in the bedroom protecting her honor. Only Latin wasn't a heroine, and he didn't have any honor.

HE TILTED his head, listening intently. There were faint, hurried sounds of motion in the living room. The subdued swish of silk, the muffled tap of a high heel. Latin got up and slid along the wall beside the door. He paused again to listen. If she wasn't on a direct line with the doorway, he had some chance of getting out and finding cover before she could hit him.

He reached slowly and cautiously for the knob and then stiffened rigidly as a latch clicked. It wasn't the bedroom door, though. It was the front door. It slammed with a final, solid thud.

Latin jerked the bedroom door open and slammed it back against the wall. He was afraid of a trick, and he didn't show himself in the doorway. He stayed flat beside it.

Voices came to him very faintly, mumbling from the hall just outside the apartment. Among them, Teresa Mayan's sounded quite clear and loud.

"Shots? Yes, I heard them plainly."

Latin came into the living room and walked across to the front door and put his ear against the panel. It sounded like there were a dozen people in the hall, all talking at once. Teresa Mayan's voice came again.

"You'd better keep watch here in the hallway. There might be a prowler around. Of course, he couldn't be in my apartment, but I'd feel safer if you'd just watch my door for a little while. It's silly, I know, but I'm so easily frightened by just the thought of things like that."

Another voice said: "Oh, I'll be watching, Miss Mayan."

Latin said some more things to himself. If he stepped out of the apartment now, there was sure to be a beef. That was the last thing he wanted at the moment. He was cornered.

After thinking it over, he shrugged casually and looked around the front room. The satin hostess coat lay on the floor in an untidy pile. Latin studied it for a second, puzzled, and then he understood. Teresa Mayan's tailored gabardine sport coat had been lying across one of the chairs. It was gone now.

She hadn't been able to get at any of her clothes in the bedroom. The hostess coat was too bulky to fit under the sport coat. She had discarded it and put on the sport coat in its place. As a costume, it was a trifle sketchy, but it would get by. She had been wearing plain black suede bedroom slippers. They were a little exotic for street wear, but she probably didn't intend to do any walking.

Latin shook his head ruefully. He braced one of the chairs under the doorknob and began to search the living room. He found some packets of love letters that made very interesting reading, but their writers had signed them with nicknames that didn't mean anything to him.

He went on into the bedroom. He uncovered an astonishing array of underclothing, all very expensive, lots of costume jewelry, and a great many more pictures of Teresa Mayan. She evidently was quite proud of her own anatomy.

He didn't find any film negative, and he moved to the bathroom. He opened the lid of the big wicker clothes hamper and stood there, rigid with surprise, staring down into the face of the man squatting inside it.

After a long time, Latin took his handkerchief from his pocket and wiped his forehead. The face of the man in the clothes hamper was a mottled bluish-red, and his eyes bulged horribly. He was dead.

LATIN LEFT him there. He went back into the living room hurriedly and picked up the drink Teresa Mayan had poured for him. He lifted it to his lips and then froze, staring down into it with a sort of fascinated horror. He was thinking of the round, brown bottles of developing fluid on the drainboard in the kitchen.

"Good God," he said in a whisper. He poked one finger in the whiskey and touched the end of it gingerly with the tip of his tongue. He put the drink down very quickly.

He remembered hearing somewhere that some sort of cyanide derivative was used in developing film. Teresa Mayan evidently also used it for a mixer. Latin's whiskey was laced with it.

"Good God," he said again, thinking of the blue face of the man in the clothes hamper.

He revised his estimate of Teresa Mayan upward ten notches. She had put the cyanide in the drink while he was in the bedroom. She had known he'd hear what she said out in the hall and that he wouldn't want to dash out and start an argument with the other tenants. He'd wait for a while, and while he was waiting, what would be more natural than to take a drink? And two bodies were just as easy to dispose of as one.

"Yes, indeed," said Latin to himself.

He went over to the telephone stand in the corner and dialed the number of Guiterrez's restaurant. The instrument at the other end got time to ring only once, and then Guiterrez's voice bellowed in his ear: "We're closed!"

"This is Latin."

"I said we're closed! We don't serve no more tonight! You come around here and start a beef, and I'll have you *arrested!*"

"Are the cops there looking for me?" Latin asked. "Are they listening to you?"

"*Yes,* you heard me! I said I'll have you *arrested,* or maybe even *murder* you!"

"Is it Walters?" Latin inquired.

"So you got a pull with the cops, have you? All right, I'll have the *district attorney's men* pinch you! And don't think they won't!"

"Thanks," Latin said. "I'll keep undercover."

He put the telephone back in its cradle and returned to the bathroom. He searched the man with the blue face and found from the contents of his wallet that his name was Donald K. Raleigh. Going into the living room, he picked up the telephone and dialed another number.

After about ten rings a hollow, tired voice said: "This is Abraham Moscowitz, the attorney who never sleeps."

"It's Latin again, Abe."

"I'm putting on my shoes right now."

"Never mind. I'm not in jail—yet. How do you feel about murder, Abe?"

"I can take it or leave it alone. Why don't you? I mean leave it alone."

"It follows me around and comes when I whistle—sometimes even when I don't. The district attorney's men are looking for me to ask me about killing Steamer Morgan."

"So you're eliminating competition now, eh? You'd better watch out for the feds. Murder is considered an unfair trade practice in some industries, I understand."

"I didn't kill Steamer. They don't even think I did. They want to hold me while they ask me about some jewels I'm not negotiating to buy back from some thieves who didn't steal them."

"That makes as much sense as a Supreme Court decision. Call me back in the morning."

"Wait a minute," Latin requested. "You mentioned that Steamer worked for a law firm named Baldwin and Frazier. Do they have any case on now involving a man named Donald K. Raleigh?"

"Raleigh," Moscowitz repeated thoughtfully. "Raleigh.... Oh, yeah. The Cataract Power Company case. It's been banging around in the courts for three years. It's got whiskers as long as Frazier and Baldwin have. Raleigh is the president of Cataract Power."

"What's the case about?"

"The same old story. There ain't no dough in the treasury and no kilowatts in the powerhouse and no customers to buy any even if there were. So the suckers want to know why. I could tell them for free. Raleigh's grandpappy and his pappy were smart men in a steal. They could grab the power rights on a river and pay off in confederate money and make the chumps like it, but he can't. He's a rumdumb. I don't think he stole the company dough—that is, intentionally. He probably spent it trying to crossbreed giant pandas and teddy bears or trying to corner the paperweight market."

"Why has the case been dragging on so long?"

"Well, naturally Raleigh doesn't want to go to jail. He will if he ever testifies. He's too stupid to lie convincingly. Even to the juries they hatch up in this state—and do we have some dillies! So the first time Baldwin and Frazier jumped him, he fixed the judge and got the case dismissed. So Baldwin and Frazier appealed that decision and got it reversed and started over with another judge that he couldn't fix. So now Raleigh is too sick to appear in court. He's been sick for six months or so. Maybe he really is, I don't know."

"He looked pretty bad the last time I saw him," Latin observed. "In fact, I think somebody may start a rumor that I murdered him."

"Did you?"

"No."

"Well, then what are you calling me for?" Moscowitz snarled. "If I've told you once, I've told you twenty times that I won't defend an innocent client! That's too hard work. If you want me to keep you out of jail, don't get pinched for things you didn't do!"

"O.K. I'll go murder somebody else right away."

"Now you're talking. Be sure you do it in front of some nice, honest witnesses. It's cheaper to buy them before than to bribe them afterwards."

"Good-bye," said Latin.

CHAPTER FIVE
LILY TAKES A LICKING

THE FIRST thin red rays of the sun hit the casement windows in the tall spire of the Château Carleton and reflected in a million jewellike pinpoints. Now, in the dawn, the streets were hushed and quiet and empty, and Latin was all alone as he walked past the front of the building and turned down the side street beyond it.

A garbage can bonged against some obstruction and raised dismal, clanking echoes, and then a man came out of the alley behind the apartment building rolling the can along expertly in front of him. He deposited it at the curb beside three more like it and paused to wipe his forehead with a luridly pink bandana.

Two men crossed the street toward him. They were Bruce and Bill, the college men. They were wearing their overcoats and white scarfs, and each carried a cellophane-wrapped florist's box under his arm. They didn't look so healthy this morning, but they were up and around.

Latin slowed to a saunter, watching. Bruce and Bill came up to the janitor and halted, standing at attention.

"Will you let us in the building?" Bruce asked.

"We want to see Miss Lily Trace," Bill added.

The janitor eyed them sourly. "You got a nerve, you two. After the hell you raised last night."

"We came to apologize for that," Bruce said.

Bill held out a ten dollar bill wordlessly.

"Well…," said the janitor uncertainly. "Why don't you wait until some decent hour to do your apologizing?"

"Miss Trace will be up," Bruce said.

"She told us she always waits up to see the sun rise," Bill explained.

"Well, all right," said the janitor, taking the bill. "But no fighting and hollering, remember. Come on and—What do *you* want?"

"I'm with these gentlemen," said Latin.

Bruce and Bill looked at him in surprise.

"I'm Miss Trace's agent," Latin explained.

"Her business agent?" Bruce asked.

Latin nodded casually. "Sort of. Lead on, MacDuff!"

"The name is MacGillicuddy," the janitor corrected.

He piloted them along the alley and down a flight of cement steps into the shadowy reaches of the apartment basement. He opened the door of the express elevator and pointed to the control panel.

"It operates itself. Just punch the buttons."

Bruce and Bill and Latin got in the elevator, and Bill pushed the button numbered 7. The elevator rose with ponderous, quiet dignity.

Bruce cleared his throat. "I hope Miss Trace won't be too angry at us. We behaved very rudely to her last night. We were drunk."

"How'd you like Priscilla?" Latin asked.

Bruce and Bill looked at each other, startled.

"The taxi driver who took you to Kate's is a friend of mine," Latin explained.

"Oh," said Bruce.

"We enjoyed her very much—I think," said Bill.

Latin nodded. "I'll tell her the next time I see her. She'll be interested to know that she looks like Lily Trace."

There was a pained silence until the elevator stopped gently. Bill slid the door back and then followed Latin and Bruce down the hall. Bruce stopped in front of the door numbered 702 and reached for the gilt knocker.

Latin pushed his hand away. "Listen!"

INSIDE THE apartment there was a rumbling thump, and then the sharp smash of breaking glass. A woman screamed in a choked, furious way.

Latin tried the door. It was locked. He slammed his shoulder against the panel. The door was thick and as solid as a stone wall. It bounced him right back.

The woman screamed again. Bruce and Bill shoved Latin to one side and hit the door together, grunting in concert. They hit hard and expertly, shoulders down, but the door was equal to them. It didn't even squeak.

Latin caught Bill by the shoulder and pulled him back. "Down that hall and around to the side! There must be a back door or a terrace to this apartment! Quick!"

Bill went down the hall at a run. Latin hammered on the door with both fists.

"Open up! Open the door!"

There was another final thump and then silence. On the other side of the door someone whimpered softly. Latin rattled the knob fiercely while Bruce breathed on the back of his neck.

The lock snapped. Latin kicked the door wide open and jumped into the apartment, crouching, the stubby revolver poised in his right hand.

"Oh, my God!" Bruce whispered.

Lily Trace was sitting down on the floor with her back against the wall and her rounded, bare legs spread out asprawl in front of her. Her hair was pulled down over her forehead, and she glared through it at them like a cornered animal. She had been wearing a black silk nightgown, but there wasn't much left of it.

"That bitch!" she said breathlessly. She was holding both hands up to her right cheek. She took the hands away, revealing four red furrows that ran from under her eye down past the corner of her mouth. She looked at the blood on her fingers and said many more things, all obscene. The room looked like someone had tried to cage a stray typhoon in it.

Bill came staggering through the rear door of the living room. He was bent painfully double, and his face was white and sick-looking.

"She—kicked me. I tried to stop her—"

He sat down on the side of an overturned chair and rocked back and forth.

LILY TRACE had pulled the remnants of her nightgown from her shoulders and was gingerly examining four more parallel red gashes that ran from her collarbone down between her breasts to her hip like a fantastic slanted bandolier. She looked up and nodded at Latin.

"Forget the jewelry gag, Latin. Get that dame for me. I'll pay anything extra it costs."

"What do you want me to do with her when I get her?" Latin asked.

"Light a cigarette," said Lily Trace. "And stick it in her eye. Or better yet—hold her until I can get there and do it myself." She wasn't fooling.

"I'll see what I can do," said Latin. "Want me to call you a doctor now?"

Lily Trace's mouth was swollen, and she grinned at him lopsidedly. "Hell, no. I've been beaten up worse than this—but not lately. The Gold Dust Twins, here, will help me patch myself up. You get out and locate that dame for me."

Latin liked her suddenly, better than he would have thought possible a half hour before. He nodded and grinned at her.

"I'll find her. I'll get in touch with you when I do. Put your face together again carefully. It's too nice to spoil."

"Well, thanks, kid," said Lily Trace. "See you soon."

Latin chuckled and went out into the hall. Three or four sleepy, awed tenants watched him as he got into the freight elevator and closed the door behind him. He punched the button for the basement and rode downward.

The janitor was nowhere in sight in the cellar, and Latin walked through it and up the flight of cement steps into the alley.

"Tweet-tweet," said a hoarse voice.

Latin stopped instantly. Inspector Walters sauntered over to him and took hold of his arm in a friendly way.

"This is another one of those coincidences," he greeted. "I was just thinking about you. I was saying to myself: 'I wonder what my old pal Latin is doing with himself these days.' And here you are. Funny, eh?"

"No," said Latin. "I thought you were going to keep the district attorney's office off my neck."

"That was before a cop reported that he spotted Steamer Morgan hanging around your joint. Where were you all night—if the answer won't shock me too much?"

"I was cornered in an apartment with a house dick and three old maids watching the door. I had to wait until they got tired and went away. I've got your murderer cornered for you now."

"That's a matter of indifference to me," said Walters. "On account of I've got *you* cornered. The district attorney's dopes were too dumb to look under those ashes in your alley, but I wasn't. Let's see you work yourself out of that hold."

"Come along," Latin invited.

MR. HAMMERSLEY was still on duty when Latin and Inspector Walters entered the enormous, austere lobby of the Gravesend Manor.

"How do you do, Inspector Walters," he said cordially.

Walters's mouth opened in surprise, but before he could make any reply, Latin said smoothly: "Good morning, Mr. Hammersley. This man is one of my subordinates. It has become very important that I see Mr. Drew at once. Is he in?"

"Why, yes," said Hammersley, "but he left strict instructions that he was not to be disturbed for any reason. He said he wouldn't answer the phone or the doorbell."

"I'm very sorry," Latin said firmly, "but we must see him. Will you give me the passkey to his apartment? You can trust my discretion."

"I'm sure I can," Hammersley agreed, handing over a tagged passkey. "Mr. Drew has apartment 404. Have the police apprehended that Latin person as yet?"

"Oh, yes," said Latin. "He's in custody right now."

He led the way to the elevator, with Walters following a step behind him.

"Impersonating an officer," Walters said grimly. "I don't mind that so much. What gets me is that you impersonated *me*—and then introduced me as my own subordinate!"

The elevator stopped at the fourth floor, and they walked down a shadowed hallway to the dark, fumed oak door that had the small silvered numerals, 404, placed in a neat slant across its middle panel.

"We'll give him a try," said Latin.

He rang the doorbell and then knocked loudly on the door with his fist. There was no answer. After waiting a moment, Latin fitted the passkey in the lock and opened the door.

The living room was square and low-ceilinged, furnished in massive, heavy mahogany. From the doorway at the left came the spattering thunder of a shower.

Latin, with Walters still right behind him, looked in the living room closet, in the bedroom and its closet, and into the kitchenette that was fitted up as a bar. He came back into the living room and pushed the bathroom door wider.

Steam misted the mirror and the chrome fittings of the sink and toilet and billowed in misty clouds against the moisture-beaded ceiling. On the far side of the room there was a sunken bathtub completely enclosed now with a slickly wet shower curtain. Water splashed noisily behind it.

Latin raised his voice: "Drew!"

THE CURTAIN shivered and billowed, and then Drew put his head around the edge of it, wiping soap and water out of his eyes.

"What the devil.... Oh, it's you. I didn't hear the doorbell. Who's that with you?"

"Inspector Walters, Homicide," said Walters.

Drew's eyes widened. "Oh. Well—well, make yourselves at home. I'll be out in just a second."

Latin and Walters went back into the living room. In the bathroom, the sound of the shower stopped abruptly, and then Drew came out into the living room, wrapping himself in a woolly white bathrobe. He looked puzzled and worried.

"Are you in trouble, Latin?"

"Somewhat," Latin admitted. "That's what I wanted to talk to you about."

"Oh," said Drew vaguely. "Well, would you like a drink? I've got some of your favorite brandy."

"Is the bottle open?" Latin asked.

Drew shook his head. "No. I seldom drink brandy."

"I'll take some," said Latin, "if I can watch you open the bottle."

"Why, yes," said Drew in amazement.

He found it in the cupboard behind the kitchenette bar. With Latin watching, he cut through the foil seal and worked out the cork.

"What did you want?" Drew asked.

Latin had the brandy in an inhaler a little smaller than a goldfish bowl. He sniffed at it appreciatively, took a sip, and rolled it around on his tongue.

"We're looking for Teresa Mayan," he said, swallowing. "Do you know her?"

"Of course," said Drew. "She's my secretary."

"She used to be your mistress, didn't she?"

"Sort of," Drew admitted.

"But she isn't now?"

Drew coughed. "Well, now and then...."

Latin nodded. "Yeah. Have you seen her lately?"

"Not for the last few days. I haven't been to my office."

"She tried to get you last night—on the phone."

"Yes," said Drew. "She wanted me to sign some important letters."

"Did she bring them over here?"

"No."

"Has she been here?"

"No," said Drew, irritated. "She hasn't been here, and she isn't here now. Look around if you don't believe me."

"We have," said Walters glumly. "Don't ask me why, though. I'm just a subordinate."

Latin said: "Did Teresa kick up a row when you gave her the old brush-off?"

Drew controlled his temper. "Yes, she did. A hell of a row, if you must know."

"But you still hire her?"

Drew shrugged. "She's a good secretary and she knows a lot about my business."

"Do you know a man named Donald K. Raleigh?" Latin asked.

DREW EYED him in silence for a long moment and then said slowly: "Yes. I know of him. I don't know him personally. He's president of the Cataract Power Company. He moved in with Teresa after I moved out. That's why she hasn't been bothering me lately."

"Did you know Raleigh was in legal trouble?"

"Just a stockholders' suit," Drew said. "It doesn't mean anything. I understand from what Teresa has said that he's stalling them. They'll get tired pretty soon."

"Those stockholders," Latin said, "got hold of a couple of lawyers who don't get tired and who—believe it or not—

are also honest. Raleigh was pretending he was too sick to appear in court. The lawyers hired a private detective to follow him and prove he wasn't. The private detective got the goods on him last night. He got pictures of him eating and drinking in Guiterrez's restaurant, and he got Raleigh's signature on a dated menu from that restaurant. Evidence like that, you can't skid around."

"Ah-ha!" Walters said, suddenly seeing the light. "So Steamer pulled his autograph collecting gag once too often!"

"Yes," said Latin. "Raleigh was too drunk to know the difference. But Teresa Mayan was with him, and she wasn't. She spotted Steamer, so Steamer ended up in the alley with his throat cut and his pockets empty."

"No!" Drew protested instantly. "Teresa wouldn't—"

"Raleigh was plenty scared when he sobered up enough to understand, after they got back to Teresa's apartment," Latin went on. "Teresa scared him some more. I don't know what she told him. It probably was convincing, and he was pretty dumb and pretty fuddled anyway. She told him he'd have to beat it—skip the country. He had assets hidden around here and there. She got his power of attorney, so she could cash in on them and send them to him."

Latin smiled thinly. "She didn't mean to do it, of course. She didn't even give him a chance to go anywhere. She put some cyanide in his farewell drink of whiskey and dumped him into the dirty clothes hamper. She had decided to move back in on you, Drew."

Drew was staring at him, fascinated. "I—I don't believe.... Why, Teresa wouldn't—"

"She went over and beat up Lily Trace to warn Lily to keep her hands off."

Drew's face whitened. "Lily!" He turned and jumped for the telephone.

"She's all right," Latin said, heading him off. "A little battered and bruised, but that's all. You better not call her now. I don't think she'd be in very good humor. After all, she knows who beat her up and why."

"Oh," said Drew uncertainly.

"All I want to know," said Walters, "is where is this here Teresa Mayan?"

"I can't figure that out," Latin said slowly. "I was sure she'd come here. She wouldn't risk going back to her own apartment until she got some reinforcements or found out what happened to me. She ought to be here now."

"Well, she ain't," said Walters.

Latin was frowning at Drew, his eyes narrowed and calculating. He looked at Drew's water-damp hair, at the bathrobe. He glanced toward the bathroom door in the same calculating way and then back to Drew again. He cleared his throat.

"May I have some more brandy?"

"Surely," said Drew. "Try it with some soda. I'll get some ice...."

HE REACHED down under the little shelf that served as a bar. Latin stepped silently forward and picked up the brandy bottle by its neck and swung it in a glistening arc.

There was a sodden smack as the bottle hit Drew's head. He bounced backward into some shelves loaded with glasses and brought them down around him in a ringing, shattering crash.

"They make these thick," Latin said, examining the brandy bottle. "It didn't even crack."

"Talk," Walters ordered dangerously. "Real fast, pal."

"Look in the bathroom," Latin said. "In the tub."

Walters went into the bathroom and came out again almost instantly. "There's a dame in there. She's dead. Drowned."

"Teresa Mayan," said Latin. "Drew was behind her all the time. She was crazy about him. She spotted Steamer at Guiterrez's or on the way there, and she telephoned Drew from the restaurant. He took care of Steamer—with her help. He fed Raleigh a cyanide drink—again, with her help. He planned all this just like I outlined it, only he was going to get the dough—not Teresa. She would do anything he said, but she wouldn't stand for Lily Trace. When she found out about that, she went on a rampage. She smacked Lily around, and she must have told Drew she'd squeal on him if he didn't quit looking in that direction. Drew had maneuvered all this business with Raleigh just to get enough money to get Lily. He wouldn't throw the prize away after he'd won the game, so he dunked Teresa in the bathtub.

"He had it all figured out that she was to take the blame for everything and then throw herself in the river for remorse over her evil deeds."

Walters had a small round tin in his hand. "She was only wearing a sport coat, and this was the only thing in the pockets. I wonder what it is?"

"Open it and see what's inside," Latin suggested.

Walters unscrewed the cover of the tin. He reached in and pulled out a long string of 36-millimeter film.

"Pictures!" he exclaimed. "Now why would she be carrying these around with her?"

"We'll never know," said Latin, pouring himself a drink. "Because that was undeveloped film, and when you exposed it to the light, you ruined it."

GIVE THE DEVIL HIS DUE

"WOULD YOU MIND MURDERING
A MAN FOR ME, MR. LATIN?"
INQUIRED THE SUAVE COUNT
FIOLO. "NOT AT ALL," REPLIED
LATIN, "IF THE PRICE IS RIGHT."
AND ON THIS NOTE OF MUTUAL
UNDERSTANDING, THE BRANDY-
GUZZLING SLEUTH JOINED
THE LITTLE GROUP WHO WERE
SEARCHING FRANTICALLY FOR
THE MISSING JUPITER ZACHARY—
TO MAKE SURE HE STAYED THAT
WAY.

CHAPTER ONE
A BREAK FOR A BUM

GUITERREZ WAS perched precariously on a high stool in front of the restaurant's main cooking range. His tall chef's hat was pushed down over one eye, and his face was creased into an expression of grimly fierce concentration. He was stirring the contents of a big aluminum kettle with a wooden spoon a good two feet long. He made each movement with as much care as an artist painting a masterpiece.

There were other people in the kitchen, quite a lot of them. Busboys and pantrymen and assistant chefs and dishwashers. They walked softly and talked in whispers and gave Guiterrez a wide berth. The old master was mean enough normally, but when he was cooking he was awful.

He looked up now suddenly and yelled: "Who the hell opened that back door?"

"I did," said Max Latin.

Guiterrez teetered on his stool, glowering. "You, you crook! Are you still running around loose? What's the matter with our police force, anyway? They hardly ever pinch you anymore. Have you bribed them all?"

"Nearly," Latin admitted. He was a tall man, lean and dark and trim-looking. He had greenish eyes that tipped a little, catlike, at the corners, and an expression of blandly cynical self-assurance. "What's that you're cooking?"

"Gumbo," said Guiterrez. "*Gumbo Guiterrez.*"

"Is it on the menu tonight?"

"It is not. It's too good for my lousy customers. It's for the waiters and kitchen help exclusively."

DICK, THE headwaiter, came in through the metal-faced swing door that separated the kitchen from the main dining room. He was a wizened little man, and he was wearing an apron that was large enough to furnish cover for three people his size.

"Listen, lamebrain," he said to Guiterrez. "Why don't you get down off that stool and act like you had some sense?"

"Go away," said Guiterrez. He ladled up a spoonful of the kettle's contents and sipped at it and then muttered to himself threateningly. He took a very small pinch of spice out of one of the cans on the shelf above the range and dropped it into the kettle. He stirred with fanatical care, still muttering.

"Look," said Dick. "I've got a special steak coming up. A five-dollar number. You're supposed to be watching it."

"Shut up!" Guiterrez screamed. "I am composing *Gumbo Guiterrez!* It's a work of genius! Nothing must interfere with my concentration!"

"The steak is for Mr. Saltonwaite," said Dick.

"Go to hell! Take Mr. Saltonwaite with you!"

"He's a good customer," said Dick.

Guiterrez turned around slowly. "How many times must I tell you that this restaurant doesn't have any good customers? They are all pigs."

One of the boards vibrated, next to Latin's ear, and he fired instantly.

"Well, they've come to the right place then," said Dick. He picked up a butcher knife and began to play mumble-ty-peg on the wooden top of the steak table. "Hello, Latin. Who's that droopy-looking dope behind you?"

Latin looked over his shoulder. "What's your name?"

"Boston," said the man. "That's what everybody calls me, I guess."

He was standing close against the back door with his shoulders hunched up close against his skinny neck, as though he were trying to take up as little room as possible. He had a draggled brownish mustache, and his lips trembled in a timidly apologetic smile under it. His eyes were a weak wavering blue. He was wearing an old suit coat fastened up the front with safety pins and overalls with canvas patches on the knees. He needed a shave and his face was dirty and his hair stuck up in clumps through the holes in his shapeless hat.

"I bet they call you worse than that sometimes," Dick observed. "Where'd you pick it up, Latin?"

"I found him out in the alley," Latin said. "He was trying to dig some food out of the restaurant garbage cans. He's hungry. Can you fix him up something decent to eat?"

Guiterrez turned his head. "Is that true, bum? Are you hungry?"

Boston nodded quickly. "Yes, sir. I guess I'm pretty hungry."

"Could you eat a lot?"

"Yes, sir. I sure could, I guess."

"I've got just the thing for you," said Guiterrez. "Nels! Put a setup there at the end of the steam table. Coffee and salad—and a steak knife."

"And a what?" Dick demanded. "Listen, stupid, are you going to give this old rummy Mr. Saltonwaite's special steak?"

"Yes," said Guiterrez, getting down off the stool and heading for the steak broiler. He pulled the door down and peered inside. "It'll be ready in a minute. Nels, hurry with that setup. Bum, go over and wash your hands and face at that sink there." He seized a long-handled fork and prodded at the sizzling steak in the broiler.

"What'll I tell Mr. Saltonwaite?" Dick asked.

"Tell him to go home. Tell him I don't like him."

"You don't even know him," Dick said.

"I don't like him anyway," Guiterrez answered. He slammed the door of the broiler and turned around and yelled: "Get out!"

"O.K.," Dick said. "I'm going. But Mr. Saltonwaite will raise hell." He pushed the swing door open and went into the front of the restaurant.

GUITERREZ OPENED the broiler and prodded the steak again, and it spattered back at him lusciously. One of the busboys rattled plates and cutlery at the end of the steam table. Boston, his face gleaming and his ragged hair slicked back, sat down there and moistened his lips in anticipation.

Dick poked the door open. "I told you," he said. "Here he is."

Saltonwaite thrust past him and into the kitchen. He was skinny and stooped and bald, with a little potbelly like a half-inflated balloon. He still had a napkin tucked into the top of the vest of his neat blue business suit. His wrinkled face was flushed with rage.

"What's this?" he demanded shrilly. "What's this, Guiterrez? Where's my steak?"

"It isn't yours anymore," said Guiterrez. "It belongs to the bum."

Saltonwaite waved his pipe-stem arms. "I ordered that steak specially! You can't do this to me, Guiterrez!"

"Oh, yes I can," said Guiterrez. He proved it by hooking the steak out of the broiler with the fork and carrying it, still spattering, across the kitchen and plopping it down on the plate in front of Boston. "Eat it."

Boston gulped. "If it belongs to this gentleman here, I wouldn't wanta—"

Guiterrez leaned over him. "Eat—that—steak!"

"Yes, sir," said Boston, frightened. He cut hurriedly into the steak.

Saltonwaite licked his thin lips, watching. "This is a crime, Guiterrez! This is outright theft!"

"Sue me," Guiterrez invited.

"My steak," Saltonwaite mourned. "My beautiful, beautiful steak that was specially ordered…." He lifted his head and sniffed alertly. "What's that I smell?"

"If it's bad, it's probably yourself," Guiterrez told him.

"Oh, no," said Saltonwaite, sniffing again. "I think… I know! It's gumbo! Yes, it is! It's cooking right here in this kettle!"

"Get away from there!" Guiterrez shouted. "Leave that alone! That's not on the menu! It's not for the customers!"

"I want some," said Saltonwaite, leaning greedily over the kettle.

"You can't have any! Get out of here!"

"No," said Saltonwaite stubbornly. "I want some of this gumbo."

"Dick," said Guiterrez in a dangerous voice. "Hand me that butcher knife."

Saltonwaite looked around with a desperately cunning gleam in his eyes. Suddenly he snatched a canister from the shelf over the range and held it tilted just over the kettle.

Guiterrez screamed like a man in agony. "Don't! Stop it! That's sugar! Don't pour it in the gumbo, or you'll ruin it!"

"I want some gumbo," said Saltonwaite, wiggling the canister warningly. "Do I get some?"

"Yes!" said Guiterrez. "Get that sugar away from it!"

"I want a lot," Saltonwaite bargained. "Two big bowls."

"Yes!" Guiterrez promised. "Yes, yes, yes!"

SALTONWAITE PUT the canister back on the shelf and patted his hands together in a dignified, scholarly way. "Please see that I am served at once. And remember—two full bowls." He strutted back through the swing door.

"You see?" Guiterrez said accusingly to Latin. "You see the kind of customers you have in your damned restaurant? I won't work here any longer! Don't argue with me! I'm through! I quit! I resign!"

"Write me a letter," Latin invited.

He pushed the metal door open and went into the front room of the restaurant, and it was like entering the violent ward of an asylum. Even this early all the closely placed tables were crowded with customers who were voraciously intent on their food. They ate whatever was put before them whether they had ordered it or not. They didn't care. They had no reason to. All the food Guiterrez served was superb. He was really almost as good a chef as he claimed to be.

Besides its food, the restaurant certainly had no other attractions. It was bare and dingy and crowded and noisier than a street fair on Saturday night. A mangy horde of waiters banged and slammed around and swore at each other and the customers. The cash register clanged and a jukebox shrieked in agony from one corner.

Guiterrez wasn't posing. He hated his customers. When he cooked something he wanted to sit and savor it and congratulate himself. He didn't want to sell it. He was an artist. He tried to make the place as uncomfortable as possible in the hopes his fans would get discouraged and stay away. They didn't.

Latin was used to the uproar, and he sat down in his special booth, the last one of the line against the wall near the kitchen door.

Dick came back from serving Saltonwaite his gumbo and stopped beside Latin's table. "That screwball in the kitchen gets nuttier every day," he observed. "One of these days they're gonna haul him off to the funny house and let him bake mud pies for the rest of his career. What do you want to eat?"

"Brandy," said Latin.

Dick took a bottle and a glass from somewhere under his voluminous apron. "Oh, I knew that." The bottle was a fresh one, and he tore the foil off the cork with his teeth and spat it on the floor. "This stuff has gone up. It costs seventeen-fifty a fifth now, so don't go splashing it around." He pulled out the cork, still using his teeth, and put the bottle and the glass down in front of Latin. "Don't you want anything else though?"

"Not now," said Latin. "Save me some of that gumbo."

"I'll put a bowl in my pocket," Dick promised. He went back into the kitchen.

CHAPTER TWO
DOWN PAYMENT ON MURDER

"**P**ARDON ME," said a gently smooth voice. "If you please. Pardon me."

"All right," said Latin, looking up. "What for?"

"For disturbing you. If you please, may I sit down?"

"Go ahead," Latin said.

The man slid into the seat on the other side of the table and sat there smiling at Latin in a courteously pleased way. He was tall and broad-shouldered and very tanned. He was so handsome he didn't look quite real. His eyes were a deeply limpid brown. He had a thin close-clipped mustache and perfectly waved black hair. He wore a tan gabardine suit and a tan shirt and a darker tan tie. They had all cost money—a lot of it.

"I am Count Fidestine Fiolo," he said. "You are Max Latin, the private inquiry agent, are you not? I am indeed very happy to meet you."

"Thanks," said Latin.

Dick came out of the kitchen and leaned over the high back of the booth. "You sure pick up some crummy characters, Latin," he observed critically. "Where'd you find this study in brown?"

"Never mind," said Latin. "Bring another glass."

Dick produced one from under his apron. "Remember what that brandy costs. Guiterrez says if you don't stop puttin' away so much, you'll have to switch to a cheaper brand. You're runnin' the joint in the red." He went back into the kitchen again.

"Have some brandy?" Latin asked.

Count Fiolo smiled charmingly. "You are so kind. Thank you, I will." He watched. Latin pour the brandy. "Are you an honest man, Mr. Latin?"

"No," Latin answered.

"Are you dishonest? I mean, actively so?"

"Yes," said Latin.

"Ah," said Count Fiolo in a pleased way. "Then we can talk as equals. I, too, am dishonest. Very dishonest. Is that hard for you to believe?"

"No," Latin admitted.

"Good!" said Count Fiolo. "We understand each other already. I wish to hire you to undertake a highly confidential task for me."

"Go ahead," said Latin, pouring himself another glass of brandy.

"All right. Have you ever heard of a man named, most unpleasantly, Ebenezer Zachary?"

"No."

"He was the president of the Planet Iron Foundry—also the sole owner."

"Was?" Latin repeated.

"Yes. He's dead, I'm happy to say. He took a long time to assume that status. I was getting most impatient. He had six strokes and still refused to die like any decent person would. I was seriously considering poisoning him when the seventh finished him. He left two sons."

"So?" said Latin idly.

"Yes. Unfortunately. Their names are Mars and Jupiter. Ebenezer made a hobby of astronomy—hence the peculiar names. Mars Zachary has a daughter named Hester—an only daughter."

"Oh," said Latin.

COUNT FIOLO nodded eagerly. "You are beginning to understand already, eh? Ah, you are very clever. The Planet Iron Foundry is an enormous business. It is worth two or three million dollars."

"The plot being," said Latin, "that you marry the granddaughter and wind up with the iron foundry."

"Correct," said Count Fiolo. "Only it is not quite that simple, I assure you. Else I would not be here, much as I enjoy your company—and the brandy."

Latin poured him another drink.

"Thank you," said Count Fiolo. "You are very kind. There are two obstacles in the way of my—ah—happiness. One of them is Hester, the granddaughter's physical appearance. She has pimples, buckteeth, and halitosis. It is really a dangerous undertaking to kiss her. But that isn't all. She is also flat-breasted and bowlegged. Frankly, the thought of marrying her appalls me. I give you my word that the prospect of it gives me nightmares and I have to drink a great deal of brandy to compose myself."

Latin poured him a drink.

"Thank you so much," said Count Fiolo. "We understand each other."

"Not yet, we don't," said Latin. "What do you expect me to do about Hester? Are you trying to hire me as a substitute?"

"No," said Count Fiolo regretfully. "No, I'm afraid that wouldn't be practical. I will have to bear that burden alone. It will be awful—but three million dollars—No, there's another matter I wish you to look into. Would you mind murdering a man—I mean, of course, as a last resort?"

"Not if the price is right," said Latin.

Count Fiolo waved his hand. "That will be taken care of, I assure you. I will be very generous with my wife's money as soon as I get it. And that's the trouble. There might be a delay before I could get it. Months, even years. That would be terrible, would it not?"

"Oh, yes," said Latin. "And you piling into bed with Hester and her halitosis night after night—"

"Please!" Count Fiolo begged, shuddering. "I cannot even bear the mention without…. Ah, yes. Some more brandy. You are so kind. As I was saying, there are two obstacles. One is Hester, and the other is Jupiter Zachary. He is Hester's uncle. Ebenezer Zachary left his whole estate jointly to his two sons with the proviso that they were not to separate it or divide it but were to run it and share it equally."

"That sounds all right," said Latin.

"No," said Fiolo. "Oh, no. Because Jupiter Zachary is what is commonly known as a stinker. He hates everybody and everybody hates him, when they can find him. Just now, they can't."

"Can't find him?" Latin asked.

"He has disappeared. That is nothing unusual. He often does. He gets mad and goes away, and then pretty soon he gets hungry and comes back home again. You see, Ebenezer Zachary kept absolute control of all his money. He gave each of his sons twenty-five dollars a week and that is all. He made them work twelve hours a day, six days a week, in the foundry to get that. He wouldn't allow them to get any other jobs. If they tried it, he would bring pressure on their employer and get them fired. He hated them and they hated him and each other other, too."

"A nice family," Latin commented.

"No," Count Fiolo contradicted. "Definitely, no. But that is aside from the point. Ebenezer left his property to them *jointly*. If either one dies, all of it goes to the other. If either one should go away, the remaining one can run things as he pleases. But if they are both here, then both have an equal say about everything."

"That would be bad?" Latin hazarded.

"But, yes," said Count Fiolo. "They cannot get along with each other at all. They do not even speak. Whatever one wanted, the other would vote against. Remember, neither can take one cent out of the profits of the foundry without the consent of the other."

"It would be a good thing then if brother Jupiter kept right on being hard to find?"

"I must be certain he does," said Count Fiolo earnestly. "I cannot risk marrying"—he drew a deep breath—"Hester unless I have that assurance. Will you find Jupiter and make sure he doesn't come back?"

"I'll give it a ring," Latin agreed.

Count Fiolo smiled and nodded. "Then it is all settled and we are in agreement. I will expect to hear from you at the earliest possible moment. Haste is vital, I assure you. I will have a great deal of difficulty delaying the wedding much longer. You can get in touch with me at the Copa Negra Club."

"Don't hurry away," said Latin. "There's a little matter of finances. We won't strike a bargain on the whole deal until I see what I can see, but let's talk about a retainer now."

"But of course!" said Count Fiolo enthusiastically. "How stupid of me! Would a thousand dollars be enough?"

"Yes," said Latin.

"I will write you a check."

"No," said Latin.

"I will give you my note."

"No," said Latin.

"I can give you fifty-three dollars and fifteen cents in cash."

"Now you're talking," said Latin.

Count Fiolo sighed. Reluctantly he produced a handsomely embossed leather wallet and took all the bills out of it. He found two nickels and five pennies in his change pocket and stacked them neatly on top of the bills.

"That's the down payment," Latin informed him. "I'll be around for some more by-and-by."

"You are so considerate," said Count Fiolo.

"Oh, yes," Latin agreed. "By the way, are you sure you can handle Hester's papa—Mars Zachary—even if Jupiter Zachary stays out of sight?"

Count Fiolo smiled. "Certainly. He is very fond of me, indeed." Fiolo pointed to the money on the table. "Besides, I am giving him bridge lessons."

Latin nodded. "I'll bet you are."

"He is so stupid," said Count Fiolo, shrugging, "that it is not even necessary for me to cheat—very much. Good night, Mr. Latin. It was such a pleasure dealing with you."

"Good night," said Latin absently.

Count Fiolo went away, and Latin sat still and relaxed in the booth, staring absently at nothing, frowning a little. After a while he held the brandy bottle up against the light to see how much there was left in it and then poured himself a carefully small drink.

"Young man."

"Yes?" said Latin.

Saltonwaite was standing beside the booth, staring down at him accusingly. He had both hands folded proudly and protectively over his small potbelly, and he was still wearing his napkin. He cleared his throat with a sharp little bark and said: "I saw you conferring with that fortune-hunting gigolo just now. What did he want?"

"Some of my brandy," Latin answered. "Do you know him?"

"I regret to say that I do. I was careful not to let him see me because he always either insults me or tries to borrow money from me or both. I disapprove of his manners and morals and appearance and intention to marry Miss Hester Zachary."

"You should tell him about it."

"I have. It has very little effect. You are Max Latin, and you call yourself a private inquiry agent, and you are the undercover owner of this restaurant."

"Well, how do I do," said Latin. "I'm glad to know me."

"This is not a matter for levity, as you will find if you proceed any further with any schemes you may have hatched up with Count Fiolo. At one time or another you've been arrested for almost every crime in the calendar, but you've never been convicted of anything."

"A man is innocent until he is proven guilty," Latin said righteously.

"I doubt if that maxim applies to you," said Saltonwaite. "I doubt it very greatly. You haven't been convicted because you're very clever, but this is the place to stop. I am an attorney, and I drew up Ebenezer Zachary's will. I warn you, it's puncture-proof. And I warn you further that if you and Count Fiolo make any attempt to alter it or change its effect you'll both be sorry. This will is going to be executed exactly as it was written. If you try to tamper with it in any way, it will be my very pleasant duty to see that you go to prison for a suitably long term."

"I'll think it over," Latin said. "Maybe I can work up a fright if I give myself time enough."

SALTONWAITE POINTED a rigid bony finger. "You will find that I am a very relentless man."

"Do you want to relentless some more gumbo?" Dick asked, coming out of the kitchen with a bowl of it in his hand.

"Yes!" Saltonwaite snapped. "Carry it more carefully! Stop shaking it like that! Don't let it get cool!"

He followed Dick away, hovering over him and the gumbo as anxiously as a mother hen with a lone chick. Guiterrez came out of the kitchen and leaned his arms on the back of the booth and stared down glumly and silently at Latin.

"Do your feet hurt?" Latin inquired.

"Look, Latin," said Guiterrez. "I don't mind minor crimes like robbery and blackmail and stuff, but murder is an entirely different kettle of fish."

Latin turned around and jerked back the moth-eaten drape against the wall at the end of the booth, revealing the shiny bright circle of a microphone. He snapped the slide switch on the cord above it.

"You're not supposed to listen in on that unless I signal you. I put that in there to get evidence in case I needed the testimony of some witnesses. I didn't rig it up just for your entertainment."

"Don't avoid the issue," Guiterrez ordered. "What about this Count Fiolo? Are you going to knock that poor Jupiter gent off like he wants you to?"

"For fifty dollars?" Latin scoffed. "Do you think I'm crazy?"

"No," said Guiterrez. "But you'll have me that way before long. Just supposing Jupiter should have a fatal accident any day now. What then?"

"Why, I'd have an alibi."

"What?" Guiterrez asked.

"At the very time the accident happens, I will be sitting right in this booth having a brandy. You'll testify to that."

Guiterrez drew a deep breath. "Do you know what happens to people who swear to phoney alibis in a murder case? They get put in jail for a long, long time."

"We have a very nice penitentiary in this state," Latin told him. "All the modern conveniences. You'll like it."

The swing door squeaked a little, and Boston put his head through the opening timidly. He looked around and saw Latin and Guiterrez and edged himself through the door.

"I'm all done now, and I guess I better be goin' along. I sure thank you, Mr. Guiterrez, for the meal. And you, too, Mr.—Mr.—"

"Latin," said Latin.

"Yes, sir. Thank you, too. I sure wish I could ask another little favor of you."

"What, bum?" Guiterrez demanded.

"Well, that gumbo," said Boston apologetically. "That sure smells mighty fine. I reckon it'd taste pretty good to a fella that was hungry."

"Are you still hungry, bum?" Guiterrez asked incredulously.

"Me? No, sir. Oh, no. I just thought it'd be awful nice if you'd give me a little of that gumbo to take along to Jupe."

"To who?" Guiterrez said.

"To Jupe," Boston repeated. "To my pal, Jupiter. That's his name."

LATIN WAS taking a drink. His hand jerked, and some of the brandy slopped on the table. Latin wiped it up carefully with his napkin.

"Jupiter," he said casually. "That's a name you don't hear very often. Is there any more to it?"

"Huh?" said Boston. "Oh, I dunno. He says his first name is Jupiter, so I call him Jupe because he's my pal. I'm pretty worried about Jupe. I guess he don't feel very good about now."

"Why not?" Latin asked.

"Well, he went out stemming—panhandling—downtown and somebody gave him four bits, and he bought four tins of canned heat and got himself in quite a stew."

"Why, that's terrible," said Latin. "That's awful. Certainly we'll give you some gumbo to take to Jupe. In fact, I'll go with you when you take it. I'm afraid Jupe might be seriously ill, and we want to see that he gets—the best of care."

"I'm beginning to feel a little sick myself," said Guiterrez faintly. "Latin, now please...."

"Get me the telephone," Latin ordered.

Guiterrez sighed and went away, dragging his heels.

"Well, now," said Boston hesitantly. "It ain't necessary to take any trouble, Mr. Latin. Jupe won't be honest-to-God sick. He'll just have a hangover. He drinks canned heat all the time. It don't seem to hurt him none."

"You never can tell," Latin observed. "Where is he now?"

"Down in our little packing-box shack by the railroad cut south of town."

Guiterrez came back carrying a portable telephone. "Latin," he said pleadingly. "Now listen—"

"Go put some gumbo in a milk bottle," Latin told him, plugging the telephone in at a switch under the microphone. "Save some for yourself."

"I don't think I'm very hungry anymore," said Guiterrez.

Latin dialed a number. The line clicked after the first ring, and a voice boomed joyously in his ear. "Hello, there! Happy's All-Night Garage! Snappy service—any time, anywhere!"

"This is Latin, Happy."

"Latin, my boy! Hooray! It's good to hear your voice! You're feeling fine, I hope?"

"Very fine," said Latin. "I want a car, Happy. One you wouldn't recognize if someone should happen to show it to you."

"Ah-ha! Dirty work, hey? That's the old pepper, Latin! I hadn't heard from you for so long I was afraid you'd turned honest on me. Why, this is the best news I've heard since Hirohito got the hives! I've got just the thing for you, my boy. A new Buick coupé registered in the name of Elmer Quinwipple. Do you know who Elmer Quinwipple is?"

"No," Latin admitted.

"Neither do I! You know why? Because there ain't any such person! I'll send it right over!"

CHAPTER THREE
BLACK OUT

THE COUPÉ fled silently across the slender span of a concrete bridge. On the other side, Latin pulled off the highway and slowed down. Gravel spattered under the fenders, and the car rocked smoothly over the washboard roughness of the road shoulder.

"About here, I guess," said Boston. "This'll be fine."

Latin put on the brakes and stopped. He switched off the bright swath of the headlights and got out. The wind was chill and thick with the promise of fog, and he turned up the collar of his light topcoat.

Boston came around the front of the car, admiring it. "Ain't never ridden in a car like this before. Sure nice. Mighty pretty, too."

"I'll tell Mr. Quinwipple you liked it," Latin said. "Have you got the gumbo?"

"Sure. Right here. Maybe—maybe I better run along ahead and just sort of prepare Jupe for your comin'."

"Why?" Latin asked.

"Well, Jupe's funny. He's got kind of a mean disposition. He's likely to sort of rear up and sass people, especially when he's got a hangover. Oh, he's got a good heart. Fine fella, Jupe is—educated, too. But he's a mite short-tempered. I think maybe he was disappointed in love or something."

"Or something," Latin agreed. "Don't worry. He'll like me. Everybody says I have a charming personality. Which way do we go?"

"Well—there's a path right beside that bridge apron. But I'd feel better if you'd let me tell Jupe you was comin' first, so he won't go heavin' rocks at us like he did the last time I brought a fella home. You could sort of sit on the bridge railing and look at the view. It's mighty pretty, Mr. Latin."

They were on the first lift of the hills, and the city spread below them in a deep semicircle following the line of the bay, like an incredibly garish, brilliantly colored blanket. The red and green and blue of neon light painted the whole sweep of the sky with their smeared colors. Automobile headlights scuttled and jumped and jittered like lively bugs. Traffic noise was a low hum that rose and fell a little in its minor key.

"I sure like that view," said Boston. "It makes a fella think—"

A siren began to keen, thin and very faint. Instantly another sounded, closer, and then another and another and another until there was no distinguishing their individual voices. They screamed without pause—on and on and on until the night began to pulsate with their warning.

"What's that?" Boston asked shakily.

"Air raid," said Latin.

Below them, the city was answering the command of the sirens. It began to black out in sections, working from the outskirts inward. The lights that formed the small squares that were blocks snapped off, and the city drew in on itself protectively. The little headlight bugs stopped scuttling around and disappeared. The neon faded thinner and thinner and was gone.

The sirens stopped. Their echoes carried a little, and then there was no sound anywhere.

"Oh, gee," Boston said in an awed whisper.

There was no city now. It was hidden, waiting.

"I never seen anything like that before," said Boston. "It's kinda scary, ain't it?"

Latin cleared his throat. "Let's go."

"Huh?" said Boston. "What?"

"Business as usual," said Latin.

THE WHITE loom of the bridge apron felt cold and smooth under his palm, and he groped downward with his foot until he located the slant of the path. It was rough with little footholds like steps kicked in it.

Latin went downward carefully, bracing himself against the cement abutment, and the night seemed to grow darker and colder around him. He reached the bottom, and gravel from a railroad bed rolled loosely under his feet.

Boston's feet thumped beside him. "Say, about that air raid. Hadn't we better sort of—sort of hide?"

"We're as safe here as anywhere else," Latin told him. "Probably safer. Which way?"

"There's a little ravine up this way."

He was a vague shambling shadow, and Latin followed him along the slick parallel gleam of railroad tracks.

"About here," said Boston.

Latin felt brush rake lightly at the skirts of his topcoat, and his feet sank a little in soft ground. The sides of the ravine were steep and high, and it was like walking in a very deep, crooked trench.

"Right beyond this bend," said Boston. "Jupe! Hey there, Jupe!" His voice echoed emptily. "He ain't showin' no light nor nothin'. I guess maybe them sirens scared him, although he really ain't a guy that scares very easy. Oh, Jupe!"

Latin could make out the faint outline of a shack pushed in against the bank swaybacked and shapeless, not much larger than a good-sized packing case.

Wood creaked and scraped against hard earth as Boston tugged at a panel that served as a door. Stiflingly thick, warm air moved against Latin's face.

"Come in," Boston said. "Watch your head. I guess Jupe ain't here. I guess maybe he went to panhandle some dough for some more canned heat."

Latin struck a match, shading it very carefully with his palms. The shadows swerved and danced along stained bare walls, swept in quick flicks across the low ceiling. The light touched the edge of a ragged pile of blankets.

"Why, there he is," said Boston. "He ain't even woke up yet. He musta got more canned heat than I thought, I guess. Hey, Jupe! Wake up!"

Latin stepped closer, still holding the shaded match. The man was sprawled on his back on top of the blankets, and the match flame reflected in twin glitters from his open unmoving eyes.

"Why, say—," said Boston, and then gulped.

Latin raised the match high for a quick calculating look around the bare room and then blew it out. He was carrying a .38 Colt Police Positive in a shoulder holster under his suit coat, and he took the gun out now and held it poised in his right hand, listening tensely.

"Say, Mr. Latin—," Boston whispered. "Jupe looked to me like he—he—"

"He's dead," said Latin.

Boston made a noise breathing. "Oh, gee. It don't seem hardly possible canned heat—I mean, he drinks it all the time, and it never did this before."

"It didn't do it this time," Latin answered. "Somebody stuck him with an ice pick."

"Wh-what?"

"Did you see that little red mark—like a big period—on his forehead just above his right eye? An ice pick did that. Somebody drove it right through his skull into his brain. If you've got a strong arm that's an easy way to kill a person."

"Oh," said Boston numbly. "An ice pick in his head.... Stickin' in.... Oh! I'm gonna—gonna be sick—"

"Quit that!" Latin said sharply. "You go and report his death. Do it right now. Here's a nickel. Go to the nearest telephone and call the police and tell them it's murder."

"I'm scared, Mr. Latin. I guess I'm so scared. I'm paralyzed. I don't wanta go out there in the dark, and there's an air raid on and a fella with an ice pick—"

"You stay here. I'll go."

"No!" Boston said quickly. "Not with—Oh, no! Couldn't we just—stay together?"

"No. Go on. Get going."

"I—I don't think—"

"Hurry!" Latin ordered.

"Oh, I'll hurry," Boston mumbled. "I'll run so fast—"

HE STUMBLED over the doorstep, and then his feet beat a raggedly thudding tattoo down the ravine. Latin waited until the echoes died, standing still, listening with his head tilted in concentration.

After a long time, he dropped the Police Positive into his overcoat pocket. He groped his way blindly across the room toward the pile of blankets and knelt down beside it and struck a match.

The dead man's face looked yellow, waxily drawn. He could have been almost any age—young or old or in the middle. He was thin and not very tall, and his eyes were a pale blue shot with red veins. He was wearing a ragged blue serge suit and tennis shoes with holes in the toes.

Latin began to search him, working very expertly and rapidly. He turned up a beer can opener, a spool of thread, a jackknife with a broken handle, and a limp sack of cigarette tobacco. The match burned his fingers, and he dropped it, swearing to himself in a whisper.

He waited for a moment, listening, and then struck another match. He hit paydirt this time. The inside pocket of the dead man's coat was fastened shut with two big safety pins. Latin loosened them and pulled out a limp dog-eared wallet. In it he found a driver's license, an identification card, a draft registration, all made out in the name of Jupiter Zachary.

Latin blew out the match and put the wallet carefully in his own pocket. Lighting another match, he continued his search. He could find nothing else at all on the dead man that would serve to identify him.

He put the last match out and started to get up, and then he froze that way, half-crouched, his head turned toward the gray-black oblong that marked the door. Very slowly he slid his hand into his coat pocket and brought out the revolver.

The seconds dragged, lengthening interminably. Latin straightened up and made the door in two catlike steps.

He slid out into the fresh coldness of the night, flattened himself against the wall of the shack.

Gravel rolled and rattled out on the roadbed, and then a blurred voice suddenly split the deep silence, shouting jubilantly: *"Oh, she'll be coming 'round the mountain when she comes! Too-ot! Toot! Choo-choo! She'll be coming 'round the—"* The voice dropped to a hoarse grumble. "Now where the hell is that ravine? Right here somewhere...."

More gravel rolled, and brush crackled. The hoarse voice swore feelingly and then shouted: "Jupe! Boston! Where are you?"

"Who's there?" said Latin.

"Huh?" said the hoarse voice. "I'm here, that's who. What *you* doin' here? You ain't Jupe nor Boston. Show a light."

Latin didn't obey. He cocked his revolver instead. The small cold click carried plainly in the stillness.

There was a quick little rustle in the air and then a *tock* next to Latin's ear. One of the boards in back of him vibrated just slightly.

Latin fired instantly. The powder made an orange flare against the night, and the echoes rolled deafeningly and redoubled as Latin fired again, shooting low at what he guessed was the center of the ravine.

The echoes drummed and faded away. Latin waited, revolver poised in his hand. There was no further sound, no movement, until faraway and faint the hoarse voice shouted: *"Oh, she'll be driving six white horses—"*

The voice faded eerily and was gone.

Latin swore to himself in a bitter monotone. He struck a match and looked at the wall of the shack. An ice pick was sticking in a board about six inches from where Latin's head had been. It was just an ordinary ice pick, the kind given away as an advertisement, and on its yellow wooden handle were the words: "Acme Ice Company—We'll Cool You Off."

"Yes, indeed," said Latin thoughtfully.

He dropped the match and crushed it under his foot. He left the ice pick where it was and felt his way carefully down the ravine to the railroad tracks. He waited for a while there, but he could hear nothing and see nothing, and finally he blundered along the cut until he located the bottom of the steep path he and Boston had come down.

He climbed laboriously up to the highway. There was no light anywhere, and the fog had crept in over the city like a vague white veil. The Buick was still parked on the shoulder. Latin walked back across the bridge and headed for the city.

CHAPTER FOUR
TELL IT TO HOMICIDE

HE HAD gone about a hundred and fifty yards when he heard the putter of a motor behind him. He stopped then, looking back, holding the revolver concealed under the front of his topcoat. Two vaguely blue slitted lights came out of the night.

"Hey, chum," said a voice. "You ain't supposed to be walkin' around in the open durin' a blackout."

Latin could see the car now. It was about the height of a wheelbarrow and no more than twice as long. It had no top. Two soldiers were sitting in the front seat—one driving and the other holding a rifle upright between his knees.

"I know," Latin said. "But this is very important."

"A matter of life and death, I don't doubt," said the soldier-driver glumly.

"Of death, anyway," Latin said. "I have to get back to the city at once. Give me a lift, will you?"

"It's against regulations," said the driver.

"So it's against regulations!" said the other soldier. "So now you want to get a promotion, I suppose? So now you're gonna be a general, huh? Maybe this bird is a fifth columnist or a parachute trooper or somewhat. We oughta ride him with us so we can watch him. Get in the backseat, chum."

Latin climbed in and sat down on the hard seat. The jeep started off with a sudden jump.

"Watch what you're doin', dummy," the soldier with the rifle said.

"The clutch slips," the driver informed him.

"So sure it slips! If it didn't you'd tear it out by the roots. And drive on the pavement!"

"It don't make no difference to this buggy where it drives."

"It makes a difference to me, though! You want I should get all my teeth shook loose?" The soldier looked over his shoulder at Latin. "We only patrol this road as far as the city limits. You'll have to get off there."

"O.K.," said Latin. "Thanks."

"You know," said the driver, "I figure this ain't a raid at all. I figure this is one of them armed reconnaissance flights, where the guys go prowlin' around to see what they can see."

"Oh, you got the dope, huh?" said the other one. "I suppose Hitler or Hirohito wrote you a letter?"

"I got brains."

"Since when? And keep on the pavement I told you!"

"Who's givin' orders?"

"I am! You want a bat with the butt of this rifle?"

A siren croaked somewhere ahead of them and then caught its breath and cut loose with a full-throated wail. Seconds later others joined it, and the whole night screamed with their sound. They stopped as suddenly as they had begun.

"One minute," said the driver. "All clear."

Lights began to pop up, and motors churned and roared as traffic started again.

"This is where we drop you, chum," said the soldier with the rifle. "The city limits are right ahead. You can catch a streetcar at the end of the line nearby."

"We should look at his identification papers," the driver suggested.

"So I suppose he wouldn't have fake ones if he was a spy? Anyway, I can tell he ain't, on account of I'm a spy expert. I can smell 'em."

"What do they smell like?"

"Snakes."

The jeep pulled up at the side of the road, and Latin got out.

"Thanks, boys. If you ever get down to Carbon Street, stop in at Guiterrez's place and have a free meal."

"What?" said the driver quickly. "What was that?"

"A free meal," said Latin. "I'm in the Reserve, and I may be called up any time now, but if I'm not there just tell Dick, the headwaiter, that Latin sent you."

"Well, man!" said the soldier with the rifle enthusiastically. "Well, hell, now! Thanks, chum!"

LATIN CAME up the street and turned into the little alley that led back alongside the restaurant. His shadow danced jaggedly ahead of him in the dimness, and then a voice said: "Latin."

Latin spun around and dropped on one knee, jerking his revolver out of his coat pocket.

"Tish and tosh," said the voice. "You're getting jumpy, Latin. I told you your conscience would catch up on you one of these fine days."

Latin stood up slowly, and Inspector Walters, Homicide, strolled out of the shadows. Walters was tall and gaunt and ugly, and twenty years of jousting with murderers of one kind and another had left him with an acid-stomach condition and practically no faith in human nature.

"You have a permit for that revolver among your souvenirs somewhere, no doubt?" he asked.

"Yes," Latin said. "Do you want to see it?"

"No. It would just make me sad. I'd like to have a short chat with you, if you can spare me a few moments."

"Come on," Latin invited.

They went in through the kitchen door of the restaurant. Guiterrez was perched on his high stool again, but he was turned the other way now, with his back to the range, his chin propped glumly in his hands. When he saw Latin with Walters he made a choking noise in his throat, and his face took on a sickly greenish color.

Latin winked at him and shook his head slightly.

"Uh!" Guiterrez gasped, making a valiant effort to recover himself. "One bum is all I feed a night, Latin. You'll have to take this one to a soup kitchen."

"There'll come a day," said Walters, nodding at him meaningly and following Latin through the swing door and into the main part of the restaurant.

The blackout apparently hadn't had any effect. The place was just as crowded and even noisier, if possible, than it had been an hour before. Dick appeared beside Latin's booth as soon as he and Walters had seated themselves. He produced the brandy bottle from under his apron and put it and one glass on the table.

"Have some?" Latin asked Walters.

"No."

"You bet he won't," Dick seconded. "This is a strictly high-class joint. We don't serve cops. You better eat something pretty soon, Latin."

"Bring me some gumbo."

"Nope," said Dick. "Guiterrez threw it out. He said it brought him bad luck tonight."

"Tell him to make some more."

"I'll tell him," Dick said, heading for the kitchen. "If you hear an explosion, it won't be a bomb. It'll be Guiterrez saying no."

WALTERS LEANED back, sighing. "I like this place. It reminds me of a zoo. Now here's a little matter I'd like to take up with you, Latin. There was an unidentified bum—known only as Jupe—murdered tonight in a little shack in a ravine back of the railroad cut on Highway 44 north of town. He was stuck fatally with an ice pick."

"I know," said Latin. "I found him."

"Why?" asked Walters.

Latin looked at him over the brandy glass. "What?"

"Why?" said Walters patiently. "Why did you find this bum?"

"I found his pal, an old guy named Boston, digging around in the garbage cans out in the alley tonight. Guiterrez gave the old guy a meal. Then Boston said he had a friend that was sick out in the shack, so I gave him some food and took him out there."

"Why?" said Walters.

Latin shrugged. "Just charity. I thought maybe Boston's pal might be really sick, and I wanted to help him if he was."

"No," said Walters judicially. "No, I don't think we can use that one. Think up another."

"It's the absolute truth. You can ask Guiterrez or Dick or anybody around here."

"I can," said Walters, "but I'm not going to. I should waste my time."

"How did you know about the murder?"

"Not from you reporting it, you can bet. Your pal Boston got himself pecked on the head with a blunt instrument and knocked six ways for Sunday. He was picked up and brought into an emergency first-aid station north of town, and he had quite a tale to tell about ice picks and stuff. He also said you were a nice fellow, so that knock on the head must have addled his brains. What were you prowling around with those two bums for, Latin?"

"I don't like your attitude," Latin told him. "It was charity, like I said. I'm practically full of the milk of human kindness."

"You're full of brandy and baloney. Do you know who killed that bum?"

"No."

"Do you plan on finding out?"

"Yes."

"Are you going to tell me when you do?"

"Maybe."

Walters got up. "All right, little man. But just remember that I know something about you that no one else does."

"What?"

"I know the reason why you never get convicted of any of these things you're pinched for. It's very simple. It's because you aren't guilty. You bend the law around like a pretzel, but you never quite break it. Taken all in all, you're generally almost honest."

"You spread that rumor around," said Latin, "and I'll sue you for slander."

"Latin," said Walters, "do you hear a little crackling sound under your feet? That's the ice you're walking on. It's getting awfully thin. You have something for me tomorrow, or it's going to break and let you down into some very, very cold water. I'm not fooling either."

"Good night, now," said Latin.

Walters nodded. "Tomorrow. Don't forget it, or you'll have a worse headache than that brandy is going to give you."

He went toward the front of the restaurant, and Dick appeared beside the booth carrying the portable telephone.

"Somebody wants to talk to you. Don't ask me why."

LATIN PLUGGED in the switch and lifted the telephone off its stand. "Latin speaking."

"Say, Mr. Latin, this here is Boston. You remember me, I guess, don't you?"

"Fairly well," said Latin. "What happened to you?"

"Well, it was sure funny. I come up that there little path by the bridge, and there was a fella lookin' inside your car. He had the door open, and he was kinda half inside and half out, and he was singin'. I swear he was, Mr. Latin. He was singin' about somebody comin' around a mountain."

"I heard him," said Latin. "What did you do?"

"Well, I snuck up on him and hollered real fierce, 'Get out of that car!' figurin' to scare him."

"Did it?" Latin asked.

"Not so's you'd notice. He come at me like a mountain cat and hit me about seven times in the head with something awful hard and knocked me down and stomped me a few times."

"Then what?" Latin inquired.

"Well, I guess he went away. I was kinda unconscious, and he wasn't there when I got up. I started staggerin' back toward town, and one of these firebomb-watchers seen me and picked me up and brought me to this here first-aid station in a schoolhouse. They won't let me out of here, Mr. Latin."

"Why not?"

"Well, they say I maybe got a concussion, and I got to lie down and be quiet. I guess I'll have to do that, Mr. Latin. Looks like they mean what they say. I'm sure sorry about all this, Mr. Latin. I hope that singin' fella didn't steal nothin' out of your car."

"No, he didn't. Everything's all right. You just relax, Boston. I'll come around and see how you are tomorrow."

"You will?" Boston asked eagerly. "You'll sure enough do that, Mr. Latin?"

"Sure enough."

"I'm mighty thankful.... Say, that nurse is takin' the telephone away—"

The line snapped and then began to hum emptily as the connection was broken. Latin depressed the breaker bar, let it up again, and dialed a number.

"Hello, there!" Happy's voice bellowed. "Happy's All-Night Garage! Service with a smile—anywhere, any time!"

"This is Elmer Quinwipple."

"Who?" said Happy. "Oh, yes! And I hope you're joyful and all in one piece, Mr. Quinwipple! What can I do for you, my good sir?"

"I left my car parked out on Highway 44 near the bridge across the railroad cut. Will you run out and get it when you're not busy?"

"Yes, indeedy! Right away, if not sooner! Will you be wanting it again tonight, my dear Mr. Quinwipple?"

"No," said Latin. "I thought I might give a fellow a ride in it, but he was sort of—called away unexpectedly. Thanks, Happy."

Latin hung up and reached for the brandy bottle. He held it very carefully over his glass and tilted it, but nothing poured out.

"Another seventeen fifty shot to hell," Dick observed, appearing with an enormous china bowl cupped in both his hands. "Say, you don't suppose Guiterrez is sick or something, do you? He didn't even throw any dishes on the floor when I asked him to make this. He just said something about giving the condemned man anything he wanted to eat for his last meal. What was he talking about?"

"I hope I don't know," said Latin.

CHAPTER FIVE
DEATH WEARS A TOP HAT

THE COPA NEGRA CLUB was on the second floor of a downtown building over a cut-rate clothing store, but anyone who didn't know that would never have guessed it was there. No sign advertised it, and its windows had been painted black on the inside so that no light could escape. Its entrance was a narrow colonial-type door with a dim blue light burning chastely over it.

Latin hammered the polished brass knocker, and the door opened instantly and swiftly. An English-style butler complete with sideburns and a swallowtail coat bowed and stepped back and bowed again.

"Please come in, sir."

The hall was small and thickly carpeted with lights tilted up against the dark-paneled walls to make the ceiling appear higher.

"Your coat, sir," said the butler. "Your hat."

Latin gave them to him, and the butler passed them along to a girl in a neat black maid's uniform and got back a brass check which he handed to Latin.

"The elevator, sir."

He pressed a button, and one of the panels slid back and revealed an elevator lined with chrome and black glistening leather. Another girl in a maid's uniform was waiting in it, and she curtsied neatly when Latin entered. The elevator rose smoothly and stopped without the faintest jar, and the door slid open.

A man in an expensively tailored dinner coat bowed impressively low in front of Latin. "A very good evening to you, sir. May I show you to a table?"

"Is Count Fiolo here?" Latin asked.

The other man stopped looking pleased. "We got a very special stairs to throw process servers down. Are you one?"

"Not just now," said Latin. "I'm—"

"My dear Mr. Latin!" said another voice. "This is such a great surprise and such a very great pleasure!"

"Is it?" said Latin blankly. "Who are you?"

The man was no more than five feet tall, and he looked as round and soft as a butterball. He, too, was wearing a dinner coat, and he teetered up and down on his toes and beamed and made pleased chuckling noises.

"But don't you remember? I am Andriev. I am the personal friend of the great *Señor* Guiterrez. Ah, many times I have eaten the deliciousness of his supreme food. You make me so happy by coming here. You shall have our very, very best. I, Andriev, promise it personally."

"I came to meet Count Fiolo."

"Yes, indeed! The Count is entertaining friends this evening. It is an occasion, you understand." Andriev winked and smirked at him confidentially. "It is to celebrate his coming marriage. His campaign is successful. It is settled. The girl is incredibly rich, but the face—" Andriev closed his eyes and shivered realistically. "The Count is very brave. I, Andriev, would not have the courage. This way, please, Mr. Latin."

He led the way along a hall and through an arched doorway into the main dining room. It was enormous. Tables were banked in endless tiers around the black polished square of a dance floor. An orchestra gleamed and purred out stately jazz, and the dancers, all bare shoulders and bald heads, twirled solemnly counterclockwise. There were no jitterbugs present. It was all as impressive and high-toned as an embassy ball and Latin, always alert to such matters, decided that the prices would be pretty impressive, too.

Andriev headed around the top of the banked tiers and was starting down the wide, deeply carpeted steps that descended to the dance floor when Latin tapped him on the shoulder.

"Does he come here often?" he asked, pointing.

"Mr. Saltonwaite?" Andriev said. "Oh, yes. He comes for the *Squab Andriev*, which is really beautiful beyond dreams. I confess to you, Mr. Latin, that it is actually *Squab Guiterrez*. The great Guiterrez gave me permission to use his recipe, and the success has been colossal. I live in constant gratitude."

Saltonwaite was sitting all alone at his table, a somber and preoccupied figure against the gayety around him. He was holding a squab in both hands and gnawing away as though his life depended on it. It couldn't have been more than two hours since he had filled up on Guiterrez's gumbo, but that wasn't cramping his style any now.

"He must have taken some exercise recently to work up that appetite," Latin observed. "Do you know how long he's been here?"

Andriev snapped his fingers imperiously. "Pierre!"

A waiter jumped to attention in front of them.

"That one," said Andriev. "Saltonwaite. How long has he been here, Pierre?"

"A half hour, sir."

"O.K.," said Latin thoughtfully. "Thanks."

ANDRIEV LED the way on down the stairs and turned in at the first tier of tables. Count Fiolo jumped up from a table that held the place of honor on a direct line across from the bandstand.

"But Mr. Latin! My dear friend! I am gratified beyond words!"

He was wearing a navy blue tuxedo, and he filled it out as exquisitely as a tailor's dummy. He looked incredibly handsome and virile and dashing, and there were at least ten women at tables nearby who couldn't keep their eyes off him. He shook Latin's hand. He beamed at him. He patted him on the shoulder proudly.

"You are so kind to honor me. And now I want to present you to my betrothed. My very own loved one, this is Mr. Max Latin, with whom I have a basis of mutual understanding and trust. Mr. Latin, this is my heart, my life. This is my glamorous future—Miss Hester Zachary."

"Oh, you," said Hester Zachary. "Now, Count, you shouldn't say those extravagant things."

"Say them?" Count Fiolo echoed. "I shout them from the housetops! I call all the world to witness the beauty I have captured!"

"Oh, you," said Hester Zachary, simpering. "I'm awfully pleased to meet you, Mr. Latin."

She was wearing, of all things, a formal gown without any shoulders straps. Latin looked twice to make sure, and it was really so. Her nose was shining brightly and her eyes boggled out in a deliriously happy daze and she did have halitosis. Her hair was pulled up on one side and down on the other.

"Is she not wonderful?" Count Fiolo demanded.

"Yes, indeed," said Latin soberly.

"Oh, you," said Hester. "You men. Mr. Latin, I want you to meet my mama and papa."

"My dear, dear parents-to-be," Count Fiolo expanded. "Mrs. and Mr. Mars Zachary."

"Charmed," said Mrs. Zachary. She was small and scrawny, and in spite of that she looked like her corset was too tight. Hester had inherited her buckteeth and her shiny nose from the distaff side.

"Are you in society?" Mars Zachary asked.

"Mr. Latin is a member of the city's most exclusive inner circle!" said Count Fiolo. "He is indeed well known."

"Yes," Latin admitted. "I have quite a record."

"We're going to get into society," said Mars Zachary. He was middle-sized and vaguely limp-looking. His hair swirled in a sticky cowlick on the top of his head, like an Indian's headdress. He had a broodingly sour expression and a manner that was furtive and defiant at the same time. He looked like he wasn't very sure he was enjoying himself.

"Don't say that," said Mrs. Zachary.

"Say what?" asked Mars.

"That we're going into society."

"Why not? Aren't we?"

"Don't argue, Mars. Will you join us, Mr. Latin?"

"Well, I don't know," said Latin. "I hadn't intended—"

Andriev saved him. He came bustling up, all smiles, and said: "My dear Count, you really must excuse me if I intrude myself. I am so honored that Mr. Latin has visited us. I took the liberty to mention it to my employer. Will you excuse yourself from this charming group and step this way with me for a moment, Mr. Latin? Will you be so kind?"

"Why, yes," said Latin. He nodded to the Zacharys. "I have a little business to attend to. I'll see you later, Count."

"Yes, indeed," said Fiolo, slightly less enthusiastic.

Andriev led the way around the dance floor and back past the long gleaming bar and knocked twice on a narrow door almost hidden by a thick blue drape that swept gracefully down from the ceiling. There was no answer to the knock, and Andriev said smoothly: "Step right in, please, Mr. Latin."

He opened the door, and Latin entered a square dark-paneled room that had no windows and was furnished only with a very small spindle-legged desk and two straight-backed chairs. The door closed softly behind him.

"Hi, Latin," said the woman behind the desk.

"Well, I'll be damned," said Latin with feeling.

"Don't boast about it. How are you, kid?"

"Surprised," said Latin.

THE WOMAN laughed. She was fat, but there wasn't anything soft about her. She was as square and solid as a block of concrete. She was wearing a tailored gray suit, and she had gray hair. There was a diamond on her left hand the size of a dime, and it was a real one. Her features were regular enough, but they'd seen some service. She winked one slightly bloodshot eye at Latin.

"How do you like my new business?"

"You don't own this dive, do you, Rosie?"

"Rosemary, if you please. Rosemary McClure Fitzgerald. Me and my partners own it, yes."

"Who are your partners?"

"About half the people in the city hall," said Rosie blandly. "I've learned a thing or two, in my time, that comes in handy when you want partners. How do you like the tony atmosphere I dreamed up? I tell you, we got strictly class here, kid. I lay it on with a trowel, and the old bald-headed bats you saw outside love it so they practically drool every time one of my waiters bows to 'em. You know I had to enroll them waiters in an etiquette school? It's a fact. It cost me fifty dollars apiece to get them learned to talk through their noses."

"It was worth it," said Latin.

"Sure. I got the idea from learning my girls to act like little ladies. Was *that* a job! Sit down, Latin. You and me are going to have a powwow. Still drink this?"

She produced a bottle from under the desk and turned it so Latin could read the label.

"You bet," said Latin.

Rosie found some glasses in the desk drawer. "You're an expensive cuss. This costs about a dollar a drink, you know that? Here."

"Thanks," said Latin. "You've had a little fender and bodywork done on yourself, too, haven't you?"

"Hell, I been hammered by every massager in town. Look, Latin, are you my pal?"

"For fun or for money?" Latin asked.

"Both."

"Yes and no," said Latin. "Make me an offer."

"All right. I'm holdin' the baby for Count Fiolo."

"How is that?" Latin inquired.

"Like this. He comes from the same neck of the woods as Andriev, one of them countries around Poland. He got out with nothing but a spare pair of pants when Hitler came in. So he came over here and sort of dragged along the bottom giving old dames bridge lessons and such. He ran into Andriev and started to hang out here. He ran up quite a bill and bounced a few checks, so I decided to give him the brush-off. Have another drink."

"Thanks," said Latin.

"But I didn't," said Rosie. "Because I discovered that about half the dames that were my tea-dance customers were comin' here on the off-chance he'd ask them for a dance. I mean, the guy slays women and no joke. So I thought I'd get my money back, and I kept him around here while I looked up a good prospect. I found what I figured was a swell one. You just met her."

"I remember," said Latin, taking a drink.

"Did you ever see the like?" Rosie said, shaking her head. "Sometimes I'd even feel sorry for Fiolo if he wasn't such a rat. What did you and he hatch up at your restaurant tonight?"

"How did you know he saw me there?" Latin asked.

Rosie said: "I've advanced him five thousand dollars. I've got his notes five for one. That baby is worth twenty-five thousand smackers to me. I keep an eye on him, and when he starts having conferences with a sharpshooter like you I begin to get the quivers. What's the gag?"

LATIN LOOKED into his brandy glass thoughtfully for a moment and then shrugged. "He's afraid Jupiter Zachary will show up and keep Mars Zachary from drawing any dough out of the Planet Iron Foundry to give to his daughter to give to Fiolo."

"Yeah. He's been itching over that. I tell him the dame will get the dough sooner or later anyway, but that don't comfort him much. He says if he is going to live with that face he has to have cash compensation right now and all the time. That will is really a heller."

"Fiolo said the property was left to the brothers jointly."

"Yeah. I got a copy out of the probate records and had my lawyers look at it. They say they never saw the likes. Saltonwaite drew it up. Do you know him?"

Latin nodded. "Yes."

"He put everything in that will but the kitchen sink. My lawyers doubt if that joint stuff is legal in a bequest, but it's so foxed up they think it would take ten years to break it. The will itself provides a whopping sum to pay Saltonwaite to fight for it if anyone tries to contest it. I think that's the reason for the funny stuff. He figured that joint stuff would make it so damned unhandy for the brothers—hating each other like they do—that sooner or later one of them would take a ring at busting the will, and then Saltonwaite would cut himself a real nice piece of cake. Did you ever see him cut a piece of cake or anything else, by the way? My God, that man can eat!"

"I noticed," said Latin absently. He had just gotten an idea, and his eyes were narrowed and greenish-looking in the dim light.

"This joint stuff," said Rosie. "I wish I'd known about that before I got Fiolo tangled up with Hester. Look, Latin, I'm starched shirt and very ritz now, and I can't afford rough stuff or to have my name knocked around in the papers. Fiolo is sure to beef on that twenty-five thousand dollars, although it's reasonable enough. I took a long chance. I'll give you fifty percent of all above five thousand you can collect on his notes to me."

Latin looked at her. "You've made a deal, Rosie."

"Jupiter Zachary is the boy to look out for—Mars is just dumb, but from what I hear, Jupiter is meaner than hell."

"Don't worry about Jupiter," Latin advised.

"I'm not. That's your job. Go away now, Latin. I don't want to know what you're going to do next. I have en—"

The lights went out. They didn't flicker or give any warning. They just went out all at once.

"Another air raid?" Latin asked.

"Hell, no," said Rosie. "We don't worry about air raids. I got this place blacked out like a tomb. Some dope pulled the main switch in the basement."

"My God!" Latin exclaimed suddenly.

HE WHIRLED around and slammed into the wall and bounced back. He found the door on his second try, jerked it open. The club was a vast black cavern with voices rising in an indignant querying babble and the orchestra still banging along slightly off-key.

Latin dove headlong into a man who grunted and said: "Here, now. No panic. Bad form, you know."

Latin pushed him away, bumped into the bar. He got his bearings and ran blindly along the edge of the dance floor until he stepped on something soft that ripped and a woman threw her arms around him and screamed in his ear.

Several other women screamed, too. The orchestra petered out with a few brassy wails.

Latin got the arms loose from his neck and pushed. He hit a railing and pinwheeled over it.

Latin climbed up over another railing and then a third. He paused tensely there, breathing hard.

"Saltonwaite!" he called. "Saltonwaite!"

There was no answer, and Latin knew he was no more than a couple of yards from Saltonwaite's table. After a second he struck a match. Saltonwaite was still sitting at the table, and he was still holding the remains of the squab in his hands. His mouth was greasy from the last bite that he had taken and that he would never taste. The yellow handle of an Acme ice pick stuck out straight from his skinny chest just over his heart.

Latin dropped the match one way and jumped the other way, drawing the Police Positive from his shoulder holster. There were people moving and swearing and screaming all around him in the darkness. He felt along the railing and found the main stairway by falling down three steps. He kept right on going down.

"Now, Hester," said Mars Zachary's voice suddenly, close to him. "Stop it."

Hester shrieked like a lost soul. Latin grabbed out in the darkness and got her by one bare bony shoulder.

"Where's the Count?" he demanded.

"He's gone!" Hester shrieked. "I kissed him and he ran awa-ay. He said he wasn't coming back—"

"Mr. Latin!" Andriev's voice wailed. "Mr. Latin, what are you doing, please?"

Latin let go of Hester and reached out blindly and got him by the throat. "Where's the back door—quick?"

"Across the d-dance floor to the right of the b-bandstand. What is the m—"

Latin put his head down and charged across the dance floor like a one-man flying wedge, leaving a profanely howling, threshing wake behind him. He tripped, got up again and went through an invisible doorway. He hit the third step down, kept his feet by a miracle of balance, and kept on going.

HE WENT through the outside door without even knowing it was there. Wind was suddenly fresh and cold in his face, and his heels clicked hard on rough paving. He whirled to his right and saw faint light from the street outlining the alley mouth. A quick shadowy figure was running that way, dodging and twisting.

Latin jerked his revolver out and fired, shooting high. "Stop!" he yelled.

The shadowy figure put on a fresh burst of speed, and then a voice in front of it said calmly: "That'll be far enough, son. Hold it."

The shadowy figure stopped, and its arm flipped up and down again, incredibly fast. All in the same split second there was the sharp rip of tearing cloth and the bursting flare of a revolver report. The shadowy figure bounced backwards and then went down in a sprawling heap.

Latin walked forward cautiously. "Walters."

"What the hell," said Walters. "This monkey heaved an ice pick at me—pinned my coat right to the wall. I ripped it getting loose. This coat cost me fifty-three dollars."

Latin knelt down by the sprawled figure. "Things like that wouldn't happen if you minded your own business and quit following me around."

"I'm minding my business when I follow you around, and don't forget it. Who is this ice-pick expert?"

"He's the boy who killed that bum down by the railroad cut tonight, then tried the ice-pick trick on me. He also just finished off a lawyer by the name of Saltonwaite."

"What's all this?"

Latin said: "It's all about a joint called the Planet Iron Foundry, which is worth a lot of money these days. It was owned by a man named Ebenezer Zachary. He had two sons who didn't like him or each other, either. The old boy had some strokes and got sort of dotty in the bean and evidently came down with an attack of the regrets. He let

Saltonwaite persuade him that the thing to do was to bring his boys together by forcing them to cooperate in running the foundry. Saltonwaite drew up a will that was supposed to arrange that, and it was really a lulu.

"You see, Saltonwaite had his eye on the profits of the iron foundry. He knew the two sons, Mars and Jupiter Zachary, wouldn't cooperate for love or money, and he had all the legal strings tied up so fancily that he was in the driver's seat. The boys would have to use him as their mutual go-between and interlocutor, and that would be very nice for Mr. Saltonwaite."

"Jupiter!" said Walters suddenly. "Jupe! Was that bum who was killed in the railroad cut Jupiter Zachary?"

"No. This bum lying here is, and he's good and dead. You nailed him right in the ticker. You see, Jupiter was just as smart as Saltonwaite and a lot tougher. He dreamed up a very nasty little scheme that would put him right on top of the heap and give him a chance to stamp on his brother's fingers. He picked out an old bum by the name of Boston and stabbed the poor guy. Boston resembled Jupiter, and Jupiter put all his identification papers in Boston's pocket so Boston's body would be identified as his. I don't think that was Jupiter's first job of murder, by any means. He's too expert with ice picks to be a beginner."

"Identification papers?" Walters said. "Let's talk about them for a minute. There weren't any identification papers on that bum in the railroad cut. Where are they?"

LATIN NODDED toward the sprawled body. "I'll bet they're in Jupiter's pocket."

"I'll bet they are, too," said Walters. "Because you just now put 'em there."

"Did you see me?"

"No," Walters admitted glumly.

"Then don't be so suspicious. Jupiter knew how dumb his brother is and how anxious he is to get some big dough so his women-folks can make a splurge. He knew Mars would jump at the chance to identify the murdered bum's body as Jupiter so he'd have a free hand at collecting the foundry's profits. Then, some fine day, Jupiter would walk up and tap his brother on the shoulder."

"Oh-oh," said Walters.

"Yes. From then on, Jupiter would sit back somewhere out of sight and collect ninety-nine percent of the profits while Mars did all the work. It was slick and quick, and if it didn't work, why, there was just an old bum dead, and who would give a damn? Not Jupiter, you can bet. Give him time to cover up, and you could never have proved that murder on him in fifty years. But his scheme went all haywire when Saltonwaite saw him at my joint. Saltonwaite knew him, but he didn't give the faintest sign of it. Saltonwaite is a slippery old devil, and he knew there was dirty work going on. Now he had Jupiter in the same crack that Jupiter had Mars."

"Hell's fire," said Walters. "What a bunch of coldblooded babies."

"And how. Jupiter had to go on with it. He mentioned his own name to me, trying to build up his murdered-bum plant, and I sat in on the game a lot quicker than he expected. He couldn't figure me out at first. He thought maybe I was really just interested in feeding a sick bum."

"Little did he know *you*," said Inspector Walters.

YOU CAN DIE ANY DAY

"NOW, MR. LATIN," INQUIRED PROSPECTIVE CLIENT MRS. GREGORY FARMER UNCTUOUSLY, "YOU'D RATHER DO GOOD THAN EVIL, WOULDN'T YOU— SOMETHING FINE AND NOBILE AND HONEST? SURELY, YOU'D HESITATE TO KILL A PERSON, MR. LATIN?" "NO," SAID LATIN.

CHAPTER ONE
UNEXPECTED GUEST

IT WAS ten o'clock in the morning, and Guiterrez was sitting on the high stool behind the check desk in the restaurant kitchen chewing the end of a pencil and spitting out the splinters with explosive disapproval. The floor around the stool was littered with crumpled paper. Two busboys were cleaning silverware, and the pastry chef and the fry cook were playing gin rummy on the metal cover of the steam table.

Dick, the headwaiter, came in through the swing door from the front of the restaurant. He was wrapping himself up in an apron the general size and proportions of a parachute. He wound it around his skinny waist three times and tied the cords in two elaborate bow-knots.

"Hi, crackpot," he said to Guiterrez. "What's with you?"

"I'm thinking up today's specials," Guiterrez snarled. "Get the hell out of my kitchen, or I'll kill you."

"Guess who's out front?" Dick invited, ignoring the threat.

Guiterrez merely glared at him.

"It's Latin," said Dick.

Guiterrez said: "I don't care if it's.... Who?"

Dick nodded confirmingly. "It's Latin. And he ain't in uniform, either."

Guiterrez got down off the stool. "I think we better look into this matter."

They went through the swing door into the main room of the restaurant. It was empty now, chairs stacked neatly on the close-packed tables. Morning sunlight coming through the plate-glass windows and doors at the front glistened on the freshly swabbed floor.

Latin's special booth was the last one in the row against the west wall, and Guiterrez and Dick stopped beside it and looked down at him.

"Hello, Latin," Guiterrez said. "Long time no see."

Latin didn't look up or answer. There was a bottle of brandy in front of him, and he poured himself a drink and sipped it slowly, staring down at the tabletop. He was

a thin man, a little better than medium height, with eyes that were a smooth, cold green. He usually had an air of jaunty self-confidence, but it was missing now. He looked glumly disconsolate.

He ran forward, trying frantically to see into the tangled mass inside the car. "My wife!" he moaned. "She was in that car!"

"You got a leave?" Guiterrez asked. "You on furlough?"

"No," said Latin.

"Are you A.W.O.L.?" Dick inquired.

"No."

"Come on, Latin," Guiterrez said. "You remember. You're in the Army now. You're even an officer. You didn't desert, did you?"

"No," Latin answered absently. "I was discharged."

"The hell you cry!" Dick exclaimed. "I didn't know the war was over!"

"Latin," said Guiterrez, "did you get dishonorably discharged? Did they catch you playin' one of your usual snide tricks on somebody? Did you cheat at cards or shoot somebody in the back or something?"

"No," said Latin. "They found out I was color-blind."

"COLOR-BLIND!" GUITERREZ repeated, astonished.

"Yes."

"I always did think you had a funny taste in ties," Dick observed, "but I never figured you couldn't help it. How come they didn't spot you when they inducted you? Didn't they give you an examination for color-blindness?"

"Yes. I memorized the charts."

"What?" Guiterrez said blankly.

Latin sighed. "They test you with charts full of colored dots. If your vision is normal, some of the dots form figures and letters. The charts are numbered. I got hold of a set and got a guy with normal vision to tell me what was on each one. Then I memorized them. I got one hundred percent perfect in the examination."

Guiterrez shook his head slowly. "You would figure out an angle. How'd they catch you?"

"They had different colored slips for different orders at the training camp. I got some of them mixed up a few times, and one of the doctors got suspicious. He sprang a new chart on me all of a sudden. I didn't do so well."

"Why didn't you bribe the doc?" Dick asked.

"Don't think I didn't try. I offered him this whole restaurant—lock, stock and cash—with you two thrown in, and he just laughed."

Dick nodded slowly. "Yeah. Them Army guys is sometimes funny that way. But what do they care whether or not you're color-blind? You can tell a Jap when you see one, can't you?"

Latin sipped his drink. "Yes, but they have different colored blinkers, signals, flags, even parachutes. Each one means something special. You might get in a jam if you couldn't tell what."

"Ummm," said Guiterrez thoughtfully. "I tell you—you could change your name and try some other doc that was usin' the old charts."

Latin looked up at him. "Got any ideas as to how I'd change my fingerprints?"

"Oh," said Guiterrez. "Yeah. There's that, ain't there?" He lifted the brandy bottle and measured the height of the liquor in it. "And it's time for you to get some breakfast in you, too. Now you're here, you got to get to work, Latin. This here doghouse restaurant has been losin' money so fast it makes me dizzy. Everybody eats too much, and I'm telling you the prices for food would make you turn green."

"Raise the prices for meals," Latin suggested indifferently.

"So!" Guiterrez shouted. "You want to be a war profiteer, is that it? Well, the hell with you! You get out and cheat somebody out of some dough so I can pay the bills by the tenth of the month, like the law says. And stay out of jail while you do it, for once! You ain't gonna use none of the restaurant dough to bail yourself out! Now sit there and shut up while I cook you a ham omelette like you wouldn't believe was possible!"

He slapped violently through the door back into the kitchen. Somebody started to tap on the plate-glass panel of the front door.

Dick said: "These early birds give me the worms." He strolled to the front of the restaurant and shouted: "No! We ain't open yet! Go away! Go home if you got one!"

A faint, muffled voice shouted back at him.

"You hear me!" Dick said. "Go home!"

Latin started to pour himself another brandy and then thought better of it and lit a cigarette instead.

"These dames," Dick muttered. "This one acts either nutty or drunk or both." He raised his voice angrily. "Beat it! Scram! We're closed!"

The tapping on the glass grew louder.

"Quit it!" Dick ordered. "You'll bust the door, you dope!" The bolt rattled as he unfastened it. "Now listen, lady. You lay off that glass and get—*ow!*"

High heels tapped emphatically, and then a woman stopped beside Latin's booth.

"**YOU'RE MAX** Latin, aren't you?" she demanded breathlessly. "Aren't you?"

"Yes," said Latin.

Dick came up behind her. "She kicked me right in the shin! Is that right, lady? You think that's polite?"

"Oh, go away!" said the woman. "For goodness' sake, I wouldn't have kicked you if you hadn't tried to stop me from coming in! Is this man really Max Latin?"

"Yup," said Dick. "And there's only one like him—we certainly hope. Now you've seen him you can go home happy, can't you?"

"Well, I certainly can't!" She plumped herself down in the booth in the seat across from Latin. "I was just surprised, that's all. I mean he doesn't look very ugly or criminal or desperate or anything like that, does he?"

"I don't know," said Dick. "Do you, Latin?"

"Every other Tuesday," said Latin. He nodded politely at the woman. "Come back then."

"What?" said the woman blankly. She was plump and short, and her brown eyes sparkled with a sort of eager, devouring interest. She was dressed in a brown tailored suit that had cost a couple of hundred dollars with or without a priority. She looked like she would organize a committee and vote on important matters at the drop of a hat. She bubbled, there was no other word for it, with enthusiasm. "Tuesday? I can't. That's Defense School night.... Oh, you're joking. You mustn't be hurt by what I said about you being ugly. After all the newspaper stories about you being in jail and accused of crimes all the time, I naturally expected.... I mean, you look *refined!*"

"Them's fightin' words," said Dick. "Watch out he don't bop you with that bottle."

"Bottle?" she repeated, looking at it. "Oh, are you drinking this early in the morning, Mr. Latin? That really isn't good for you, you know. Don't you think I'd just better put it aside for a little while...."

Guiterrez came out of the kitchen carrying a platter with a fluffy yellow omelette on it.

"Now, who the hell is this?" he demanded. "Dick, I told you I don't want no customers kickin' around here before one o'clock."

The woman switched around to beam at him. "Oh, you're Mr. Guiterrez, aren't you? I've heard so much about you. Always so lovably gruff and with a heart of gold and such a wonderful cook!"

Guiterrez gaped at her. "Who, me?"

"Lovable," Dick whispered, stunned. "Heart of gold."

"And such a beautiful omelette!" the woman exclaimed. "The very sight of it makes me hungry. Can you cook me one just like it?"

Guiterrez made choking noises. "Yes, I can! But, by God, I'm not going to! This is my extraspecial, triple *de luxe* edition, cooked personally by me, Guiterrez, to keep Latin from seeing little green men from drinking too much brandy in the morning. I positively don't hand it out to customers—and particularly dames."

LATIN WAS smiling in spite of himself. "Go cook her one," he ordered.

"I will like hell!" Guiterrez snarled. "I quit! You hear that, Latin! Phooey on you! I'm through! I resign!"

"Cook her an omelette first," Latin said.

"Now that's the way it goes," Guiterrez shouted. "You ain't here more than five minutes before you start drivin' me nuts! I'm gonna sue the Army! Phooey!" He slammed back into the kitchen again.

Dick produced napkins and silverware and a cup of coffee for Latin. "Have you got a name, lady?" he asked the woman patiently.

"Oh dear, yes!" she said. "Isn't that stupid of me? I was so interested in all of you that I forgot to introduce myself.

Mr. Latin, I'm Mrs. Gregory Farmer. Have you ever heard of me—or rather, of my husband?"

Latin shook his head, chewing on the omelette.

Mrs. Farmer edged closer, looking very earnest. "He's a manufacturer, Mr. Latin. He makes plastics, and he's awfully clever and successful at it. He has a factory just outside of town. The company he owns is called the Bay City Chemical Products. It's a *big* factory. Surely you've seen it?"

Latin shook his head again.

Guiterrez came out of the kitchen with another omelette. "I was savin' this for myself, but I suppose you don't mind takin' the food right out of my mouth. Here!"

Dick produced another cup of coffee.

Mrs. Farmer tried a mouthful of the omelette. "Oh! Oh, my! This is divine! I'm so glad I decided to consult you, Mr. Latin. You've made me feel much better already."

"That ain't Latin," Guiterrez told her. "That's my extra-special, triple *de luxe* omelette."

"Don't let us keep you two from your work," Latin said.

"So now he insults us!" Guiterrez said to Dick.

Dick curled his upper lip. "As if we'd want to listen to anything he had to say!"

Guiterrez went into the kitchen, and Dick strolled up to the front of the restaurant.

"You wanted to consult me?" Latin said to Mrs. Farmer.

She nodded eagerly. "Yes, Mr. Latin, you wouldn't hesitate to kill a person, would you?"

"Depends on who he is," said Latin, "and on how long you want me to hesitate."

"But that's so *wrong!* Oh, that's a terrible attitude for you to take!"

"Nope," said Latin. "I know lots of people who need killing."

"Oh, but think of the suffering you inflict. And think of the *moral* side of the question! Wouldn't you much rather do good than evil?"

"No," said Latin.

Mrs. Farmer looked hurt and really incredulous. "You—you *like* to act in an unlawful way?"

"Sure," said Latin.

"But suppose someone came in and offered you a chance to do something fine and noble and honest. What would you do, then?"

"Throw them out," said Latin. "And go on eating this omelette."

"Oh!" said Mrs. Farmer breathlessly. "But—but I'm willing to pay you."

"That's a horse of another color," said Latin. "I'll even be honest for pay—if it's enough. What do you want me to do?"

"Well—if there were a person—a horrible, unscrupulous person—who was menacing the happiness and the very *life* of a person you loved, what would you do?"

Latin pointed an imaginary gun and said: "Bing."

"Shoot them?" Mrs. Farmer gasped, horrified. "Oh, but no! You couldn't!"

"Oh, yes I could. What's his name and where does he live and what's he worth to you dead?"

"It—it's a woman!"

Latin shrugged. "Then the price is much cheaper. If he was a guy, he might shoot back at me."

"Mr. Latin!" said Mrs. Farmer. "Please! You're just going at this all wrong. You must let me explain!"

"Go ahead," Latin invited.

Mrs. Farmer drew a deep breath. "Mr. Latin, I love my husband. He's just the most wonderful, dear person in the world. He's suffering terribly, and I want you to help him."

"Help him suffer?" Latin asked.

"No! Please be serious! This—this is the most serious and vital thing in my life. He *is* my life! And we've always been divinely happy. And now he can't sleep and he can't eat and he's so wan and pale and worried all the time. It—it breaks my heart, Mr. Latin!"

"What's the matter with him?" Latin inquired.

"It's that woman and her awful paper! Just dinging and dinging at him every day and saying nasty, insulting things and calling him a traitor and a fifth columnist and an obstructionist and a slacker and a war profiteer and—and—"

"That's enough," said Latin. "That would even make me lose a little sleep—providing it was true."

"It's *not* true! It's just all lies!"

"LET'S SEE," Latin said thoughtfully. "So far we've got a dame and a paper. Is it a newspaper?"

"Well—yes. I suppose you could call it that. It comes out weekly, and it's called *Defend Our World*."

"Is it published here? I never heard of it."

"Their editorial offices are on the fourth floor at 411 Court Street. It's just a little office. The paper circulates among defense workers in the war factories all through this district. It has departments about each factory with gossip and personals and all that. I don't think it has any general circulation—on newsstands or anything, I mean."

"And the dame owns it?"

"I don't know. She's the editor. Her name is Gertrude Glenn, and she's a horrible, messy, sloppy sort of a person. She has dyed hair."

"That's bad," Latin agreed. "Why does she pick on your husband?"

"I don't know, but she's got to stop it, because it isn't fair!"

"Why does she claim he's a fifth columnist and whatnot?"

"Because his factory isn't producing the capacity it has been assigned by the government. I don't know much about that part of it, but the factory makes all kinds of plastic articles that they substitute for metal because it's lighter and cheaper."

"But not enough of them?"

"It isn't Gregory's fault!" Mrs. Farmer wailed. "He works so hard and such long hours, and he worries so! He can't get the materials that he needs. They're all on priority, and they have to be assigned to each factory in just the quantities needed, and there are delays and delays and bickering, and Gregory just nearly goes mad! And then that woman says it's all his fault and that he's doing it on purpose to hold up the war effort and help Hitler!"

"Is he?" asked Latin.

Mrs. Farmer's eyes brimmed over. "Oh, Mr. Latin!"

"All right, all right," said Latin quickly. "He isn't. In fact, I know he's a fine fellow and a great patriot. What do you want me to do about it?"

"I want you to make her stop! I want you to make her leave Gregory alone before he—he gets so desperate he does himself some harm. It's awful, Mr. Latin! Sometimes I think he might—might—"

"Might," Latin finished, nodding. "How do you figure I'm going to stop this Glenn doll?"

"Well—," said Mrs. Farmer, swallowing hard. "Gregory is a marvelous and wonderful man, and his life is being ruined, and—and you would be accomplishing something—"

"Fine and noble," Latin agreed. "But how?"

Mrs. Farmer sat up straight. "You make her stop, that's all! I tried to talk to her, and she was just nasty and sneering and superior. I—I don't even care if you *hurt* her! I don't! Gregory means everything in this world to me, and I'm not going to have him treated that way!" She opened her big patent leather purse. "There! That's all I could save out of my household money. Will it be enough?"

Latin didn't attempt to count the crumpled bills. "I think so," he said.

Mrs. Farmer got up out of the booth. "Oh, and here's my card. You—you'll call me?"

"Yes," said Latin.

"And—and be firm with her, won't you? I mean, *really* firm."

"All right," said Latin.

"Good-bye, Mr. Latin. It was a pleasure to meet you. I'd read so much about you, but I never thought—Well—good-bye."

"Good-bye," said Latin.

CHAPTER TWO
REVENGE!

DICK LET her out of the front of the restaurant, and Guiterrez came in from the kitchen and leaned over the back of the booth. Latin was straightening out the bills Mrs. Farmer had given him, and Guiterrez watched, moving his lips silently as he counted.

"Whee!" he said, when Latin was finished.

Latin looked up at him. "Twelve hundred bucks," he said slowly. "She saved this out of her household money. She must be a lot smarter at buying food than you are."

"So now you're calling me a crook!" Guiterrez snarled. "O.K., then. Hand over some of that dough so I can meet the payroll around here."

"Maybe I can use it to grow some more," Latin said, putting his bills in his pocket. "Dick, bring me the telephone."

Dick came over carrying the portable telephone, and Latin plugged it in at the concealed switch behind the drape that covered the wall at the end of the booth.

"Now look, Latin," said Guiterrez. "Fun is fun, but you ain't going to try to chisel that poor dame, are you? After all, she's tryin' to help her husband out of a jam, and even if she is maybe a little silly, she's a nice, decent sort of a doll."

"Run away and play house," Latin said, dialing a number.

"I wonder how you sleep nights!" Guiterrez exploded. "There'll come a day! You wait! You'll see! One of these times you get put in jail, you ain't never gonna get out again! And will I laugh! Ha, ha, ha!"

"Go away," said Latin absently.

A voice in the telephone said: "Good morning. This is the *Daily Blade*."

"Let me speak to Les Blaine."

"Who is calling, please?"

"This is his wife's boyfriend."

There were two sharp clicks, and then a voice said angrily: "Why, damn you, if you think this is funny, you wait until I lay my hands—"

"Hi, Les," said Latin. "This is Max Latin."

"You're a damned liar. Latin is a lieutenant with the motorized infantry at Fort Crail."

"Not anymore, he isn't," Latin denied.

"Latin! What's the matter? You didn't go and try any of your chiseling...."

"No!" Latin snarled.

"Oh. Well... I mean, what's the trouble, pal?"

"They found out I was color-blind."

"Oh, hell! After all the trouble you took? Well, couldn't you slip somebody a small bill...."

"I tried," said Latin.

"I'm sorry, kid. But honestly I can't do anything for you with the Medical Corps...."

"That's O.K., Les. I'll think of something. In the meantime, what can you tell me about a paper called *Defend Our World?*"

"Why?"

"I'm after some dough, of course. Do you want to tell me, or shall I ask somewhere else?"

"Don't be so huffy. I'll tell you, but—but she's a hell of a nice gal, Latin."

"Who is?"

"Gertie Glenn. She edits the sheet."

"Do you know her?" Latin asked.

"Sure. She used to work for the *Blade.* Did sob-sister and fashion stuff."

"Did she get fired?" Latin inquired.

"Yup."

"For what?"

"Sleeping too late."

"With whom?"

"Aw, Latin. She really is nice. She's a big, sloppy gal, and she's honest, just lazy. They warned her about fifty times, but she never could turn up less than two hours late. She likes her sleep. So they finally had to give her the bounce. Then she picked up this defense paper. She's doing all right from what I hear."

"Does she scare easy?"

Les Blaine laughed. "You've got the wrong number, kid. Gertie would just laugh if Superman and Boris Karloff came and gibbered at her as a duet. You can't scare her. She's got a sense of humor."

"I'll be seeing you, Les," said Latin. He depressed the breaker bar on the telephone and stared thoughtfully at the stained ceiling for a moment. Finally he dialed another number.

THE RECEIVER buzzed once, and then a voice chortled cheerfully: "Hello! Hello! This is Happy's Twenty-four-Hour Garage! Service any time, anywhere! How can I serve you, friend?"

"This is Latin, Happy."

There was a long pause, and then Happy said cautiously: "Beg pardon, friend. What was that you said?"

"This is Max Latin."

"Latin! Lieutenant Latin! Well, throw me down and stomp on my face!"

"Not Lieutenant anymore, Happy."

"Hell's fire, Latin! You didn't let 'em *catch* you, did you? You don't mean to tell me that after you dodged the police for ten years, you'd let a bunch of Army rumdumbs put the old who's-that on you? You ain't going to get shot at sunrise or anything, are you, Latin?"

"I hope not," said Latin. "But you never can tell. Listen, Happy, I'd like to get in touch with those two birds who were indicted for that torch-torture murder six months back. I want them to do a little job with me."

"Oh, no," said Happy unhappily. "Not them two."

"Yeah."

"No, Latin. Them two are very uncivilized. Honest, you wouldn't like 'em at all."

"A hundred bucks apiece," said Latin. "For one little job that won't take an hour."

"Latin," said Happy, "them two ain't nice people. I give you my word. You know how they are, don't you?"

"That's why I want them."

"I don't like this, Latin. I advise you against it."

"Send them over," Latin ordered. "Send that black Buick coupé over, too. Get them here as fast as you can."

"Oh, Latin," said Happy. "Oh, my. I hope you ain't gonna be as sorry as I think you're gonna be."

LATIN SAT and waited for an hour. He used up a full package of cigarettes and finally drank the rest of his bottle of brandy. He decided he would have some more cigarettes and some more brandy, too, and he opened his mouth to shout for some and then closed it again.

"How do you do?" said the young man who was watching him from over the top of the next booth.

"All right," said Latin.

The young man smiled at him. He could—and did— smile very nicely. He had incredibly regular teeth and a thin, pencil-line black mustache and a tan that spelled a lot of money, or Palm Beach, or perhaps both. He was wearing a hat with a feather in it and a belted, swingback suit with padded shoulders. He came off his perch and slid into the seat opposite Latin.

"You're Max Latin, aren't you?" he asked. "I think it's thrilling to meet you, and I'm doubly flattered that you asked for us."

"Where's the rest of us?" Latin asked.

"Oh, you mean Raymond? He's in the kitchen, of course. You see, we weren't sure about you. I mean, that horrible grand jury indicted us for some stupid murder or other, and we just can't take any chances.... My name is René, by the way."

"How do you do, René?" Latin said soberly.

"It's such a pleasure to know you.... Oh, here's Raymond now.... Raymond, I know you didn't find anything in the kitchen that was at all suspicious, and I've been having a very nice chat with Mr. Latin.... May I present Raymond, Mr. Latin?"

"How do you do, Raymond?" said Latin.

Raymond was small and sleek and blond. He looked exactly like René except that his mustache was light and the feather in his hat was a different color.

"No cops," said Raymond. "No hide-outs."

"That's nice," said René. "I was sure we wouldn't have to deal with that sort of thing—not with a person of Mr. Latin's integrity."

"A dictaphone," said Raymond.

"Oh, dear," said René. "Not really."

Latin had both his hands spread flat on the table. "Behind the drape," he said, jerking his head toward the end of the booth. "I use it for evidence when I need witnesses. It's not turned on now—I don't think."

"You look, Raymond," René said.

Raymond leaned over and pulled the drape aside. The microphone of the dictaphone made a bright, metallic circle. There was a slide switch on the cord above it, and Raymond tested it with his thumb, snapping his nail against the microphone and listening expertly.

"It's off now," he said. "It was off while we were talking."

"Well, of course it was," said René. "Mr. Latin trusts us, and we trust Mr. Latin. There was a price mentioned for our services, Mr. Latin. It was two hundred dollars."

Latin smiled thinly. "It's in my wallet."

"Of course," said René. "And you carry your wallet in your—inside pocket of your coat, don't you?"

"My God," said Latin.

René smiled at him. "You won't mind, I'm sure, if Raymond extracts it from your coat?"

"Oh yes, I will," said Latin flatly.

"Of course," said René. "Surely. We haven't had the good fortune to deal with men of your caliber lately. That grand jury.... Really so annoying.... It's just a formality, Mr. Latin, but may we see the money?"

Moving very slowly and carefully, Latin took out his wallet and counted out twenty ten-dollar bills. He had four left—in his wallet. René and Raymond watched him put them back in the bill pocket.

"Yes," said René thoughtfully.

"Yes," Latin echoed. "Are you going to sign up for me or agin me?"

René laughed musically. "For you, of course. You mustn't be suspicious of us, Mr. Latin. We are very loyal—indeed."

"Indeed, you'd better be," said Latin.

"How can we serve you?" René asked.

"Sure," said Raymond. "Name it."

"A small piece of change for you boys," said Latin. "I want a girl scared, and badly. She doesn't scare easy. She's a newspaper girl and sort of toughlike. Her name is Gertrude Glenn, and she runs a newspaper on the fourth floor at 411 Court Street."

René looked at Raymond and laughed.

"What's funny?" Latin demanded.

"Nothing," said René. "Really. It's awfully quick and easy money, that's all."

"Wait until you earn it."

"Surely," said René. "If we take it, we'll earn it. We don't cheat. How badly do you want her hurt?"

"Not at all," said Latin.

"Oh, now," said René. "We've been so delightfully open and aboveboard about all this, and it's *your* restaurant and *your* dictaphone...."

"I'm going with you."

"Oh, dear," said René.

"No," said Raymond.

Latin pulled the stacked bills toward him.

René laughed, delighted. "Of course, Mr. Latin. You're going with us, and you're the—ah—boss. You want this dear girl frightened. We will certainly do our best."

"No shooting," said Latin. "No knives."

René looked shocked. "Why, of course not."

CHAPTER THREE
SINISTER INTERVIEW

THE BUILDING at 411 Court Street had housed a bank on its ground floor in its better days, but now the bank's premises were occupied by a bicycle repair shop, which might have been a sign of the trend of the times. The building was constructed of red brick, four-stories high, and it had an air of battered but grim defiance of the elements and the years.

Latin rolled the Buick coupé into the graveled parking lot beside it, and Raymond got out of the car immediately and headed back through the lot.

"Hey!" said Latin. "Not that way."

"It's all right, really," said René. "He'll meet us upstairs in Miss Glenn's office."

Latin got out of the coupé. "Do you always go in places that way? One in the back and one in the front?"

René nodded. "We find it so much more convenient."

He and Latin went around to the front of the building and into a narrow, tiled lobby that had formerly been the foyer of the bank. There was one elevator, and the operator was sitting on a stool beside it picking his teeth disconsolately with a match. He was an old man dressed in baggy blue coveralls.

"Goin' up?" he asked, sighing.

Latin nodded. "Four, please."

"Ain't nothin' up there but that there durned newspaper for defense workers."

"O.K.," said Latin, getting in the elevator.

"They don't want to buy nothin'," said the operator.

"Up," said Latin.

The operator sighed and got off his stool. He closed the elevator door with a clang, and the cage wheezed slowly upward, trembling as though it had palsy. It stopped a foot short of the floor, and the operator opened the door.

"You'll just get throwed out, but I ain't gonna wait for you."

He slammed the door behind them, and René and Latin went down the dim, straight corridor toward the double frosted-glass doors facing them. One of the doors bore the legend: *DEFEND OUR WORLD*, and the other: *EDITORIAL OFFICES—ENTER*.

Latin opened that door, and he and René stepped into a long narrow office with a long table piled high with newspapers against one wall and a straight bench against the opposite one. There was a railing at the back, and behind it a very small, thin girl with thick, horn-rimmed spectacles was pounding frantically on a typewriter. A man was sitting on the bench with a newspaper in front of his face.

"Oh, Raymond," said René. "You should be more careful. That newspaper is upside down."

Raymond folded the paper and dropped it on the floor. "It's lousy any way you look at it," he said. "There's just the two dames here. This one and the one in the office in back. There's no interoffice speaker. The one in back buzzes the one in front when she wants her. There are no other occupied offices on this floor."

THE SMALL girl had stopped typing and was staring at the three of them with her mouth slightly open. "Is—is there anything you wanted?" she asked in a faint voice.

"Yes," said René, going through the gate in the railing. "Isn't it nice of you to ask? What's your name, my dear?"

"It's—it's Lucy. What do you want?"

"We want to interview your employer. It's most important, Lucy."

Lucy started to edge out of her chair. "I'll tell her…."

"No, you won't," said René, smiling. "We're going to give her a lovely surprise."

"You can't—go in."

René chucked her under the chin. "Now, Lucy."

"She's going to scream," said Raymond. "You'd better choke her a little bit."

"Oh, no," said René. "That wouldn't be nice. And Lucy is going to cooperate with us, aren't you, Lucy?"

Lucy made little wordless noises.

"Of course," said René. "Now just get up, my dear. And open the door of the private office. Right there. That's it, my dear. And just step in ahead of me…."

Latin slid in through the doorway behind them into a huge, square, barren office with a big desk in the middle of it and papers and parts of papers and snipped out articles spread all over the floor. There was a scummy jar of paste on top of the desk, and the woman behind it was stirring it absently with the eraser end of a lead pencil.

"Beat it, Lucy," she said, without looking up. "I'm thinking."

"May we watch you?" René asked. "It'll be so interesting for us. We've never seen anyone think."

The woman's head jerked up, and a lock of her metallically yellow hair fell over one eye. She was big, but she was gracefully big, and not fat. She was wearing a green dress that had spots on it that weren't all put there by the patternmaker. Her arms were bare, and they were firm and rounded and faintly tanned. Her eyes were narrowed and brown and humorously tolerant, and she had a peaches-and-cream complexion that she hadn't bought in a beauty shop.

She smiled slowly and calmly and then nodded and said: "Hi, chums."

Lucy said: "Miss Glenn, I—I tried to keep them out, but—but—"

"It's O.K., kid," said Gertrude Glenn. "Who's the end man for this minstrel show, boys?"

"The name is Latin," Latin said. "Max Latin."

"I've seen it," said Gertrude Glenn. "In police records. What can I do for you, chiseler?"

"Miss Glenn!" Lucy broke in breathlessly. "The other two! When I saw them together—I recognized…. They're the torch murderers!"

Gertrude Glenn looked from René to Raymond and then back again. She wasn't smiling now.

"They are!" Lucy babbled. "Their pictures were in all the papers! They're the ones who b-burned that old lady's feet to make her tell them where she had hidden her money!"

"Yeah," said Gertrude Glenn slowly.

Lucy gulped. "And when she wouldn't tell them, they threw gasoline on her and s-set fire to her!"

"Just a newspaper exaggeration," said René pleasantly. "It was a case of mistaken identity. We were acquitted at once, you know."

"You wouldn't have liked the old doll, anyway," said Raymond. "She kept parrots and poodles."

"Or so you've been told," said René.

Raymond nodded. "Sure."

Gertrude Glenn's face had paled slightly. "I don't like this, Latin. What did you bring these two here for?"

"To take a look at you," said Latin.

"It's been a pleasure, too," said René.

"What do you want?" Gertrude Glenn demanded.

Latin said: "Lay off Gregory Farmer. Entirely off. Don't mention him again in your paper."

Gertrude Glenn didn't show any surprise, but her full lips thinned just slightly. "And if I do mention him?"

René sat down on the corner of the desk, swinging one leg gracefully. There was a snap, and he was holding a burning match between his thumb and forefinger. He stared at Gertrude Glenn over the flame, smiling. When the match had burned down near his fingers, he dropped the end into the paste pot, and it went out with a sputtering hiss. A thin spiral of smoke curled upward.

"Get it?" Raymond asked.

Gertrude Glenn nodded stiffly.

"Remember it," said Latin.

"Oh, I'll remember it," said Gertrude Glenn.

"Let's go, boys," said Latin.

"You and I will," said René. "Raymond will stay here for just a second."

"No funny business," said Latin.

"Oh, dear me, no," said René. "You heard what Mr. Latin said, Raymond."

"I got ears," said Raymond.

RENÉ AND Latin went out through the front office and down the corridor to the elevator. Latin rang the bell, and the grill opened at once.

"I told you I wasn't gonna wait," said the operator, "but I did. I knew you'd get throwed right out. That Miss Glenn is a mighty handsome woman and nice, too, but she can sure be hard-boiled. Did she take a poke at you?"

"No," said Latin. Then he added thoughtfully: "Not yet."

"She's very interesting," said René. "I'll be looking forward to any further business dealings with her."

"Don't get ideas, son," Latin said flatly. "This is where you two bow out. Just remember that I'm not an old lady and that I keep gadgets around that bite a little deeper than poodles or parrots."

"Mr. Latin," said René. "Please. You can rely on us. We are much too clever to want trouble with you."

They walked out of the building and around to the parking lot. Raymond was sitting in the Buick coupé, waiting for them.

Latin said: "I'll leave you here. Take the Buick back to Happy's Garage and leave it there."

"Good-bye, Mr. Latin," said René. "Thank you for calling us. It has been a very great pleasure to meet you. Hasn't it, Raymond?"

Raymond yawned. "Oh, sure."

René slid under the wheel, and the Buick rolled smoothly out of the parking lot and down the street. Latin stood staring after it for a second and then shrugged his shoulders with an uneasy little jerk and started along the street the other way, looking for a taxi.

WHEN LATIN came into the restaurant through the back door, Guiterrez was sitting on his stool behind the check desk again. He had chewed his original pencil completely up and was well started on a second. The discarded paper under the desk resembled a lopsided snow drift.

"Look here, Latin," he said belligerently. "Just hold still for a moment while I give you some facts."

"All right," said Latin. "What?"

"Them two guys that come here. That René and Raymond. Them torch murderers. Them two fellas is awful. They made a bonfire of that poor old dame. I don't mind so much them other crumbs you pal around. Even cops I can take in small doses. But at torch murderers, I draw the line. I'd as soon have Hitler and Hirohito kicking around my kitchen."

"They won't bother you anymore."

"That's what you say, and this time you better not be lying. I tell you, with them guys and me it is strictly nix. They give me the creeps. And say, there's a guy that's called you sixty-five times in the last half hour."

Dick came into the kitchen. "He's at it again, too. He sure sounds like he's in pain. Where'll you take it, Latin?"

"In the booth," said Latin.

He went into the empty front room of the restaurant and sat down in his booth. Dick brought the portable telephone, and Latin plugged it in.

"Yes?" he said.

The voice on the wire was high-pitched and almost incoherent with frantic anger. "Now you're not going to stall me off any longer! I want to talk to Max Latin!"

"You are," said Latin.

"What? Is this Max Latin? Well, what in God's name do you think you're doing?"

"Wasting my time," said Latin. "Good-bye."

"Wait! Latin! Don't you dare hang up on me! This is Gregory Farmer!"

"Never heard of you," said Latin.

"Oh, yes you have! There's no use lying! My wife confessed to me that she hired you to frighten Gertrude Glenn! Oh, she's a fool and a simpleton and an interfering busybody, and you're nothing less than a criminal! I'm going to have you arrested!"

"Go ahead," said Latin amiably.

"Oh, for God's sake, Latin! Will you listen to reason for a moment? My wife and you, between the two of you, have just made a complete mess of everything!"

"Is that so?" said Latin, mildly interested. "How?"

"I had everything arranged until you blundered into it with your stupid threats of force! You fool, don't you understand that I'm a respectable businessman? I suppose you've never dealt with anyone like that!"

"Oh, you'd be surprised," said Latin. "But what's the beef?"

Farmer made gulping sounds that were audible even over the telephone. "I will not stand for any such activities as you've been engaging in! I want you to drop the case! Get out! Leave it alone! Just forget it!"

"I couldn't do that," Latin said. "My conscience would bother me. I've been retained."

Farmer shouted: "You've been retained! You—you— Can't you see the horrible position this puts me in? As though I would countenance the use of threats of force against a woman! As though I would hire murderers.... Oh, this is ghastly!"

"Well, of course," said Latin, "if you really don't want me to handle the case, I could bow out if I were compensated for all my time and thought...."

"Compensated!"

"Bribed, I mean," Latin explained.

"Why, you—you incredibly insolent.... Oh, all right! *All—right!* How much?"

"A thousand dollars would make me very happy."

"What! A thousand dollars!"

"Or even two," said Latin.

FARMER MADE hoarse, breathing sounds over the telephone. "One thousand! It's agreed. You're to leave this business alone—completely alone! You're not to meddle in it in any way! You're not to communicate with my wife! Do you understand all that?"

"Sure. Get the thousand in hundred dollar bills. Take the numbers down if it'll make you happy. Put the bills in a plain envelope and send it by messenger to the restaurant here. Have the messenger give it to my headwaiter. His name is Dick."

"How well you arrange these matters!"

"I've had practice," Latin assured him. "There's a tag on my offer. I want you to answer two questions. How did you find out about your wife hiring me?"

"Through Gertrude Glenn, of course! She called me up and told me just what you'd done and just what she was going to do about it."

"Is that so?" said Latin. "And what was she going to do about it?"

"You'll find out," said Farmer grimly.

"Probably," Latin agreed. "And now, how did you arrange to have her stop picking at you before I stepped into the picture? You said you had."

"I don't know whether it applies anymore or not! I arranged it in the obvious and honest manner—a way that would never occur to you. I've succeeded in getting a supply of the materials I needed. Now I can meet the production schedule the government has assigned me, and naturally there won't be any reason for Miss Glenn to criticize me anymore. That is, unless you have succeeded in making her so angry that she will do it anyway."

"Yeah," said Latin absently. "How did you arrange to get a supply of those materials?"

"That's none of your damned business!" The line cracked sharply as Farmer hung up.

Dick was leaning against the back of the booth. "Did I hear something about a thousand dollars?"

Latin nodded absently, scratching his ear.

"I got to hand it to you, Latin," said Dick. "I sometimes think I am a little on the immoral side myself, but you pass me so fast it gives me chilblains. It's a pleasure to watch you work. After this day's labor, I think you better prime yourself with a bit of brandy." He took a bottle and a glass from under his apron and put them down on the table.

"I'm not through yet," said Latin. He took out his billfold and withdrew the card Mrs. Farmer had given him. It had a telephone number on it, and he dialed the number.

The phone at the other end rang twice, and then a coldly formal voice said: "This is the Gregory Farmer residence."

"May I speak to Mrs. Farmer, please?" Latin asked.

"Mrs. Farmer is indisposed."

"Just tell her that Max Latin is calling. I think she'll want to talk to me."

"One moment, please."

THERE WAS a long pause, and then Mrs. Farmer gasped in a choked, thick voice: "Oh, Mr. Latin! Oh, dear!"

"Hello, Mrs. Farmer," Latin said. "Is there something the trouble?"

"Oh! Mr. Latin, Gregory is just furious at me! He n-never talked to me like that in all the years we've been married! He *swore!*"

"I can't imagine it," said Latin. "Why would he act in such a wicked way?"

"He said I had s-spoiled everything he had arranged about—about that Gertrude Glenn. He said he was going to increase his pro-production at the factory and she wouldn't have s-said those things about him anymore, but now perhaps she w-would because you had made her so angry! Mr. Latin, what will I do? You don't—don't think Gregory will *leave* me, do you?"

"No," said Latin judicially.

"Oh, if he did, I'd just die! I'd just die! I just couldn't stand living without Gregory!"

"Did he tell you how he was going to increase his production?"

"What? Oh, Mr. Latin, how can you talk about things like that when my whole marriage is at stake? Of course he didn't tell me! He knows I don't understand about business. All I do is just make him happy and give him a perfect, comfortable home and—and now maybe he won't even *want* me to!"

"Don't be downhearted," Latin advised. "I'm on your side, you know."

"No! No, no! Please, Mr. Latin! Don't do anything more! Don't say anything to Gregory! Oh, please!"

"All right, Mrs. Farmer," Latin said, with a little sigh. "Forget it. And good luck."

He hung up.

Dick was still leaning against the side of the booth. "Why didn't you put the bite on her—make her pay you for quitting like you did the old man?"

Latin shrugged. "I'm slipping."

Dick nodded. "She is a nice dame. I bet she clucks around after that husband of hers like a mother hen. Yeah, I guess we can get along without any more of her dough. It's too much like stealing pennies from a blind man."

The telephone buzzed.

Latin picked it up and said: "Latin speaking."

"This is Happy, Latin. My God, get over here, right away! Quick!"

"Sure, Happy," Latin said. "Hold everything. I'm on my way." He dropped the telephone back on its cradle and jerked his head at Dick. "Go out and whistle for Dude's cab. If he isn't at the stand, nail another cab if you have to roll in the street in front of it. Hurry!"

Dick took one startled look at his face and ran for the front door.

"Guiterrez!" Latin yelled.

Guiterrez poked his head through the swing door. "Now what the hell...."

"Get me a gun," Latin said. "Right now."

Guiterrez disappeared instantly.

Dick came back to the booth. "Dude's on his way."

Guiterrez popped through the swing door. He was carrying a flat Colt .32 automatic and an extra magazine in one hand and a pink slip of paper in the other.

"Here. Here's the license for it."

Latin slid out of the booth. He dropped the magazine and the license in his left-hand coat pocket and the gun in his right.

"Your hat," said Dick, handing it to him. "What is it, Latin?"

"Happy's having trouble."

"It's them two damned torch murderers!" Guiterrez shouted. "I told you! I warned you!"

Latin was headed for the front of the restaurant.

"Latin!" Guiterrez said, his voice suddenly shaky. "Be careful, will you please, you damned fool? Don't tackle them two birds—"

Latin slammed the restaurant door behind him just as a battered green cab rolled up at the curb. The driver had a long, exotically bent nose and a grin that showed that all of his upper front teeth were missing.

"Hi, keed!" he greeted. "Hey, how's my old Army gettin' along—"

"No time, Dude," Latin said, ducking into the backseat. "High-flag it. And burn some rubber. Happy's Garage."

"Hold your hat, baby," said Dude.

CHAPTER FOUR
INVISIBLE KILLER

HAPPY'S GARAGE was in the commercial district at the lower end of Flandin Street. There were no houses along these blocks, except a few stray tenements that hadn't yet been crowded out. Warehouses and machine shops and bottling plants lined up in long, dreary rows with the vacant lots between them grown high with dried, soot-heavy weeds. The air rumbled and thundered uneasily with the roar of trucks and the constant pound-pound of heavy machinery.

"Park in front across the street," Latin said. "And keep awake. I might want to go away fast."

"Yeah man," said Dude amiably.

He swung around in a U-turn and nosed the cab in against the curb. Latin got out and walked quickly across the street. Happy's Garage was a narrow, low building constructed of whitewashed bricks with soot streaked down from its eaves like jagged black icicles.

Latin walked down the cement ramp into the long, shadowy interior. The air was heavy with the odor of gas fumes and the sharp, thin smell of auto paint. There was no one in sight anywhere.

"Happy!" Latin called.

Happy came out through the whitewashed door at one side. He was short and very round, and he wore a pair of white coveralls with the name "Happy" stitched across the chest in red tape. His plump face was a sickly yellow now, and his blue eyes looked round and wide and worried.

He didn't say anything. He beckoned silently with his forefinger and indicated the whitewashed door. Latin followed him through it into a little cubbyhole of an office furnished only with an old desk, a water cooler, and a couch that had once been the backseat of an automobile.

René was sitting on the couch. He wasn't wearing his hat, and his smooth hair was rumpled stickily. He was bent forward, holding both hands on his abdomen, staring at the floor between his neat shoes. He looked up at Latin and smiled in a painful, strained grimace. There was blood on his teeth. He looked down again at the floor. He was breathing in short gasps.

Latin looked at Happy. Happy punched himself once in the stomach and once in the chest with his thumb and then held up two fingers and shrugged meaningly.

"Did you call a doctor?" Latin asked.

René grunted and then said thickly: "No. No doctor."

Happy formed words silently with his lips. "No use."

Latin drew a deep breath. "What happened?"

"I was under a car in the back end," Happy said. "I hear these shots, but I don't think nothing of it. They got a lot of new kid truck drivers around here who like to pull the spark and blast their engines and play like they're a machine gun or a dive bomber or something. Then the Buick rolls in the garage and smacks a parked car, and this one gets out of it."

"Where's Raymond?"

Happy took a piece of wastepaper from his hip pocket and wiped his forehead. "He got one right between the eyes. I parked the Buick in the back of the garage. He's in it yet."

"Can you talk, René?" Latin inquired softly.

René bent a little further forward. "Caught us just as I was—turning into the garage. Not close to us. Didn't see anyone. Several shots—very close together." He looked up at Latin, his eyes horribly dilated. "Oh, isn't this disgusting!"

He leaned forward and kept on leaning until he fell off the couch. Latin and Happy both jumped to catch him, but he slid limply through their hands and rolled on his side on the floor, his eyes wide open and staring. Latin knelt beside him and felt his pulse.

"Dead," he said, standing up.

"He's been dead for twenty minutes," said Happy. "He just now found it out. Hell, he was hit twice right dead center. The guy that shot 'em was usin' a rifle, Latin. The bullets went clear though the Buick end-for-end. I can't patch holes like that, and besides, the upholstery is full of blood and brains."

LATIN TOOK out the folded bills he had gotten from Mrs. Farmer and put them on the desk. "Better run the car out in the country and set fire to it. I'm certainly cleaning up money fast on this deal. I should have paid some attention to what you said."

"Well, hell," said Happy. "I ain't always so smart about these matters."

"Can you get rid of these two?"

"Yeah. I'll dump 'em somewhere. They can't trace the Buick back to me. Even if they do, I can prove I rented it out. I'll cover you."

"I won't forget it," said Latin.

"What was the deal?" Happy asked. "What did you want these birds for? Like I said, they ain't civilized. They really did set fire to that old dame, you know. They got off because there was six women on the jury. René and Raymond could look real sweet and mild and innocent if they wanted, and the dames figured such nice, well-bred boys wouldn't commit such a horrible crime. It ain't the first time they got off on that gag, either."

Latin said slowly: "There's a little blat of a newspaper giving the hotfoot to a guy, and his wife wanted me to throw a scare into the editor. The editor is a woman. I figured René and Raymond would really give her a fright and without getting rough about it. I didn't want to push her around or anything."

"Did they scare her?" Happy inquired.

Latin jerked his head to indicate René's body. "It doesn't look much like it, does it?"

Happy blinked. "You don't mean you think the dame— the editor—took this whack at 'em?"

"I think she had a finger in the pie. I must be getting soft in the head. I botched this whole thing. I had plenty of warning, too. I was told she didn't scare and that she could be plenty tough—so I went right ahead anyway. I couldn't wait to investigate. I had to poke my neck out."

"You better pull it in again," said Happy. "You better sign a nonaggression pact with this editor."

Latin nodded absently. "Yeah."

Happy was watching him. "What's on your mind, Latin?"

"The more I think about this, the more I think I stepped into something speedy. I believe I'll just look around a bit here and there."

"I'd make it there, if I was you," said Happy. "I'd make it a long ways away from here."

Latin pointed toward René. "How soon can you get rid of this and the other?"

"Couple hours, unless you don't want 'em found. If you want 'em dumped in the bay, I got to wait until night."

"I think they'd better be found. Clean up things as soon as you can, because if I make any slips somebody might come around to see you. Did those shots raise any commotion around here?"

"Naw. Like I said, there's so much backfiring and pounding and noise on the street it would take an invasion to make people notice anything. I mean, maybe they might look out the front door or something, but they wouldn't be very curious. I didn't see nobody prowling around."

"O.K. I'll see you later. Thanks, Happy."

"Service with a smile," said Happy, winking.

LATIN WENT out of the office and up the ramp to the garage entrance. Dude was sitting in his taxi across the street, watching, and Latin flipped a hand at him reassuringly. He waited for a truck to rumble past and then started across toward the taxi.

He was in the middle of the paving when the first bullet knocked his hat off and the second went past his face so close that he could feel the hot sinister breath of its passage. He dropped on his knees and then sprawled flat on his face. Another bullet drove a long gouge in the asphalt beside him, and a fourth hit six inches closer to him and screamed away in a ricochet.

Latin rolled frantically, threshing his arms and legs. He hit the curb and heaved up to his hands and knees. Another bullet made a leaden-silvery smear on the sidewalk in front of him. Latin lunged headdown for the garage door, and just before he got there a bullet hit one of the end bricks and crumbled it into dust.

Latin dove into the gloom of the garage. Happy's face was a pale, scared circle staring at him.

"My G-God, Latin," said Happy.

Latin moved sideways until he was in the shelter of the thick brick wall. He took out his handkerchief and wiped his face. His hands were shaking.

"Talk about your nerve!" said Happy, getting control of himself. "That guy just lay there and waited after he blew at René and Raymond. He wanted to see was we gonna call the cops or rouse the neighborhood or something. When we didn't, he just blasted at you. You don't claim a dame would play tricks like that, do you, Latin?"

"No," said Latin. He coughed and swallowed hard. "No. Whoever it was didn't know me. They weren't sure it was me when I arrived. But they knew you'd call me, and when the taxi waited and I stayed quite a while and no one else came...."

"Blooie-blooie," Happy finished. "Well, where is that guy hangin' out is what I want to know? I don't want him takin' potshots at me."

"I didn't even hear the shots," said Latin.

"You was busy, pal. I heard 'em. They was a little muffled, but they was there. Hey, your taxi driver is gone."

"I wouldn't wonder," said Latin.

He moved closer to the door and peered out cautiously. Apparently the shots had caused no excitement. Two heavy trucks thundered past, and then a man came out of the lock shop across the street and looked both ways, squinting under his palm. He saw Latin and called: "Hey! Did you hear some shots?"

"No," said Latin.

"It was them damned trucks again," said the man. "Them kid drivers do it on purpose. I'm gettin' tired of it. I'm gonna complain to the police, that's what."

He went back in his shop and slammed the door. Feet made a little shuffling sound at the back of the garage. Latin jumped sideways and ducked behind the hood of a parked car. Happy dodged back inside his office.

Latin waited, breathing silently through his open mouth. He had the Colt .32 balanced in his right hand, ready for a snapshot.

"Hey, Latin," Dude said.

Latin rose slowly from behind the car. "You'd better yip a little sooner next time. I'm nervous."

"Ha!" said Dude. "Are you nervous! I never see such a fancy dance as you just did in the street. Say, do you know what that was?"

"I had an idea that was someone shooting at me."

"Oh, sure," said Dude. "I mean you know what they was shootin' with?"

Happy came cautiously out of his office. He was carrying a sawed-off shotgun under his arm, and he sighed with relief when he saw Dude.

"What were they shooting with?" Latin asked.

"An Army rifle. I recognized the sound right away. Only this wasn't no Springfield. This was one of them new Garands. Automatic-like. Just pull the trigger and aim, only this bird didn't aim good."

"Pretty good, I think," Latin contradicted.

"Naw. He shoots at your head. That's bad when you're shootin' at over a hundred yards at an angle and the other guy is movin'. If it hadda been me, I woulda shot at your belly, and I woulda hit it, too."

"Do you know where he was?" Latin demanded.

"Sure. I spot him right away. He is upstairs in that empty warehouse down by the corner. He shoots down over the roof of the next building. I don't want to argue with this baby, but I think I maybe better get a look at him to see who he is—in case you wanta know—so I bust down the alley and circle around. He moves too fast, though. He's gone. But I catch a kid that sees him, and this kid says he is a tall guy with dark glasses and a golf bag. The rifle is in the golf bag, I bet. Anyway, this guy drives a black Ford coupé that is nice and shiny. The kid naturally don't get the license number, but there it is for what it's worth."

"Thanks, Dude," said Latin.

"Is this party a friend of yours, Latin?"

"No," said Latin.

"Then you better hunt him up and sort of have a word or two with him."

"I had that in mind," said Latin. "I guess it's safe to move out now, if the guy is gone. Come on, Dude. I'll be seeing you, Happy."

"I hope so, Latin," said Happy. "I sure hope you'll be seeing me when we meet the next time and that I won't just be seeing you—on a slab."

THE RESTAURANT was open for business now and there were quite a few customers—nearly all of them men—seated at the crowded tables, eating and arguing noisily. Latin came in through the front door and stopped at the cashier's desk. He took a fifty-cent piece out of his pocket and rapped twice with it on the top of the glass counter.

Dick appeared at his elbow. "What, chum?"

"Get these people out of here," said Latin.

"Hey, listen!" Dick protested. "These guys is all vice presidents and stooges like that—the ones that can afford to take a long lunch and pay for it. They're good customers."

"Get them out," Latin said. "And lock the doors. We may be having some trouble pretty quick. Dude's out in back. Tell Guiterrez to feed him."

Dick shrugged. "O.K., mastermind."

Latin went back and sat down in his booth. He paid no attention to Dick's maneuvers or the protests of the partially fed customers. He was still sitting there, staring blankly at the empty table in front of him, when Guiterrez and Dick stopped beside the booth.

"Latin," said Guiterrez. "Dude tells me that somebody took a whack at you with a rifle."

"Dude talks too much," said Latin.

"Sure," Guiterrez agreed. "But what about them two torch butchers—René and Raymond?"

"Kaput," said Latin. "They got liquidated."

"Same guy?" Dick asked.

"Yeah."

"Who?" Guiterrez inquired.

"It's funny," said Latin. "I know his name as well as I do my own. It's right on the tip of my tongue, but I just can't think of it at the moment."

"Now don't get nasty," said Guiterrez. "I was only asking. Do you know they still got a police department in this town?"

"So what?" said Latin.

"So a pal of yours was in to look you over. Inspector Walters from Homicide."

Latin looked up quickly. "When?"

"One seventeen to one forty-one," said Dick.

"Did you tell him I wasn't here?"

"He didn't ask," said Guiterrez. "He looked. He *knows* you wasn't here."

"Hell," said Latin. "That shoots it. I thought I had an alibi for about that time if I needed it. Dick, go bring me the telephone."

Guiterrez said slowly: "Latin, I been thinking."

"Do tell," said Latin.

"You're sure sharp these days. I mean, I been thinking about this rifle-shooting business. I can't think of nobody who would take a crack at you—and miss. If they knew you at all, they'd know you'd never stand still for that. If they shot at you, they'd make damned sure they hit you someplace fatal. They'd know that if they missed you'd hunt 'em down if it took you fifty years, on account of you're so damned mean."

"Why don't you go bake a cake?" Latin asked.

"All right. But I figure it must be somebody that's cracked or some stranger in town. Now there's a clue for you."

"Goody-goody," said Latin sourly. "I'll put it under my pillow and sleep on it. Scram."

"I sure wish you'd stayed in the Army," said Guiterrez, going back into the kitchen.

DICK BROUGHT the telephone. "There's a guy on the wire here, Latin. He talks like he's been eating soap. Do you want to speak to him, or shall I cut him off at the switch?"

"I'll talk to him." Latin plugged in the telephone and lifted the mouthpiece from its cradle. "Yes? This is Max Latin speaking."

"Ah, Mr. Latin." The voice was sonorous and smooth, and its owner rolled out his syllables as though he were tasting each one and enjoying it. "My name is Preston—Jasper Preston."

"I believe you," said Latin.

"I'd like very much to talk to you, Mr. Latin. My office is at 540 Court Street. Drop around."

"Why?" Latin asked. "I'm busy now."

"Not nearly as busy as you will be if you don't come and see me."

"Oh," said Latin. "I get it. Could you tell me what it is you want to talk about?"

"About a newspaper called *Defend Our World.*"

"That's a coincidence," Latin remarked. "I was just thinking about the paper. What connection have you with it?"

"I own it."

"Well," said Latin, "that's news. You said your name was Preston? Do you do anything else besides own *Defend Our World?*"

"Of course, Mr. Latin. It is only one of my minor interests. I am a priorities promoter."

"A what?" Latin inquired.

"A priorities promoter. I advise people—businessmen and manufacturers—who find it difficult to obtain strategically scarce goods or commodities. I'm an expert on rationing and such matters."

"I'll come over and see you," Latin promised.

"I'd advise it—and soon. Good-bye, Mr. Latin."

Latin put the telephone down and nodded at Dick in a surprised and thoughtful way. "Get me the directory."

Dick brought it to him, and Latin thumbed through the leaves until he located the number he wanted. He picked up the telephone and dialed. After a moment a polite voice said: "This is the Bay City Chemical Products."

"May I speak to Mr. Gregory Farmer, please?" Latin asked.

There was a click, and then another voice said: "This is the main office."

"May I speak to Gregory Farmer?" Latin repeated.

There was another click, and then a third voice said: "This is Mr. Farmer's secretary. May I help you?"

"I'd like to talk to Mr. Farmer. This is Max Latin speaking."

"Mr. Farmer is on an inspection tour of the plant just now. He'll be in shortly. Will you call again?"

"Wait a minute," said Latin. "Maybe you can help me. Mr. Farmer has had some recent business dealings with a man named Jasper Preston, hasn't he?"

"No, he hasn't," said the voice instantly.

"Thanks," said Latin. He replaced the telephone and winked at Dick. "I think maybe we've got something."

"What?" Dick asked skeptically.

"Suppose there was a newspaper that circulated among defense plants and defense workers. Now naturally, just in the course of events, you'd put in something now and then about how things were going. No figures, of course. Just in general. Some plant was doing all right—some plant not so good. In fact, if you wanted to, you could needle a plant owner plenty about how he was running things—especially if he wasn't producing the amount he was supposed to be.

And you'd want to if you owned the newspaper and were a priorities juggler. In fact, if you needled the guy enough you might give him the idea that he'd better come around and see you about getting the proper amount of raw materials."

Dick shook his head. "Nobody could promise to get you raw materials if there ain't enough to go around."

"You could *promise*," Latin contradicted.

"It don't seem to me that would be honest," said Dick.

Latin nodded. "I think you've got something there. Keep your eye out for a guy with an envelope. I'm going to drop down to Court Street and prowl around a bit."

"Don't walk across any rifle ranges," Dick advised.

CHAPTER FIVE

MAN TRAP

THE BUILDING at 540 Court Street was in much better shape than the one further up the street that housed *Defend Our World*. It was larger, and it had an air of dignified prosperity, and the elevator attendant was a brisk young man in a snappy blue uniform. He jumped to attention when Latin appeared and said: "May I help you, sir?"

"I was looking for Jasper Preston," Latin said.

The attendant bowed. "Step right in."

He took Latin up to the third floor, opened the door with impressive courtesy, and said: "It's Number 203. First door on your left."

"Thanks," said Latin.

The door he had indicated had nothing on it except the numeral itself—not even a name. Latin opened it and went into a very small, very neatly furnished office with appropriately blended deep green drapes and carpet. There was a blonde girl behind the shiny desk in the corner. She had a very frank, very pleasant smile.

"May I help you, sir?" she asked.

Latin nodded. "My name is Latin. I wanted to see Mr. Jasper Preston."

"Certainly. Wait just one moment, please."

She went through a door at the side and then came back out again almost immediately.

"He'll see you now, Mr. Latin. Step right in, please."

Latin walked slowly into another office. It was as small and as nicely furnished as the outer one. A man with red, smooth hair and very nice teeth sat behind the big, flat desk facing the door. He indicated the leather-cushioned chair in front of the desk and said: "Won't you sit down, Mr. Latin?"

The door into the outer office closed behind Latin, and he sat down cautiously in the chair.

"It was nice of you to drop in," said the red-haired man.

"Yeah," said Latin absently. He drew a deep breath and then smiled suddenly. "Say, I've got an important phone call to make. I just remembered it this moment. It's rather private, or I'd call from here. But it'll only take me a second. If you'll just excuse me, I'll be right back...."

He got up out of the chair and started for the door.

"The door is locked," said the red-haired man. "And you're not going anywhere. Sit down."

LATIN SAT down again, looking disgusted. "It's getting so you can't turn around anymore, without falling over a fed."

"My name is Brighton," said the red-haired man. "And I'm from the Department of Justice. But I'm very interested in finding out how you knew that."

Latin shrugged. "The elevator operator and the secretary looked a little too good to be true, and you don't look like Preston sounds over the telephone. When you've been around about so long, you get so you can smell copper. You're no cop from this neck of the woods, and you look smart, so I figured you'd be some sort of a federal man."

"Good observation," said Brighton. "Suppose you tell me now why you wanted to see Preston."

"Oh, I just thought he might have a job for me."

"Doing what?"

"This and that and the other."

"Did he contact you? Did he ask you to come here?"

Latin looked surprised. "No."

"Where did you hear about him?"

"From a fella named Smith I met in a bar."

"Thanks for your help," said Brighton sarcastically. "You might find it would pay you to be a little more cooperative." He looked over Latin's shoulder at the door into the outer office. "Yes?"

The blonde girl came in and put several sheets of paper on his desk and went out again quietly.

"Pardon me for a second," Brighton said, reading the writing on the papers. He looked up after a moment. "This is quite interesting. Like to hear it?"

"Oh, sure," said Latin amiably.

Brighton read slowly aloud. " 'Max Latin. Holds a license as a private detective but calls himself a private inquiry agent. Has a very shady reputation, which he uses as a business asset to attract clients who wish services of doubtful legality. Operates from a place called *Guiterrez's Restaurant,* which he owns and uses as a headquarters. This man is a very shrewd operator with an extensive knowledge of the law.' "

"I hardly recognize myself," said Latin.

Brighton read from another page: " 'Max Latin. Criminal Record. He has been arrested for murder, first and second degree, manslaughter, blackmail, perjury and subornation of perjury, compounding a felony, bribery, intimidation of a witness, conspiracy to defraud, and maintaining a public nuisance.'"

"That last one was a bum rap," said Latin.

Brighton read on: " 'He was not convicted of these nor of any other crimes. The cases were usually dismissed for lack of evidence. It is the Department's opinion that the dismissals and the other acquittals were justified. Latin was not guilty of any of the crimes charged against him.'"

Latin sat up with a jerk. "What?"

Brighton ignored him. "'Latin operates in an unorthodox and unethical manner and carries on a constant feud with the police and the district attorney, and it is our opinion that he thinks it is good publicity to get arrested from time to time in order to get his name in the papers.'"

"Say!" said Latin indignantly. "I'm going to sue somebody in a minute! That's nothing but a dirty lie. I spend all my time committing crimes, but I'm just so smart they can't catch me."

Brighton nodded gravely. "This is just an opinion—unofficial. We investigated you quite some time ago." He turned the last page, read it silently, and then looked up at Latin. "Why aren't you in uniform and with your military unit?"

"I'm taking a vacation," Latin answered.

"Yes?" said Brighton.

THE BLONDE girl came in as quietly as before and laid another slip of paper on the desk and went out again.

Brighton read from the paper and then smiled slightly. "So you tried to trick the Army Medical Corps into believing you weren't color-blind?"

Latin sighed. "I wish I had your sources of information. You certainly find out things fast. And how do you know that girl is coming in when she does?"

"A trick," said Brighton. "It's done with mirrors. Why did you come to see Preston?"

"I told you. Just drumming up business."

Brighton nodded at him seriously. "Don't play games with us, Latin. You won't get your name in the papers, but you will get put in jail. And if we put you there—you'll stay."

"I'll be careful," said Latin. "I wouldn't—"

A loud and angry voice sounded suddenly in the outer office: "Don't you lie to me, young lady! I know damned good and well he's here! And I'm going to see him!"

Brighton pressed a black button beside the desk blotter.

"Young lady!" shouted the angry voice. "You get out of the way! I'm going in—"

Another masculine voice said something in a smooth murmur.

"What?" said the angry voice. "Who are you to ask who I am, and where did you come from? What?... F.B.I.! Well, why didn't you say so? I'm Inspector Walters of Homicide, and this is my bailiwick, so don't wave that badge at me!"

The second voice murmured again.

"I want to see Max Latin!" said Inspector Walters. "That's who I want to see! I know he's in here! I've got as much jurisdiction as you have!... It's none of your business why I want to see him!... What! Can't! Who says I can't see him? Hey! Quit that! Let go of me! You can't do this—"

A door slammed heavily, and then there was silence.

"Do you know him?" Brighton asked.

"Inspector Walters?" Latin asked. "Oh, sure. He's an old friend of mine."

"He didn't sound very friendly."

"He's got indigestion," said Latin. "He gets upset very easily. I hope your men don't hurt him—fatally. By the way, where is Preston? In jail?"

"No," said Brighton. "He's at large—temporarily. I think he must have the same sort of instinct you have. We've had the girl outside and the elevator operator and a couple of other special agents planted in the building for the last week. Preston doesn't use his office much—except as a headquarters. He circulates around a lot. He was here for a while today, but something made him suspicious. He told the girl he was going to the washroom down the hall, and he did, because the elevator operator was watching him. But he kept on going. He went out the window and down the fire escape. We'll pick him up in a few hours."

"What do you want him for?" Latin asked.

"He says he is a priorities promoter. He claims he can obtain rationed or restricted goods in any quantity if you pay him a twenty-five percent commission. If he can do that, we want to know where he gets them. If he can't, we want to know why he's saying he can."

Latin shook his head. "It's quite a problem."

"We'll find the answer," said Brighton, without any doubt in his voice. "And Preston, too. And you—if you've been dealing with him."

"I haven't," said Latin. "Never saw the man in my life. That's the truth. Can I go home now, please?"

"Yes," said Brighton. "I'll be seeing you again."

"Not if I see you first," said Latin.

He went out of the private office and nodded politely to the blonde girl.

"I've been dismissed," he told her.

She smiled at him. "I'm glad."

"Me, too," said Latin.

HE WENT out into the hall. The elevator was waiting for him.

"You've got a system around these parts," he said to the attendant.

"Oh, yes," said the attendant. "Do you like it?"

"No," said Latin. "Did you poke Inspector Walters in the snoot before you threw him out—I hope?"

"It wasn't necessary," said the attendant. He closed the elevator grill and took Latin down to the first floor.

Latin went to the front door and looked out into the street cautiously. Inspector Walters was standing on the curb directly across from the building, waiting with a sort of grim malignance.

Latin went back to the elevator again. "Is there any other way I can get out of here?"

"Yes," said the attendant. "Through that door and downstairs into the basement. You'll see the door into the alley right opposite the stairway."

"Thanks," Latin said.

He went through the door and down a dim flight of stairs. Sunlight gleamed through a wide doorway ahead of him, and Latin crossed the basement to it and went up a cement runway to the alley.

"Hello, you rat," said Inspector Walters. He was a gaunt man with a lined, hardbitten face and a sourly cynical expression. "I knew if I let you see me in front, you'd run out the back. You're under arrest."

"For what?" Latin inquired.

"For murder. What do you think of that?"

"I think it's terrible. Will anything I say be used against me?"

"You're damned right it will."

"I just wanted to know," said Latin. "Who did I murder this time?"

"A couple of guys by the name of René and Raymond Jones, Potter, Carlson, Benson and what-have-you."

"Are they a vaudeville team?" Latin asked.

"No. But they're a team—a nasty one."

"How do you know I murdered them?"

Walters came up and punched Latin in the chest with his forefinger. "I know your tricks. These two guys were wrapped up in a big piece of paper and dumped in front of a dog-food factory on the South Side. That sounds like one of your stunts."

"You flatter me," said Latin.

Walters punched him in the chest again, harder. "Who murdered those two rats, Latin?"

"I thought you were going to pinch me for it."

"I am—unless you tell me who did it."

Latin pulled at the lobe of his ear thoughtfully. "I've got sort of an idea.... How would you like to take a walk with me?"

"I wouldn't. My feet hurt."

"It's only a block or so," said Latin. "Come on. Maybe we'll stir something up for you."

"Where are we going?"

"To buy a newspaper."

"Why?" Walters demanded.

"I can read," Latin said. "Even if you can't. Are you coming?"

"I wish to hell you'd stayed in the Army," said Walters bitterly. "I had a little peace and quiet while you were gone."

CHAPTER SIX
SNAKE IN THE GRASS

WHEN LATIN and Walters came into the narrow lobby of the building at 411 Court Street, the old man in the baggy blue coveralls was still on duty at the elevator. He sighed gloomily and nodded at Latin.

"You're sure as hell persistent, ain't you?"

"What?" Walters barked sharply. "Has this man been here before?"

The old man blinked at him mildly. "Says what?"

"You heard me! Has this man been here before?"

"Which man?"

"*This* one!"

"What's his name?"

Walters leaned over him dangerously. "Are you going to answer my question?"

"No," said the old man. "Are you gonna ride in my elevator or ain't you?"

"Get in!" Walters snarled, shoving Latin into the elevator and getting in after him.

The old man closed the door and worked the control lever. The elevator went upward, wheezing and trembling. It stopped at the fourth floor.

"How do you know where we wanted to go?" Walters snapped.

"I can read minds," said the old man. "Providin' the other guy's got one for me to read. I couldn't do much with you in that line. Get out of my elevator."

Walters got out, hauling Latin after him. "I'll have you fired for your smartcracks, you old fool!"

"The hell you will," said the old man. "I own the building." He slammed the door in Walters's face.

Walters made seething noises in his throat and then suddenly turned on Latin. "Well! What are we standing here for? Where are we going?"

"This way," said Latin mildly.

They went down the hall to the double frosted-glass doors and through them into the outer office of *Defend Our World*. The small girl in the horn-rimmed glasses was shaking her head with reluctant firmness at the tall man who was leaning over her desk.

"You can't see her," she said.

The tall man gestured in a harassed way. "But I've *got* to see her! I want to apologize! I want to explain the circumstances to her! Good God, she can't just condemn me unheard like this! Why, I even brought my wife along. She's waiting in the car outside. *She's* going to apologize!"

The small girl kept right on shaking her head. "Miss Glenn doesn't want to see you. She told me not to let you—" The small girl caught sight of Latin, and instantly she opened her mouth and shrieked at the top of her voice: "Miss Glenn! Miss *Glenn!* He's here again!"

THE DOOR of the inner office burst open, and Gertrude Glenn appeared. Her full lips were tightened grimly, and she was carrying a dime store butcher knife with a shiny blade a foot long in one capable hand.

The tall man started toward her. "Miss Glenn, please! You've got to let me explain—"

The small girl shrilled: "Shall I call the police, Miss Glenn? Shall I?"

Gertrude Glenn waved them aside, glaring at Latin. "Well? What do you want now?"

"This is Inspector Walters of the Homicide detail," Latin told her quickly.

Gertrude Glenn smiled without humor. "You sure pal around with funny people, kid."

"Miss Glenn," said the tall man. "Won't you please listen to me for a moment? It was all my wife's doings. She'll tell you so herself. She's waiting out in my car. She's—"

"Shall I call the police, Miss Glenn?" the small girl asked anxiously.

Walters had reached the boiling point. "Shut up!" he yelled. "All of you! Now what's going on here? Why did that girl start screaming when she saw Latin?"

"Latin!" the tall man echoed. "Is this Max Latin? I've been looking for him! I'll show him—"

"Back off," said Walters flatly. "Who are you?"

"My name is Gregory Farmer!" The tall man's voice was choked with fury. He was so mad he was shaking.

He was very thin and stooped, with deeply creased lines in his face. His hair was a dingy gray, and the skin on his face looked yellowish and unhealthy. "My wife hired Latin to threaten Gertrude Glenn! He brought a couple of murderers up here and threatened to torture her!"

"Well, well!" said Walters, beaming in sudden triumph. "You're Gertrude Glenn, huh? Did Latin bring a couple of guys up here and threaten you?"

"I've got some news for you," Latin said.

"You shut up," Walters shouted.

"*You* shut up," Gertrude Glenn advised. "This is my office. What's your news, Latin?"

Latin said: "There's a guy by the name of Preston who has an office a block down on Court Street."

Gertrude Glenn nodded. "Sure. I know Jasper."

"The F.B.I. is swarming over his joint like bees right now. They want him—but bad."

Gertrude Glenn watched him narrowly. "What's that to me?"

"The F.B.I. is going to find out that he owns this paper, and when they do they'll be right over to see you."

"No, they won't. Because he doesn't own it."

"What?" Gregory Farmer exclaimed. "What's that? He doesn't own your paper?"

Gertrude Glenn shook her head. "No. He advanced me some money to get it started, and I gave him a note and a mortgage on my car and clothes and life insurance and everything else to secure it. But the paper's mine. He hasn't anything to do with it."

"He doesn't own…," Gregory Farmer said incoherently. "Why, he told me he owned it and that if I didn't pay him…. I mean, I don't understand…."

"Neither do I," said Gertrude Glenn. "What are you talking about, anyway?"

LATIN WAS smiling. "I had an idea you weren't the type to mix in a racket like Jasper's. He was using your paper as a threat and a lever to force manufacturers to hire him as an agent to buy rationed materials for them. That's why the F.B.I. is after him. I don't know whether he could actually obtain the materials through black-market operators and ration bootleggers, or whether he just shook dough out of the manufacturers by promising to get the goods and threatening to have you slam the guys in your paper if they didn't come across. In either case, the F.B.Iill snatch him."

"He's lucky if they do it before I lay hands on him," said Gertrude Glenn.

Latin nodded at Gregory Farmer. "You paid Preston to get you some materials, didn't you?"

"No!" Gregory Farmer shouted furiously. "You mind your own business, damn you! You promised you wouldn't meddle in my affairs any further!"

"You promised something, too."

"I sent you that envelope! Now you keep your word!"

"My God!" said Latin, suddenly remembering. "Let me use that telephone!"

Without waiting for permission, he leaned over and grabbed the telephone from under the small girl's nose and dialed the number of the restaurant.

Guiterrez answered at once. "This dump is closed. Don't ask me why, because I don't know. It's just another bright idea thought up by the crackpot crook that owns the place."

"Open up for business," Latin ordered. "Right now."

"Oh, it's you," said Guiterrez. "Well, just why in hell was we closed?"

"Because somebody was looking for me," said Latin. "With a rifle. I didn't want him walking in an' popping bullets around among the customers. He's sort of wild on the aim."

"He could shoot all my customers and see if I care. Dick says there is a guy wants to get in touch with you very badly. You're to call this guy at Vestor 8-3435 and ask for

Dunstead. Dick says this guy talks like he had been eating soap and that you'd know who he meant."

"Good!" Latin exclaimed. "Swell! Tell Dick to watch for an envelope. Open up the restaurant right now."

He broke the connection and dialed Vestor 8-3435. The telephone at the other end rang several times before a voice answered very cautiously: "Hello?"

"Is Mr. Dunstead there?"

"Who wants him?"

"This is Max Latin."

"Oh." The voice smoothed out into the oily tones of Jasper Preston. "I'm going to make you and that damned client of yours damned sorry for this little trick you pulled on me."

"What client?" Latin asked. "What trick?"

"Gregory Farmer. He turned me in to the F.B.I."

"He's not my client," Latin said, turning to stare at Gregory Farmer curiously. "Are you sure he's the one who turned you in?"

"You bet, I'm sure. And he's going to be sorry."

"How would you like me to take the heat off you?" Latin inquired.

"How?" Preston said skeptically. "You can't bribe or scare the F.B.I."

"I've got connections in Washington. I can have them pulled off the case, but it will cost you plenty."

"I'm not stupid enough to shell out on any song and dance like that—without knowing a whole lot more about it."

"O.K.," said Latin. "I'll give you proof. Come over to the restaurant tonight about nine. Bring some dough."

"I'll be there."

Latin broke the connection and nodded to Gertrude Glenn. "What is Preston's office phone number?"

"Tucker 6-5212," she said.

"Say, what are you up to?" Walters demanded.

"Wait a minute," Latin said absently, dialing the Tucker number.

"Hello?" said the pleasant feminine voice.

"I want to speak to Mr. Brighton. This is Max Latin."

"One moment, please."

Brighton said: "Hello, Latin. What do you want?"

"Jasper Preston just called me up and hired me."

"To do what?"

"Run you out of town."

"That's very interesting," said Brighton. "When are you going to start?"

"Never," Latin told him. "Preston will be at the restaurant at nine o'clock tonight."

"So will we. Thanks, Latin."

Latin put the telephone down. "Get the idea?" he asked Walters cheerfully.

"What a dirty double-crosser you are," said Walters.

"I don't cut corners in front of the F.B.I.," said Latin. "They're not as dumb as ordinary cops." He pointed his finger at Gregory Farmer. "So you're the one that started this little fandango by reporting Preston to the F.B.I."

Gregory Farmer nodded. "Yes, I did."

"Then what was all that you told me about getting more materials from somewhere?"

"That was to keep you from prying into my affairs."

Latin nodded. "Fair enough. There's just one other thing I'd like to know. Are you actually—"

CHAPTER SEVEN
PHONEY DEATH

THE WHOLE building shivered suddenly. From outside there was a hollow, heavy thunder of sound as ominous as a bomb blast. Window glass tinkled, and faint excited shouts came from the street.

"What the hell—," said Walters.

Latin turned on Gregory Farmer. "Didn't you say your wife was waiting outside—"

"My wife!" Farmer shouted incoherently. "That Preston! He called me up at the factory and threatened…."

He jumped for the door with Latin right behind him. They ran down the hall together, and Gertrude Glenn and Inspector Walters crowded out of the office and came after them. Ahead of them, the elevator grill was just closing.

"Hold it!" Latin yelled.

The old man opened the door again. "I knew you'd be out in a hurry. Miss Glenn, if you're gonna stick somebody with that knife, will you kindly wait until you get 'em outside my building first?"

Gertrude Glenn and Walters and Gregory Farmer were in the elevator now, and Latin slammed the grill shut and then reached over the old man's shoulder and pulled the operating switch over as far as it would go. The elevator dropped like a plummet.

"Hey!" the old man protested, jiggling the switch frantically. "You wanta bust my neck and my elevator—" The hydraulic brake caught, and the elevator slowed and shuddered and stopped at the street floor with a wracking jar-Latin jerked the grill open. "Where's your car?"

Gregory Farmer didn't answer. He ran through the lobby and out the front door and round the walk toward the side of the building. At the entrance of the parking lot, he stopped short and made a little moaning sound. Latin and Walters and Gertrude Glenn paused beside him.

A milling group of people shouted and gestured around the twisted, smoking ruin of an automobile. Broken glass glittered on the gravel.

"My wife!" Gregory Farmer moaned. "She was in the car! That Preston—"

He ran forward, shoving spectators heedlessly out of his way, and the other three followed him. Farmer was trying frantically to see into the steaming, tangled mass inside the car.

"My wife! She—she—"

"Gregory! Gregory, dear!"

Farmer spun around, his mouth open. Mrs. Farmer was coming toward them across the lot.

"Gregory, dear!" she repeated. "You were so long I went across the street to get a soft drink. Something happened to the car. It just blew up."

Farmer stared at her, his eyes horribly dilated.

"Gregory!" said Mrs. Farmer. "What's the matter, dear? I'm all right."

"*That's* what's the matter," said Latin.

THE SPECTATORS circled them in a pushing, peering crowd, trying to hear and see, excited by the tensity of the group.

Walters got hold of Latin by the lapels of his coat. "I'm tired of playing shill for your one-man band. You start talking and make some sense. What's this all about?"

"Let go," said Latin, batting his hand away. "I've still got a couple of questions I have to know the answers to."

He nodded to Gertrude Glenn. "Is Farmer short on his production schedule at his factory?"

"Why, I don't know," she answered blankly.

"Haven't you been calling him names in your paper because he hasn't been fulfilling his defense orders?"

"No," said Gertrude Glenn.

"Why, she's lying!" Mrs. Farmer exclaimed. "She's been printing terrible things about Gregory!"

"Did you ever read any of those terrible things?" Latin asked her.

"No," said Mrs. Farmer. "Gregory told me about them."

"Yes," said Latin. "Gregory has been telling lots of things to people lately for one reason and another. He wasn't worried about his factory, because it's getting along fine. He wasn't worried about being called names, because nobody was calling him names. He was worried about Gertrude Glenn." Latin nodded at her. "How long have you known him?"

"Three or four months. I wrote up his factory in the paper. I met him at that time."

"Seen much of him since?"

Gertrude Glenn hesitated for a second and then shrugged. "He's been pestering hell out of me. Calls up or comes around a couple of times a day."

"Has he been making any progress?" Latin asked.

Gertrude Glenn jiggled the butcher knife warningly. "Don't crack wise about me. I don't play around with married men, and I've told him so six hundred times."

"That was why he was worried," said Latin. "He wasn't going to get anywhere with you as long as he was married. He couldn't divorce his wife because he had no reason to. He knew she wouldn't divorce him. So he decided to become a widower." Latin pointed to the wrecked automobile. "He almost did."

"That's a filthy lie!" Gregory Farmer shouted.

"Nope," said Latin. "You planted a time bomb in your car and told you wife to wait in it. It's lucky for her she got thirsty."

"Gregory," said Mrs. Farmer faintly.

"Don't believe him!" Farmer yelled at her.

"You had it planned nicely," said Latin. "You had to provide the police with a suspect for your wife's murder. That was Preston. He contacted you in the course of his priorities' racket. You turned him over to the F.B.I. You knew he'd make threats against you. He runs off at the mouth a lot. You were going to claim he murdered your wife trying to get you. You thought he owned *Defend Our World*, and you intended to put pressure on Gertrude Glenn by threatening to turn *her* over to the F.B.If she wasn't more cordial. That's why you were willing to do anything to keep me from prying into the business. You didn't want me messing up your plans."

FARMER SHOOK his fists. "Young man, I'll have you arrested for criminal slander!"

"Wait until I get through," Latin advised. "You shot René and Raymond and tried for me. Your factory is on

Bellevue Avenue near Flandin. When Gertrude Glenn called you up and told you about René and Raymond and me, you beat it right over to Flandin and laid for us. You called me from some hot dog stand or drugstore near there while you were waiting. You were crazy mad because you thought I'd queered you permanently with Gertrude Glenn and because you thought I might have found out something I would tell your wife. The only thing I don't know is how you knew where to find us."

"I told him," said Gertrude Glenn, staring at Farmer with a sort of horrified revulsion.

"How did *you* know?" Latin demanded.

"Raymond told me—after you and René had left. He asked me for a date."

Latin stared incredulously. "A date?"

"Yes. He said he had money and a brand-new car, and how would I like to go somewhere? I said he'd probably stolen the car, and he said he hadn't either—that it was rented from Happy's Garage on Flandin Street, and I could call up and ask if I didn't believe it. When I called up Farmer, I was plenty burned up, and I told him all about it."

"That rat," said Latin. "Well anyway, that's how Farmer knew where to catch us. He shouldn't have used a Garand rifle, though. They're hard to get hold of now. But if you owned a defense plant, you could easily steal one from one of the soldiers who were guarding the plant."

Farmer's gaunt face was dark with congested blood. He spun around and dove into the crowd. The spectators split away from him for a startled second and then closed in again. Farmer went down under a dozen writhing bodies. Walters yelled angrily and jumped on top of the pile.

"Gregory," Mrs. Farmer whimpered unbelievingly. She swayed and then crumpled down on the gravel in a neat, limp heap.

Gertrude Glenn knelt down beside her and lifted her head gently. "Don't you think you've done enough dirty work for one day?" she snapped at Latin.

"Yes," Latin admitted. "I tank I go home now."

CHARITY BEGINS AT HOMICIDE

A HYPHEN HAD ONLY BEEN A
MARK TO SEPARATE "BRANDY"
FROM "GLASS" TO MAX LATIN
UNTIL THE GUY CALLED CARTER-
HEASON, STRICTLY FROM
KIPLING, STEPPED INTO LATIN'S
HEADQUARTERS CHEZ GUITERREZ
WITH A STRANGE TALE TO TELL OF
THE LATEST GOINGS-ON OF THE
"CHARITY" RACKET.

CHAPTER ONE
CHARITY BEGINS
AT CHANNEL ISLAND

GUITERREZ WAS waiting. He was not waiting patiently, but then he never did anything very patiently. He was walking up and down on the sidewalk in front of his restaurant with his tall chef's hat pushed down over one eye, his hands clasped behind him and his long, slightly soiled apron swishing snakily around his ankles. In the dimmed lights that came through the restaurant windows he looked like a shadowy Satan with a stomach ache.

"Hello," said Max Latin.

Guiterrez jumped a foot. "You!" he yelled. "Haven't you got any regard for my health? Do you want to scare me to death? Would you like to see me drop dead here in the gutter?"

"It's not a bad idea," said Latin. "Why don't you?"

"Just to please you?" Guiterrez sneered. "Hah! I can see myself. Listen, you crook. I've been waiting for you. I want to ask you a question—and no lies. Did you get to England while you were in the Army?"

Latin was wearing a tailored blue topcoat and a dark blue rolled-brim hat, and he blended into the shadows as though he belonged to them. He was thin and a little above medium height, and he had a blandly confi-

As the two men plunged through the shattered glass, he saw
Maxine Lufor lying on the floor with an ugly wound in her back.

dential smile that didn't mean any more than the ones they
paint on Kewpie dolls. His eyes were greenish and tipped
a little at the corners, and they never smiled at all.

"No," he answered. "I told you I never got further than
the basic-training camp. They found out there I was as
color-blind as Grant's Tomb and shipped me home."

"Were you ever in England before you got in the Army,
then?"

"No."

"Latin, did you commit any crimes in New Zealand or Australia or South Africa?"

"No," said Latin, "but I recall a little matter of some jewels smuggled across from Canada if that will help you any."

Guiterrez slapped himself on the forehead. "Oh-oh!"

"It was all a mistake," Latin soothed. "The customs authorities made an error."

"Well, the error has caught up with you."

"So?" said Latin. "How do you figure?"

Guiterrez tapped him on the chest impressively. "Sherlock Holmes's younger brother is sitting in your booth right this minute. I didn't like the looks of this baby when he came in, and when he asked for you, both Dick and I tried to give him the brush-off. Latin, you couldn't brush this number off with an antitank gun. He just sits. I think you better take a powder."

"Let's see what he wants first."

"Latin," said Guiterrez, "I don't think you're gonna like English jails. They're damp, and you catch cold easy."

"I'll take a chance. Come on."

HE OPENED the door, and the noise rolled out like the overflow from a jam session in a boiler factory. Guiterrez's place was never noted for its air of quiet refinement. The customers were hardy souls who took what came and thrived on it as long as it included substantial portions of Guiterrez's cooking, which was really almost as good as he thought it was.

Latin and Guiterrez worked their way expertly through the uproar and the writhing, close-packed tables to the last of the row of booths that ran along the side wall.

"Well, I found him for you," said Guiterrez. "The service you get in this dump is amazing. Even crooks we serve for supper."

"I'm Max Latin. Did you want to see me?" Latin said.

The man in the booth was so typically upper-class British that he looked faintly unreal. He had a long bony face burned brick red by the sun and a close-clipped, gray, military-style mustache and gray shaggy eyebrows. His eyes were a light blue, and he looked pained when he smiled.

"Ah, yes," he said. He got up, awkward and bony in the narrow booth, and extended his hand. "Carter-Heason, here. Will you sit down?"

Latin slid into the seat across the table. A small and wizened waiter in an apron so big that it could have, and apparently had, been used for a tent, skidded to a stop beside the booth and said: "You want to give him the good brandy, Latin?"

"Certainly," said Latin.

The waiter produced a bottle from under his apron.

Latin looked at Guiterrez. "Is there anything keeping you here?"

"I just wanted one last look at you before you got that prison pallor," Guiterrez told him. "Good-bye, Latin, you louse. It was nice knowing you." He slammed through the swing door into the steamy bedlam of the kitchen.

CARTER-HEASON RAISED his shaggy eyebrows at Latin. "Were you planning on going somewhere?"

"Guiterrez thinks you're going to arrest me."

"Arrest you?" Carter-Heason said blankly. "But why?"

Latin shrugged. "Lots of people do."

Carter-Heason looked vague. "Oh, I see. No, I assure you the thought hadn't entered my mind. I came here to do business with you. I was told that this was your office. That was some of your American humor, I imagine."

"No. It is my office."

Carter-Heason made a little flustered gesture. "I meant no offense, really. Entirely your affair where you conduct your business, of course. But this establishment is rather—ah—confusing...."

"Sometimes that helps in my business," Latin said. "Now what can I do for you?"

"Oh, yes. Now I've heard that you have a reputation for engaging in certain—ah—sharp practices. Please don't be offended, old chap. My information might be entirely wrong."

"It's not wrong," Latin said.

"I see. And I've heard, on very good authority, that you have been remarkably successful at engaging in these practices."

"Yes," said Latin.

"I've been told that although you've been arrested innumerable times, you've never been convicted."

"That's right."

"Well," said Carter-Heason. He sipped his brandy, smiled weakly. "Well…"

Latin chuckled. "Come right out with it. Do you want to hire me?"

"Ah!" said Carter-Heason, relieved. "Yes, as a matter of fact, I do. You see, it's not exactly…."

"Honest," Latin finished.

"Well…."

"Is it, or isn't it?" Latin asked. "After all, you should know."

"That's just the trouble, old chap. I don't."

"I'll soon tell you," Latin said. "Just tell me all about it."

"**THAT WOULD** be best, wouldn't it? Right. Have you ever heard of the Channel Islands?"

"Channel Islands," Latin repeated. "They're small islands in the English Channel, aren't they? Close to the French coast?"

"Right. They were occupied by the Germans in the early part of the war."

"What about them?"

"There's a chap by the name of Fortwyn going about here and there in America collecting funds for the relief and rehabilitation and reestablishment of the interned residents of these islands after the war. Very good thing.

Very admirable. The people of the islands have a cultural background that is their own and unique and well worth preserving, and there's no doubt but what they've been battered about considerably by the German occupying forces."

"What's the beef, then?"

"Eh? Oh, I see. Fortwyn is a British citizen." Carter-Heason added as an afterthought: "So am I, you know."

"Never would have guessed it," Latin said. "I gather you don't like this Fortwyn character."

"No," said Carter-Heason judicially. "I don't. In fact, I don't completely trust him."

"Ah," said Latin. "Now we're coming to pay dirt."

"Yes. As you say. Now the funds that Fortwyn is collecting are to be administered after the war."

"Maybe," Latin suggested.

"That's the crux of the matter," Carter-Heason admitted. "He has a small group of his own. He is not connected with any other organized charity or war-relief society. That does not, of course, mean that his methods or motives are in any way questionable."

"Does he keep books?" Latin asked.

"Yes. Very excellent ones. I've inspected them. Several times."

"Did he squawk?"

"Eh? Object, you mean? Well, in a way. I mean, the first time he seemed cordial enough, but he grew distinctly cooler when I came back."

Latin nodded. "Yeah. Did the books seem to be on the square?"

"Oh, yes. Administrative expenses were very small—investments excellent. The idea is that the funds are to be kept in trust for use on the islands after the conclusion of the war."

"In whose trust?" Latin asked.

Carter-Heason sighed. "An incorporated trust company, of which Fortwyn is the president of the board of directors. There are two other directors. One is his secretary, the other is the accompanist of his singer—a piano player."

"Oh-oh," said Latin.

"That was my impression," Carter-Heason said ruefully. "There's nothing obviously wrong with the arrangement. Fortwyn makes no effort to conceal it. It has the advantage of keeping down administrative expenses."

"It also has the advantage," Latin observed, "of allowing Fortwyn to vote to do any damned thing he pleases with those funds any time he pleases. His two stooges would naturally back him up. He could walk off with the treasury the day peace was declared or any day before that he happened to think was convenient. And then you could have fun chasing him."

"Right," said Carter-Heason.

"How about the F.B.I.?"

Carter-Heason shook his head gently. "There is absolutely nothing wrong with Fortwyn. He is not committing any crime. On the contrary, he is engaged in a very praiseworthy task. He is a valid British citizen, and he has no record whatsoever of any business chicanery. There can be no question here of any governmental interference. There are no grounds for official action."

"So you came to me."

"Right," said Carter-Heason.

"Here I am."

CHAPTER TWO
TOP HAT, WHITE TIE
AND—FRAUD

CARTER-HEASON GRUNTED uncomfortably. "Well, I'd like you to—ah—chisel at him. Is that the correct word?"

"Close enough," Latin said absently. "You mean you want me to put the bite on Fortwyn in a heavy way. If he pays off rather than risk a beef with me and the authorities in opposite corners, then you'll know there's something smelly about his charity deal. Is that it?"

"Yes. I think that covers the ground very succinctly."

Latin frowned down at his brandy. "This could be a little dangerous. You picked me because I've got a reputation that Fortwyn could check on easily. The cops and people like that keep an eye on me for the same reason, you know."

Carter-Heason nodded. "Frankly, old chap, I think it's damned dangerous. I don't see how you're going to avoid being jailed for one reason or another. I wouldn't have asked you to do it if I could have thought of any other plan. Of course, I can offer you a considerable financial remuneration."

Latin looked up. "Who's paying?"

"I am."

"I can easily find out."

"I know it. You are welcome to make any inquiries you wish. I really am paying."

"Why?" Latin asked.

Carter-Heason looked embarrassed. "Well, you see they won't accept me for service—not any service anywhere. Had a little trouble with fever years ago. Bad heart and that sort of silly stuff. So I've been doing my best to promote friendly feeling between this country and Britain. Not connected with any official organization or any of that. Just bungle around in my clumsy fashion and try to act amiable."

"I see," said Latin.

"This chap Fortwyn may be all right, but if he's not it's a very nasty thing he's doing. Cheating Americans who are generous enough to give to his charity is bad enough in itself, but if he should turn out to be a crook it would certainly not make the Americans involved feel very friendly toward the British in general. Sort of biting the hand that feeds you and all that."

"I see," Latin repeated. "How heavy can you go with the cash?"

"I have two hundred pounds on hand. That surely will do for a retainer, won't it? I don't mean that to be all, of course, but it will take me a little time to raise the remainder, whatever that is."

"How will you raise it?"

"I was going to mortgage my pension."

"Pension?" Latin said.

"Yes. For Colonial Service."

"Skip it," said Latin. "I'll handle it. Maybe I can pick up a penny or two as I go along, and anyway I'm not very busy at this point."

"Well, old chap, I can't really—"

"You can send me cigarettes while I'm in jail. Tell me more about Fortwyn. How does he operate?"

"Very cleverly. I mean that whether he's honest or not he's quite efficient. He has this small group that travels with him from one city to the next. It consists of the secretary I spoke of—Isabel Grey—and the accompanist who is her fellow director, named Perwinkle, and Maxine Lufor, who is a singer. Fortwyn's idea is to contact some top-drawer social clique in each city and make them the more-or-less exclusive sponsors of his island charity."

Latin nodded. "You have to have a top hat and tails before you can contribute, eh?"

"Well, yes. In a manner of speaking. Fortwyn doesn't solicit gifts from the general public. In fact, he hardly solicits at all in the general understanding of the word. Things are so arranged that people are very glad to contribute for the social prestige as well as for the future of the Channel Islanders. He puts on a dinner at the home of some socially prominent person. The socially prominent person invites the guests he—or usually she—selects. They make such contributions as they wish. The expenses of the dinner and whatnot are deducted, and the charity gets what remains."

"Sounds good," Latin commented.

"**IT IS.** Fortwyn does the thing up well. Aside from the dinner, he furnishes entertainment. Maxine Lufor sings folk songs indigenous to the island and some early English folk songs. She's very good. Perwinkle plays their folk dances and, of course, accompanies Maxine Lufor. Isabel Grey exhibits handiwork and other goods produced on the islands. She is a native of the islands and can answer any questions as to how the inhabitants live and work.

Fortwyn gives a little lecture illustrated with some first-rate lantern slides."

"Where have they landed in this town?"

"With a Mr. and Mrs. Jeffers Hayes. I understand that his is an old and rich banking family, and that they are very prominent socially among the older and more conservative people. The dinner and entertainment is scheduled for their Manxton Park estate tomorrow night. I'm really sorry not to give you more warning than that, but I hesitated a long time before I could nerve myself up to come at all."

"I'll make out," said Latin. "Is the Fortwyn party staying out at Manxton Park?"

"No. At the Hanford-Plaza Hotel. I'm staying there, too, incidentally."

"Are you haunting them?" Latin inquired.

Carter-Heason chuckled. "As a matter of fact, I imagine that is their impression. I'm even going to the entertainment at the Hayeses tomorrow night. They didn't wish to invite me, or rather, Fortwyn didn't wish to have them. But I have—ah—social connections myself."

"I'll see you there."

Carter-Heason looked surprised. "You mean.... I mean.... Well, is that all?"

"For now. Unless you want another brandy."

"No, thanks, really. I do wish I could offer you something for your time and trouble, not to mention the risk. After all, you don't even know that I'm telling you the truth about all this."

"I'll find out," said Latin. "Won't I?"

"Well, yes. I imagine so." Carter-Heason stood up. "This has really been most interesting. I had no idea—"

Dick, the waiter, popped up beside the booth. "You want something, chum?"

"Eh?" said Carter-Heason, startled. "Oh, no, thanks. I was just leaving...."

"Cheer-o," said Dick. "Toodle-oo."

"Yes," said Carter-Heason. "Good night, all."

VERY STIFF, very straight, withdrawn into his own dignity and ignoring all the uproar, he made his way to the front door and went out.

Guiterrez came through the swing door and leaned over the back of the booth, wiping the sweat off his face with the end of a towel he had wrapped muffler-style around his neck.

"Well?" he demanded. "What kind of a down payment did you shake him for?"

"Nothing," said Latin.

"A fine businessman you are," said Guiterrez. "If he didn't come to pinch you, he must have come to hire you. There sure as hell ain't anybody silly enough to pay social calls on a sharpy like you. So why'd you let him waltz out of here just on a promise to pay?"

"I didn't. He didn't promise."

"I don't like the sound of that," Guiterrez stated.

"Me, neither," Dick seconded. "Hold it up and let us see it, Latin."

"This is a charity job."

"Charity!" Guiterrez shouted. "Charity begins at home, don't you know that? What about us? Look at poor Dick, here. He's hungry, he's sick, and he ain't got no soles on his shoes!"

Latin nodded at Dick. "Run over on your bare feet and get me the telephone." He nodded at Guiterrez. "You go out and get me something to eat."

"I wonder why I put up with this," said Guiterrez, slamming back into the kitchen.

Dick came back with the portable telephone, and Latin plugged it in at the concealed switch behind the drapes against the back wall of the booth.

"Want anything else?" Dick asked.

"Yes. I want to be alone."

"Swish," said Dick. "That was the noise I made disappearing."

Latin thought for a moment and then lifted the handset and dialed a number. The telephone at the other end didn't have time to complete its first ring before there was a snap on the line, and a voice said breathlessly: "Yes? Yes? Yes?"

Latin said: "Is Toots Carr there?"

"Oh, yes! Hold the wire, he's right here. Toots—*Toots!* It's for you.... This is it! Hurry!"

Latin looked mildly surprised. Through the receiver he could hear a faint banging and then the crash of some furniture overturning and then the hurried stamp of footsteps. A hoarse masculine voice said eagerly: "Yes, sir! Yes, Your Honor! This is him—I mean, me. I mean, this is Toots Carr."

"THIS IS Latin, Toots. What's all the business?"

"Who—Latin? Oh! Get off the wire, Latin. I'm expecting a vital call. Quick! Good-bye."

"Hold it," said Latin. "Who's going to call you?"

"The president of the United States, that's who! Now go away, Latin. This is serious!"

"Why is the president going to call you?"

"Because I sent him a telegram and asked him to. Now, Latin, please. He might be tryin' to get me this very minute. Hang up!"

"Why did you send him a telegram, Toots?"

"Because I'm gonna have him burn the ears off of my damned draft board, that's why! I'll show them guys! I got no time to talk, Latin. Good-bye."

"Wait now, Toots. Be reasonable. It's after one o'clock in Washington. Do you think the president works all night as well as all day?"

"Huh? Oh, yeah. That's right. I guess he'll call me up first thing in the morning, then."

"No doubt," said Latin. "What's the matter with your draft board?"

"Why, them guys is criminals, that's what. They're a set of fifth columnists! You know me. You know who I am. I am positively the best safe-puffer in the business, that's who. I can take a vault door off and lay it down as gentle as a baby in a cradle. You know that yourself, Latin. Am I right?"

"Sure," said Latin.

"O.K., O.K. So that's what I tell them dim bulbs on the draft board. I tell them I see some of these Nazi tanks in the newsreel. You think if I can open up a Class-A bank vault I can't top off them cans? I say to these dopes: 'Let me in, and I will strew the insides of them zinc tubs from here to Calcutta.' That's what I say."

"What did they say?" Latin asked.

"Them criminals! They say I am 4F, and that I can't get in."

"You look pretty healthy," Latin observed. "Why the 4F—are you sick?"

"I ain't no sicker than Superman! They got that on me, them rats, because they claim I am morally unfit for duty. How do you like that? So maybe the cops do claim I done a few tricks here and there. So maybe I was in Leavenworth and Alcatraz and a couple other boffs. So what? How about that guy they're fightin', huh? How about Hitler? I suppose he was never in jail!"

"You've got something there," Latin admitted.

"Wait until I tell the president what them guys is doin' to me! He'll fix them babies. Oh, just wait! I'd like to see their faces when he gets through."

"Sure," said Latin. "In the meantime, can you tell me where Tatsy Stevens is?"

"He's stashed away in some cow-country tank for fifty years or more."

"Where's Bill Lutz?"

"He got himself hung, the dope."

"How about Clarence Carlson?"

"Aw now there's a sad case, Latin. You know how he used to worry about the Feds always steppin' around behind him and givin' him dirty looks if they even caught him at a dime store jewelry counter? I say to him: 'Clarence, you should ought to turn honest like me and get yourself right with all them laws.' But, no. Clarence just went on worryin' until he caught himself stomach ulcers and croaked. Why are you asking about these characters, Latin?"

"Well, Toots," said Latin, "this is confidential."

"Oh, sure. Absolute. You know me, Latin."

"Yes. Well, there's some big stuff being buzzed off lately. Jewelry mostly. All strictly hush-hush. The guy doesn't fence it. He goes around behind and sells it back for a percentage. He's smarter than fire. I've got a tip he's on the loose and close. I want to put out a wire to let me negotiate for him, but I don't know who he is."

"Gee," said Toots.

"It would be money in the bank. He's a fancy man at his business. I checked all the highflyers, and it's not one of them if your dope on Tatsy and Bill Lutz and Clarence is straight."

"It sure is, Latin. Gee. I wonder who it is?"

"The only one I can think of is Maurice Peters."

"Who was that, Latin?"

"Maurice Peters. You've heard of him. He's from across."

"Oh," said Toots vaguely. "Yeah."

"He's been doing damned well in London. You know, when there were a lot of bombs dropping sometimes there'd be an extra bang—only that one wouldn't be a bomb. It would be Maurice knocking a safe around."

"Gee!" said Toots. "Yeah, I remember him now. Sure! He's something. You think he's over here now, Latin? Do you really?"

"Must be, I guess. Listen around, will you?"

"Sure. You bet!"

"And don't cough any of this. It's strictly under the bed. That Maurice Peters is quick and nasty. I don't want a guy like him thinking I'm trying to smear him."

"I won't breathe it, Latin. No, sir! Anything I hear, I'll give you a ring."

"Good night," said Latin. "Give my regards to the president."

CHAPTER THREE
S.O.S. FROM 18R

HE HUNG up and poured himself another brandy. He looked just slightly amused.

Dick stopped beside the booth. "You ready to eat yet, or do you figure on drinkin' yourself into a stupor first?"

"Get me the telephone directory."

Dick went out into the kitchen and came back with the directory.

Latin looked up a number and dialed it. The telephone at the other end rang several times, and then a nasal, insolently superior voice said: "This is the Jeffers Hayeses residence."

Latin said: "Let me speak to Mr. Hayes, please."

"Who's calling?"

"This is Max Latin."

"One moment."

Latin waited. After a while the superior voice came back and said: "Mr. Hayes doesn't know any Max Latin. May I ask what your business is with Mr. Hayes?"

"Tell him it's a matter of some stolen jewelry and that he'd better come to the phone because I'm much easier to talk to than the police."

"Stolen jewelry?" the superior voice said, startled. "Police? One moment, please."

Latin waited some more, and then a wheezily impatient voice said suddenly: "What? What, what? What's this?"

"This is Max Latin. Have you ever heard of me?"

"No!"

"You should read the crime news. I specialize in—ah—recovering stolen jewelry for people. For a suitable reward, of course."

"What nonsense! I haven't had any jewelry stolen."

"No," Latin agreed. "Not yet."

"Eh? What, what? What do you mean, sir?"

"You're having a party tomorrow night," Latin said. "There'll be quite a lot of important people there, wearing important jewelry. If their jewelry was stolen at your home, you'd feel pretty mortified, wouldn't you? You'd want to do everything you could to insure its return, isn't that right?"

"Stolen....My home....What? No one would dare! Just what are you talking about?"

"I'm putting in my bid ahead of time," Latin explained. "After the jewelry is stolen, just give me a buzz, and I'll see what I can do."

"After..." the wheezy voice said, stunned. "After the jewelry is stolen....Here! The insolence! Why, I'll have you arrested. I'll have you put in jail. Calling me up and telling me....Why, why, this is fantastic! I'm going to inform the police at once. I'll have you prosecuted to the fullest extent of the law."

"You do that," Latin said. "I'll be looking forward to it."

He broke the connection before the wheezy voice could work up another head of steam.

GUITERREZ OPENED the kitchen door. "Are you gonna eat this stuff, or am I gonna throw it away?"

"Bring it on," said Latin.

Dick appeared with an armful of napkins, silverware, plates, coffee, salad and soup and dumped them all
helter-skelter on the tabletop. Latin arranged them in the
proper sequence and started eating.

The telephone buzzed softly, and Latin picked it up and
said: "Yes?"

The voice was a faint, broken murmur. "Is this—is this
Max Latin?"

"Yes," said Latin.

"Did you talk to a man named Carter-Heason?"

"Yes. Can you speak a little louder? I can't hear."

"No. I'm afraid. If they heard…. Oh, you've got to help
me! Please, please!"

"Sure," said Latin. "What are you, and where are you?"

"Isabel Grey. At the Hanford-Plaza."

"I remember. You're Fortwyn's secretary. What's the
matter?"

"I spoke—I spoke about the funds…. The money we're
collecting…. I didn't know—didn't realize…. Oh, I'm so
afraid! Oh, please come! I can't talk anymore."

There was a click, and the line went dead. Latin listened
for a moment more and then put the telephone back on
its stand slowly. Absently he pushed away the remains of
his soup and salad and picked up his glass of brandy. He
looked at it thoughtfully and then put it down untouched
and picked up the cup of coffee instead.

"Trouble?" Guiterrez asked.

"I wouldn't be at all surprised," said Latin. He finished
the coffee and stood up. "Keep the home fires burning."

IN ITS brief but bawdy history the Hanford-Plaza
Hotel had seen some spectacular goings-on. It had been
in receivership since the day it opened, and it had never

failed to default on its bonds. But this present crisis was something no one could possibly have foreseen. The place was making money.

The lobby was stacked three-deep with people who had rooms and people who didn't have rooms but wanted them and people who didn't have rooms but had given up hope and gone to sleep any handy place. The clerk huddled behind his desk and watched it all with awed and helpless dismay.

"Hey," said Latin. "Have you a party by the name of Fortwyn staying here?"

"I don't know," said the clerk.

"How's for looking it up?"

"Oh, yes," said the clerk numbly. "Yes. I could do that, couldn't I?" He consulted the file of registry cards. "There's a Reginald Fortwyn and party in Suite 18R. That's on the eighteenth floor."

"O.K. How about a party named Carter-Heason?"

The clerk looked again. "In 1751. That's the seventeenth floor. You—you don't live here, do you?"

"No."

"Oh, you're lucky. You can't imagine."

Latin left him and went over to the elevator bank. He eased himself inside, and the cage ground wearily upward.

"Eighteen," he said, when the operator looked at him out of bleary red-rimmed eyes.

"I'll take you up," said the operator, "but you may have to walk down. I'm gonna quit any minute now."

"Having trouble?" Latin asked.

"Hah!" said the operator. "I don't mind 'em swearin' at me and stickin' their elbows in my back and their fingers in my eyes, but I'm gettin' damned sick of having to run this thing with people sittin' in my lap. Here's your floor."

"Happy landings," said Latin.

HE WALKED along on silent deep blue carpeting until he came to the door numbered 18R. Latin rapped a small bronze knocker sharply. There was no answer. He rapped again and then tried the knob. It turned easily and smoothly under his hand, and the door opened quietly in front of him.

Latin stepped through it into a small, formal foyer. He went on through an arched doorway into a combination reception and living room. The Fortwyn party evidently did themselves well. The lights were on, and everything was bright and clean and glistening, but the room was empty.

There were closed doors to Latin's right and to his left. He picked the left and walked over and opened that door.

"Oh," he said. "Pardon me."

It was a small room, hardly larger than a hall closet, and it had been fixed up as a temporary office with a tall steel filing case and a small desk table with a typewriter on it. There was a woman sitting behind the desk. Her head was down, resting on her folded arms beside the typewriter. She was a small woman, dressed in a black tailored suit, and her gray hair had been clipped short.

"Pardon me," said Latin, more loudly.

The woman's body sagged dejectedly, and her shoulders slumped as though she were crying. In spite of the gray hair she looked remarkably like a schoolgirl who had just been scolded by her teacher. She didn't move or raise her head.

Latin took a silent step closer and touched her gently on the shoulder. He stood rigidly still then, looking down, for about five seconds. After that he let out his breath in a long sigh and slid his hand under the woman's chin and lifted her head. Her eyes were gray and glassily dilated. She wasn't breathing, and the blood had soaked through and made a glossy purplish sheen on the front of her dress.

Latin let her head fall back on her arms again. He glanced carefully around the little office and then stepped quietly backward out into the reception room and closed the door. He took out his handkerchief and polished the knob carefully. Just as carefully and quietly he went back across the reception room, through the foyer, and out into the hall.

He considered for a moment. The door had an automatic night latch on it. Latin snapped that into the lock position and then closed the door, staying outside. Then he hammered loudly with the knocker.

"Fortwyn!" he shouted.

He waited for a moment and then pounded on the door panels with both fists and threw in a couple of kicks for good measure and then waited again. The door opened suddenly and violently.

"What's the meaning of this?"

"Well," said Latin mildly. "Goodness me. Hello."

CHAPTER FOUR
LIFE—AND DEATH AT THE
HANFORD-PLAZA

SHE WAS sultry and sensational. She was wearing a greenish padded housecoat that matched her eyes, and golden strap slippers that matched her hair. She was just about the right height, and there was nothing wrong with the rest of her proportions. She couldn't have been more than twenty-two or -three at the best, and her best was something.

"What's the idea of making all the noise?" she demanded.

"I wanted to get in," said Latin.

"Well, where's Miss Grey? She's supposed to answer the door. Miss Grey!"

"Never mind," said Latin. "I'd rather talk to you, anyway. I bet you're Maxine Lufor, aren't you?"

"How did you know? Who are you?"

"I guessed," said Latin, "and I'm Max Latin. Let's you and I call each other Maxie, shall we?"

"No! What do you want, anyway?"

"Just business," Latin said. "But it's not important at all. It can wait if you'd like to invite me in to have a dish of tea or something."

"I wouldn't invite you to have a dish of dog food. Go away!" She tried to slam the door. "Take your foot out of that door. Go away!"

"Maxine!" another voice said. "Maxine, dear! What on earth is the matter?"

The door opened wider, and a man looked out over Maxine Lufor's shoulder. He had a face as round and flat as a pie tin and a rosy red complexion and popped eyes that were blue and wide and bloodshot. He was dressed in a tuxedo, and his chest ballooned out pouter-pigeon-style under a glistening expanse of starched white shirtfront. His voice boomed and raised modulated oratorical echoes.

"Eh! What is this?"

"He was beating on the door," Maxine Lufor explained. "So I came to see what he wanted."

"Well, what does he want?"

"To get funny," said Maxine Lufor.

"Now, fellow," said the fat man. "I'm Reginald Fortwyn. Who are you, eh?"

"I'm Max Latin."

"Well, what is it that you want?"

"I want to see you."

"Why?"

"Business," said Latin.

"Oh," said Fortwyn. "Well, you'll have to make an appointment with my secretary. Where is she? Miss Grey! Oh, Miss Grey!"

"Maybe she went to the little girl's room," Maxine Lufor suggested.

Fortwyn said: "Miss Grey never... I mean, I told her specifically to stay here and see that I wasn't disturbed. I'm sorry, my man, but I'm frightfully busy now and—"

"It won't take long," Latin said. "I hear there's going to be a robbery at the Hayeses place tomorrow night."

"You hear.... *What?*"

Latin nodded. "Robbery. Jewel robbery. You know, that'd be bad. I mean, people might not think it was just a coincidence. You know how people are when they get robbed. Unreasonable. Since the party is being given for your benefit, they might dream up some sort of connection between you and the robbery."

Fortwyn stared with his mouth open. "Do I understand you to say.... Are you from the police?"

"On the contrary," said Latin.

"Well, how do you know there's going to be a robbery?"

"I don't," said Latin. "I've just got a hunch, but my hunches are generally pretty accurate. I'd count on this one if I were you."

FORTWYN GOGGLED at him incredulously. "I believe you are insinuating that you have some secret information. If you know anything about a proposed robbery and don't inform the police, you are an accessory!"

"Oh, sure," said Latin. "Being an accessory is one of my hobbies, but I don't think you'd enjoy it."

"Eh?"

"I'm trying to explain that if a robbery took place the rumor might get around that you were an accessory. That would have a bad effect on your reputation—and your receipts the next time you put on a shindig."

"What—what are you suggesting I do?" Fortwyn asked groggily.

"Pay me," said Latin.

"Pay you?"

"Sure. For a reasonable fee I will guarantee that there won't be a robbery."

"Won't be...? See here! Why, that's nothing more than blackmail!"

"No," Latin denied. "Insurance."

"Oh, no!" Fortwyn shouted. "Oh, no, indeed! You are threatening to arrange a robbery and implicate me in it unless I pay you money not to. Why, I've never heard of such monstrous insolence. I'll have you arrested. Maxine! You heard his proposal. Look at him closely so you can identify him. I want another witness. Find Miss Grey! Hurry up. Look for her!"

Maxine Lufor stepped back inside the suite. "I'll see if she left a note in the office."

Fortwyn pointed a pudgy finger at Latin. "Don't you try to get away, fellow! I'm going to see that you answer to the authorities—"

Maxine Lufor screamed horribly.

Fortwyn swung around, the rosy red of his complexion fading suddenly. "What is it? Maxine! What—"

She screamed again.

"Good-bye, now," Latin said pleasantly.

Fortwyn ignored him. He lumbered back inside the suite, calling anxiously: "Maxine! What is it? What did you see?"

Latin turned a corner in the corridor and walked on along to the stairs and went down them to the seventeenth floor. He was whistling softly and thoughtfully to himself. He went along the hall on the seventeenth floor until he came to the room numbered 1751. He rapped with the bronze knocker.

THE DOOR opened at once, and Carter-Heason said: "Well, old chap. This is a surprise. Come right in."

The room was small and narrow, and it had none of the shiny luxury of the Fortwyn suite. There was a man sitting in the chair that was crowded in between the bed and the one window. He was a thin man with narrow shoulders and hair that looked startlingly black in contrast to the smooth pallor of his face. He wore thick horn-rimmed glasses and a blue suit that was shiny at the seams.

"This is Mr. Perwinkle," Carter-Heason said. "He is employed by Fortwyn. If you'll remember, I spoke to you about him. This is Max Latin, Perwinkle. He is helping me investigate Fortwyn."

"You're the accompanist," Latin said.

Perwinkle looked up gloomily. "Piano player," he corrected. "General all-around stooge and patsy."

"Mr. Perwinkle is—ah—dissatisfied with his job and his employer," Carter-Heason explained. "He shares my suspicions of Fortwyn's honesty."

"The guy is a crook," said Perwinkle. "He is also a rat, if that matters."

"Can you prove it?" Latin asked.

"No."

"We were having a conference on that matter," Carter-Heason said. "Mr. Perwinkle indicated that he would cooperate with me in investigating Fortwyn, but we are in a quandary as to just where to start."

"That old blowbelly is as smooth as they come," Perwinkle stated. "I know he's crooked, but he never makes a misstep, and he carries more oil than a tanker. He can explain anything."

"I was just up talking to him," Latin said. "We didn't get anywhere. That's quite a nifty number he has singing for him."

"You should try to play the piano for her," Perwinkle said. "The last time she got off the beat she crowned me with a vase and claimed it was my fault. Of course, the old boy took her part."

"Is he that way about her?"

"Yeah, man. She snaps her fingers, and he hops. It's the only thing he is silly about, but if I were she I'd take it pretty easy. I bet the old guy would really blow his top if he thought she was taking him for a ride, and believe me he can be rough and tough when he gets a mad on."

"Do you think he's a crook because you don't like him," Latin asked, "or have you got any good reasons?"

Perwinkle moved his narrow shoulders disconsolately. "I just know. He's not doin' this for fun. He's taken in plenty. It's all nicely invested now, but I'm damned sure it isn't going to stay there. I could quit, but if I do, I automatically get myself fired from the board of directors of that phoney trust company of his, and then I never would find out what goes on."

"How about Isabel Grey? Is she in it with Fortwyn?"

"Aw, no. Izzy's straight. She's got all kinds of relatives hanging out in those islands, and besides that she's a nice old gal. She's smoothed old Fortwyn down lots of times when he's been on my tail. She's kind of dumb, though. She thinks Fortwyn is the greatest man alive—on account of him claiming to collect all this money to help her relatives and friends and all. I've tried to talk to her about this and that, but she won't hear a word against him. She just looks shocked that I could even think—"

THE DOOR in back of Latin opened suddenly, bumping him forward.

"Here, now!" said Carter-Heason indignantly. "This is a private room! What do you mean, breaking in this way? Who are you?"

"I'm Detective Inspector Walters," said the man in the doorway. "Homicide. And if you keep people like Latin in your room, you've got to expect people like me to come in after them."

"Hello, Walters," said Latin. "You're not looking very well these days."

"I'm not feeling well, either," said Walters. He was a tall, thin, gauntly bitter man with the sourly disillusioned air of a person who has been disappointed in human nature so regularly that he has become insulated. "So just tell me what you know about that murder on the eighteenth floor and don't waste my time trying to act innocent."

"Murder?" Latin repeated. "On the eighteenth floor? This is very surprising, Walters. Are you absolutely sure of your facts?"

"I can generally tell a corpse when I see one. Start talking, Latin."

"Who was murdered?" Latin asked.

"A dame named Isabel Grey, as if you didn't know."

"What?" Perwinkle gasped. "Did you say Isabel Grey? Izzy?"

Walters looked at him. "Yes. Who are you?"

"Perwinkle," he said numbly. "I play the piano.... Izzy—dead? Murdered? Who—who would do a thing like that?"

"If you'll shut up," Walters told him, "I'll go ahead trying to find out. What did the dame want when she called you on the telephone, Latin?"

"Called me?" Latin said blandly.

Walters's eyes narrowed dangerously. "Are you denying that she did?"

"Oh, no," Latin answered. "Come to think of it, she did. It slipped my mind. She just asked me to drop around and see her sometime."

"Why?"

"Oh, I expect she wanted me to make a slight contribution to the Channel Islands charity."

"And you were so anxious to do it that you whipped right up there in the middle of the night?"

Latin nodded. "I'm hell-bent on charity."

"Ha, ha," Walters said sourly. "Now, look here. That wasn't any ordinary call she made to you. How do I know? Because she didn't want to take a chance on making it from the suite upstairs. Instead, she went down to the lobby and called from one of the booths. The clerk noticed it. Now what did she have to say that was so important?"

"That's all," said Latin. "Just asked me to drop around."

"You liar. You were right outside the door when her body was discovered."

"Yes," Latin agreed, and repeated with emphasis: "Outside."

WALTERS POUNCED. "How did you know when the body was discovered?"

"Deduction," Latin said. "Maxine Lufor let loose with a loud halloo while I was standing in the hall talking to Fortwyn. I mean, people scream for no end of reasons, but when you mentioned a murder, I sort of tied it up with that. But just remember I was outside in the hall the whole time I was there, and incidentally, the door was locked."

"I don't think it was incidentally," said Walters. "I think it was on purpose—your purpose."

"Oh, now, Walters," Latin said. "You're just being silly. You know you couldn't prove a thing like that."

Walters leaned forward. "You were inside that suite!"

"Shame," said Latin. "Do you think I'm the sort of person who would enter people's rooms uninvited?"

"I know damned well you are!"

"Let's not bicker," said Latin. "You'll get all excited and give yourself indigestion. Let's talk about something pleasant for a change."

"Blaah!" said Walters explosively. "Who is this skinny bird here?"

"This is Carter-Heason. He's British."

"What are you doing in his room?"

"He's a stranger to the city, and I just thought I'd drop in with a word of welcome. Make him feel at home and all that."

"Is that true?" Walters demanded.

"Certainly," said Carter-Heason. "Look here, old chap. I don't know a great deal about your legal procedure in this country, but I think you're going a little too far when you barge into my room in this impolite manner and treat my guests as though they were some sort of criminals."

"Criminals!" Walters echoed. "Some sort! Latin is *all* sorts of a criminal! If there's any crime in the books that he hasn't committed it's just because he's been too busy to get around to it. Hey, wait a minute. You with the cheaters. What'd you say your name was?"

"Perwinkle."

"You belong to the outfit upstairs, don't you? Aren't you the guy that plays the piano for the dame with the stream-lines?"

"Yes," Perwinkle admitted.

"What are you doing here?"

"Just visiting Carter-Heason."

"What for?"

"We were just talking about music."

Walters looked at Carter-Heason. "What do you play?"

"I don't. I'm a student of the Art."

"Nuts," said Walters. He turned back to Perwinkle. "Where were you for the last hour?"

"Right here," said Perwinkle. His eyes bulged suddenly behind the glasses. "You don't think I—I...."

"I don't know," Walters answered grimly, "but don't think I won't find out. Now, Latin. Get a grip on this and remember it. I just got on this case. Not five minutes after I arrive, I hear your name. So I checked up with the desk clerk and came here to find you. I don't know what it's all about yet, but if you're in it, it's bound to be sour. You stick around where I can find you." He pointed a finger at Carter-Heason. "As for you, you're in bad company. People that play with Latin end up behind the eight ball if not in a coffin. Four-eyes, you trot along with me."

"Me?" Perwinkle wailed. "But I don't know anything about.... I haven't seen Izzy since dinner! I went to the picture show and came right up here and stayed here. I can prove—"

"Less noise," Walters ordered. "Out. Get going back upstairs. We've got lots to talk about."

He grabbed Perwinkle's skinny arm and shoved him through the door. He turned back to nod grimly at Latin and Carter-Heason.

"I'll see both of you—later."

He slammed the door.

"Extraordinarily unpleasant character," Carter-Heason commented. "I don't believe I approve of the American police."

"They get in my hair, too," said Latin.

Carter-Heason frowned in a worried way. "I'm confused. In America, violence happens so—so violently. This murder, so unexpected....I fear I might have some responsibility. You see, I've spoken several times to Miss Grey as well as Perwinkle. She couldn't help but know that I was suspicious of Fortwyn and have been for some time. She wouldn't, as Perwinkle said, hear a word against Fortwyn, but do you suppose she found out something or said something to him?"

"Maybe," said Latin. "I've got to run along."

"Where are you going?"

"Home," said Latin. "To get some sleep. I have an idea we'll have a big night tomorrow. I'll see you then."

CHAPTER FIVE
MURDER GOES
HIGH CLASS

YOU DON'T see the really big limousines very much anymore—the Cunningham and the Rolls and the Mercedes-Benz—all glitter and weight, with an insatiable thirst for gas. Their owners save them for special occasions. But this was one, and here they were, parked in a sleek gleaming line up the curve of the long drive. Latin walked along, admiring them, until a man stepped suddenly out of the shadow and said: "That's far enough."

"Hello, Walters," Latin said. "How's murder?"

"Looking up," said Walters, "now that you've arrived. What are you doing here?"

"I'm expected at the party."

"Let me see your invitation."

"I didn't say I was invited," Latin told him. "Just expected. What have you found out about Isabel Grey's death?"

"Plenty. Where is Maurice Peters?"

"Who?" Latin asked.

"Don't act dumb," Walters ordered. "I want to know where Maurice Peters is."

"Don't know him," said Latin.

Walters breathed deeply. "Look, smarty. You're not the only one who gets around. I know all about Maurice Peters. He's a hotshot from London, and you've got a tip that he's going to pick off some jewelry at this party. This Carter-Heason with his dopey suspicions of Fortwyn gave you just the chance you needed to poke your nose in. You put the bell on Jeffers Hayes so that if Maurice Peters walks off with something you'd get the chance to negotiate to get it back. Then you turned right around and put the shake on Fortwyn, so if Maurice Peters should change his mind, then you'd take credit for preventing a robbery and get some dough on that angle. Both ends against the middle. That's you all over, Latin."

"I never heard such nonsense in all my life," said Latin. "I don't believe there is any such person as Maurice Peters."

"Well, I believe there is. And what's more, I believe you're going to point him out to me. Because if you don't, you know what's going to happen."

"What?" Latin inquired.

"I'm going to personally escort you to jail. And you won't slide out with any accessory charge this time. You laid yourself wide open. If any jewelry is missing from this party tonight, you're going to be charged with stealing it. You're a principal, and I can prove it by the testimony of Hayes and Fortwyn."

"In that case," said Latin, "I'd be only too glad to help you in any way I can, but I don't really think I can point out Maurice Peters to you."

"I really think you'd better," Walters said, taking a firm grip on his arm. "Come on."

THE HOUSE was white and austere and imposing, spread majestically across the top of its private knoll. The curtains were drawn tight across its many windows, and only a few stray gleams of light escaped, but the place was alive with the shadowy, busy bustle of people. As Latin and

Walters came up the drive and up the wide front steps to the veranda, they could hear the faintly nasal whine of a string orchestra and the muffled *bumble-bumble-bumble* of many mixed conversations. There were about eighteen resentful-looking chauffeurs standing in a row beside the front door in the custody of an even more resentful-looking uniformed policeman. Walters marched Latin up and down in front of the row.

"Well?" he said inquiringly.

"Well, what?" Latin asked.

Walters gave his arm a jerk. "I told you to drop that stupid act! Is any of these birds Maurice Peters or any relation to him?"

"Not that I know of," said Latin.

"Come on inside, then."

Walters opened the front door and hauled Latin into a big, spectacularly shiny hall. A tall, darkly sinister butler bowed to them in icy greeting.

"How about this number?" Walters demanded. "Is he Maurice Peters?"

"Nope," said Latin.

"The name," said the butler, "is Hoggins, in case the information remotely concerns you. May I have your invitations, if you please?"

"No," said Walters. "We'll blow our own horn."

He pulled Latin on down the hall and through a wide, curtained archway. The drawing room and dining room and reception room extended before them like a luxurious movie set in triplicate, crowded with fat women under full sail in evening dresses and fat men in tails and with well-bred hauteur clustered around so thickly you could spread it with a putty knife.

"Just take your time," Walters ordered.

Latin looked. "That bloated bird in the corner is a crook if I ever saw one."

"I know it," said Walters. "But his name is not Maurice Peters, and he's not here to steal jewelry. He's the president of the Chamber of Commerce. Look again."

"There's a bar over there—"

"I know that, too, but you're not going to get any closer to it. Quit stalling."

A tall, lathlike man with a sun-reddened bald head and fishy gray eyes moved out of the crowd and said: "Ah, Inspector. Glad to see you paying such close attention to your duties. Anything I can do for you?"

"No, thanks," Walters said. "Mr. Jeffers Hayes, I'd like you to meet Max Latin."

Hayes said absently: "Pleasure, I'm sure—" His voice deepened to a croak. "What? What, what? Who?"

"Max Latin," said Latin. "Hi."

Hayes recoiled. "You—here! In my house.... Inspector Walters! What do you mean by bringing this—this person here? What, what? Explain yourself, sir!"

"He's looking over the people," Walters said. "He's going to point out Maurice Peters to me. Peters is the thief we expect is here."

Hayes swallowed hard. "Looking over.... Expect.... What? *Thief!* Inspector, these people are my guests. My guests! Do you think I'd invite a thief to my home? What utter nonsense! Take this man away from the premises."

Carter-Heason came up to them and said: "What-o? Having trouble?"

"No!" Hayes snarled. He glared haughtily at Carter-Heason and then spun on his heel and stalked rigidly away.

CARTER-HEASON SMILED pleasantly. "Sour sort of a chap, isn't he? Very resentful that he had to issue me an invitation to this affair. Boring, isn't it?"

"Why did he have to issue you an invitation?" Walters asked suspiciously.

Carter-Heason shrugged. "Oh, I imagine the British consul put in a word for me. Charming fellow, Rodney. Known him for years. Have a spot to drink?"

"Yes," said Latin.

"No," said Walters. "And I'm keeping an eye on you, Carter-Heason. Ever hear of a man named Maurice Peters?"

"Don't believe so," said Carter-Heason. "Is he a friend of yours?"

"No!"

"I see. Aren't you a homicide detective, by the way? Expecting a murder?"

"It could happen," Walters answered grimly. "Come on, Latin."

They went back into the hall and down the length of it and through another door into the gleaming, narrow butler's pantry and the restaurant-size kitchen beyond. There was a policeman sitting and eating an apple in front of the kitchen door.

"Stand here," Walters said. "Just watch them as they go back and forth. Everybody here, Kelly?"

"Yup," said Kelly, eating more apple.

"I don't see any familiar faces," Latin said.

"O.K.," said Walters. "Upstairs, next."

They went back through the butler's pantry and up the servant stairs to the second floor. There was a wide hall that branched back both ways from the main stairway, and Walters chose one of the doors along it and knocked.

"This is the ladies' dressing room."

A cute, pert blonde maid looked out at them. "You can't come in here!"

"I don't want to," said Walters. "I just want Latin to look at you."

"And am I glad to," said Latin. "My name is Latin, and if you should drop into Guiterrez's restaurant some night—"

"Come on!" Walters snarled. "I've got better things to do than clown around with you. This is the gents' dressing room. Take a look at the valet and—"

There was a shrill, throbbing scream.

"I know that voice," Latin said. "It belongs to Maxine Lufor."

"Stay here!" Walters snapped.

HE POUNDED on down the hall, and Latin ran right after him. They turned a corner, and the hall ended ahead of them in a glass-paneled door that gave out onto a sun deck with a high white-plaster wall. There was a second door to the right of the glass door, and it snapped open now, and two struggling figures caromed out of it and bounced against the wall opposite.

"Here!" Walters yelled. "Stop that! What's going on here?"

The larger of the two figures swung two awkwardly chopping blows at the smaller and knocked him back across the hall. This one was Perwinkle, and he tripped and went down in a sprawl.

"Get him!" the larger man shouted. "He murdered Maxine! I saw him! I saw him!" He pointed a rigid, shaking finger. "He murdered her—stabbed her!"

"Here you!" Walters barked. "Fortwyn! Hold it, now! What's all this?"

Fortwyn's round face was reddishly bloated. He made choking sounds in his throat and then ripped away the starched collar of his dress shirt. His eyes bulged.

"Look at him!" Perwinkle shrieked. "Look! Her blood is on his shirt!"

There was a dark smear across the white front of Fortwyn's shirt. He looked down at it, still making those animal choking sounds in his throat, and then kicked savagely at Perwinkle. Perwinkle got him by the leg, and the two of them slammed back into the glass door and knocked it open with a thunderous clatter of broken glass.

"Fortwyn!" Walters bawled. "Stop that! Put up your hands!"

The two men rolled out on the porch floor over the crunching glass, and Walters dove through the shattered door after them.

Latin stopped to peer through the door in which they had first appeared. Beyond it was a dressing room, evidently half of a bedroom suite. There was a small piano in the corner, and the chair in front of it had been tipped over on its back. Maxine Lufor was lying face down halfway between the piano and the door. Her hands, with their long predatory-red nails, were reached out ahead of her clutching the carpet like agonized claws. Her face was hidden in the sleekly tumbled gold of her hair, but nothing could conceal the deep and ugly wounds between her smooth, bare shoulder blades. Blood was smeared wet and thick in the silk of her evening gown and more of it clotted the blade of the slim hunting knife lying on the rug by her feet.

CHAPTER SIX
CHARITY REMAINS
AT HOME

THERE WAS a rumbling thump from the sun deck and the rattle and slap of a chair going over. Latin ducked back into the hall and through the glass door in time to stumble over Walters.

"Knocked me down!" Walters panted thickly. "Smacked me. Why, the guy's nuttier than a fruit cake! Get him, Latin. Down those stairs!"

Latin ran the length of the sun deck. Stairs went down steeply here into the patterned formality of a small, closed garden. Fortwyn was running headlong across it toward the thick, iron-studded door in the wall at the far side. Perwinkle was right behind him.

Latin was halfway down the stairs when Fortwyn reached the big door. He grabbed the wrought-iron catch and wrenched at it, but the door didn't open. Fortwyn swung around, his face shiny and twisted with desperation, and Perwinkle tried to tackle him.

Fortwyn picked him up and threw him a good ten feet into a close-trimmed privet hedge and then followed it up, trying to kick him. Perwinkle rolled frantically to get out of the way and came up to his knees grasping one of the border stones in both his hands. It was a smooth, white-painted boulder half the size of a man's head. Perwinkle swung it up at full arm's length, squarely into the middle of Fortwyn's face.

It made an ugly chucking sound like the blade of an axe cutting into hard wood. Fortwyn bounced back and hit the wooden door with the length of his body. He bounced forward again and went down flat on the rolled white gravel of the path. He squirmed a little there and then was still.

Perwinkle had lost his balance when he swung with the boulder. He hitched frantically backward now, half sitting, half on his knees.

"Look out!" he panted. "He—he's crazy as a mad dog! He'll get up and—and...."

"He won't get up," said Latin.

Perwinkle began to shake all over. "I didn't—I didn't mean.... I rolled on that stone, and when he came for me, I just—just—"

"You just gave him what he ought to have had," said Walters grimly, coming up to them. "Now just what the hell started him off, anyway? What's this about a murder?"

Perwinkle fought for control. "We—Maxine and I—were practicing a new number. They put a piano in that room up there for us. He, Fortwyn, came in all of a sudden. He looked funny, but I didn't pay a lot of attention. He was always griping about something. He said he wanted to talk to Maxine alone, so they went into the bedroom that's attached to the room where the piano is. I could hear them yelling at each other in there."

"Yelling about what?" Walters asked.

"Same thing as usual. Money. Some things she had charged to Fortwyn's account. I didn't get all they were saying, because I wasn't paying much attention. I just figured it was another of their rows. They kept shouting louder and louder, and then all of a sudden she yelled for me. I jumped up, and then she ran out of the bedroom with him right after her."

"Well?" Walters said sharply.

Perwinkle gulped. "It was like a—a nightmare. He had a knife in his hand, and he stabbed—and stabbed...." Perwinkle's face was greenish, and he shook his head mutely, unable to finish.

"Why would he kill her for charging stuff to his account?" Walters inquired.

"You should ask me," Latin told him.

"I should," Walters agreed dangerously, "and I am. Why?"

"IT'S SIMPLE," said Latin. "Carter-Heason thought Fortwyn was a crook. Carter-Heason was right. He doesn't know how to investigate things like that, and all he could do was poke around, but that was plenty to make Fortwyn nervous. He didn't know when Carter-Heason might accidentally stumble across something. Fortwyn was doing his dirty work with some fancy double bookkeeping. He had sold Isabel Grey on the idea that what he was doing was the right thing to do. I don't know what line he gave her, but from all accounts she was a sort of believing soul and he was a smooth talker.

"That was O.K. until Carter-Heason let them know that he was hiring me. Isabel Grey thought that the thing to do was to explain to me just why the double bookkeeping was necessary. I'd understand, since I had nothing against Fortwyn personally, and everything would be smooth. When Fortwyn found out she meant to do that he went into one of his tantrums and stabbed her."

"Fine," said Walters. "But what about Maxine Lufor, or have you forgotten that?"

"No. Carter-Heason had scared Fortwyn. Fortwyn didn't dare take a chance on stealing a penny of that charity fund while Carter-Heason was watching him. He didn't have any money to give Maxine Lufor. They fought about it, and finally she got mad and up and charged stuff that he couldn't pay for without dipping into the charity fund. That really set him off. I imagine she added to it tonight by refusing to return the stuff she had charged."

"Yes," said Perwinkle. "Yes. She did say she wouldn't take anything back. I didn't know what she was talking about then."

"O.K.," said Walters. "Just one more thing. Let's hear you talk your way around this. Where is Maurice Peters?"

"In your imagination."

"Huh?" said Walters blankly.

Latin said: "I know Toots Carr is not only stir-crazy but punch-drunk from having too many safes drop on his head. I also know he's a stool pigeon. I knew that if I called him up and talked about Maurice Peters, the terrific safe artist from London, Toots would talk himself into believing there actually was such a person and that Toots knew him. Then he would run around and tell you."

Walters made a strangling sound. "Why, you—you— What in hell did you do that for?"

"I wanted to have some sort of a proposition to talk to Hayes and Fortwyn about. I wanted to get in here tonight. I did. And thanks a lot for your personally conducted tour of the premises. I'll make out alone from now on. I know where the bar is."

IT WAS nine o'clock the next night when Latin threaded his way through the close-packed tables in the restaurant and stopped beside his personal booth.

"Sorry if I'm late," he said. He slid into the seat next to Carter-Heason. "How do you feel now?" he asked Perwinkle.

"Oh, all right," Perwinkle answered glumly. "I was just bruised a little. But I can't get the whole damned dirty business out of my head."

"No wonder," Carter-Heason told him. "Ghastly affair. Fortwyn never recovered consciousness. Died on the way to the hospital. Good thing."

Perwinkle shivered. "Not for me to think about."

"Don't let it worry you," Carter-Heason said. "Only thing you could possibly have done. Good job."

"What have you decided to do about Fortwyn's Channel Islands charity?" Latin asked.

Carter-Heason said: "I can settle it up with Perwinkle's help. We'll turn the funds over to some British or United Nations charity and let them administer the thing."

"I don't know what I'm going to do after that," Perwinkle said.

Latin said pleasantly: "I think you'll hang."

THE NOISE in the restaurant seemed to ebb and flow around the sudden silence in the booth.

"What was that?" Carter-Heason said slowly.

"Perwinkle killed Isabel Grey and Maxine Lufor as well as Fortwyn," Latin said. "Perwinkle saw a good thing, and he edged in on the party. Hasn't it occurred to you that he was a director of Fortwyn's trust company—the only one left? When you and he added up the funds, you'd have found about ninety percent of them missing. You'd have blamed that on Fortwyn. Actually Perwinkle would have had the dough in his pocket. That's exactly what he meant to do the whole time."

"You're a damned liar," said Perwinkle evenly.

"Not this time," said Latin. "Fortwyn was just what he appeared to be—a big fat blowhard. You played him like you play your piano. Maybe he meant to run out with those funds and maybe he didn't. Anyway, you got there first. Isabel Grey suspected you. She was afraid of you, too. It was you she meant to tell me about, not Fortwyn. You were in the lobby when Isabel Grey made her call to me. She saw you. That's why she was afraid to say any more. She beat it back upstairs, but you got there ahead of her. You stabbed her and ran down to see Carter-Heason."

"You make me laugh," said Perwinkle contemptuously.

"O.K. Go ahead. You stabbed Maxine Lufor because you knew you'd never get away with a dime without giving her a big part of it. Then you called in that poor boob of a Fortwyn and accused him of doing it. You even wiped some blood from the knife blade on his shirtfront. You had evidence that he and Maxine had quarreled violently. Naturally the shock and the accusation and the evidence against him scared Fortwyn green. All he could think of was to shut you up and run. You saw that he didn't run far. I think you had a gun on you all the time. I think you'd have shot him if you hadn't been able to nail him with that rock."

"I had a gun on me all the time," Perwinkle said. "I have one now. It's under the table. If either one of you makes a move, I'll kill you. You can't prove any of this stuff, but you could get me held for investigation. I wouldn't like that because those funds have already been transferred to a place where I can get hold of them. All I need is the time to do that. You're going to give me that."

Latin shrugged indifferently. "I pass."

"Well, you can't do this, you know," said Carter-Heason.

"I thought I might have trouble with you," said Perwinkle. "I have a small bottle of a private preparation of my own in my pocket. I think you're going to drink it and become violently ill and go to the hospital. That would be a good reason for you not attending to settling up the charity funds. I'll do it for you. I'll take care of Latin in some other manner."

"Do you want that poison served with a glass of water?" Guiterrez asked, leaning over the back of Perwinkle's seat.

Perwinkle's breath hissed through his teeth. He jerked his head back, looking up and over his shoulder. In the same split second Dick stepped around the end of the booth and swung expertly with the bottle he was holding by the neck.

The bottle hit Perwinkle on the temple and shattered in a wet, glittering spray. Perwinkle's thin body uncoiled slowly, and he rolled out of his seat and collapsed full-length on the floor.

Latin nodded at Carter-Heason. "There's a dictaphone behind the drape at the end of the booth. They could hear everything he said in the kitchen. Get the telephone, Dick. I'll call up Walters and give him a thrill."

"Oh, no!" Guiterrez snarled. "Just wait a minute, now. Dick, you search this bird on the floor first. He ain't gonna get out of this dive without payin' for the bottle of brandy you smashed over his dome. Latin can take jobs for charity, but I'm a businessman!"

www.ingramcontent.com/pod-product-compliance
Lightning Source LLC
Chambersburg PA
CBHW031334020726
47499CB00005B/1258